Sex, Drugs, Rock'n'Roll:

Stories to end the century

....

EDITED BY SARAH LEFANU

The editor would like to thank Juliet Annan, Steve Aylett and Stephen Hayward for their help.

'The Achieve of, the Mastery of the Thing' by Laurie Colwin was first published in her collection *The Lone Pilgrim*, New York, Knopf, 1981. Reprinted by permission of Donadio & Ashworth Inc, Literary Representatives.

'The Story of No' by Lisa Tuttle was first published in *Slow Hand: Women Writing Erotica*, edited by Michele Slung, New York, HarperCollins, 1992. Reprinted by permission of the author.

'Autopsy' by Ivan Vladislavić was first published in his collection *Propaganda by Monuments and Other Stories*, Cape Town, David Philip, 1996. Reprinted by permission of the author.

Library of Congress Catalog Card Number: 97–067085

First published 1997 by
Serpent's Tail, 4 Blackstock Mews, London N4
and 180 Varick Street, New York, NY 10014

Phototypeset in 10pt Times by Intype London Limited

Printed in Great Britain by Mackays of Chatham

For Christopher

Remember what the Dormouse said
– Jefferson Airplane

Contents

Introduction by Sarah LeFanu   ix

Michèle Roberts   *A Bodice Rips: A Novel in Seven Chapters*   1

Steve Aylett   *Sampler*   19

Ursule Molinaro   *Amazons in the Night City*   36

Philip Hensher   *A Chartist*   42

Janice Galloway   *help*   52

John Saul   *Honeymoon*   72

Bonnie Greer   *Stillness*   81

Nicholas Royle   *Trussed*   89

Lisa Tuttle   *The Story of No*   101

Ivan Vladislavić   *Autopsy*   116

Laurie Colwin   *The Achieve of, the Mastery of the Thing*   128

Christopher Hope   *Gone*   150

Diana Hendry   *Just Breathing*   163

Joyce Carol Oates   *A Woman is Born to Bleed*   171

Michael Carson   *Postcards of the Hanging*   176

Cherry Wilder   *Friends in Berlin*   188

About the Authors   219

Introduction

....

'Sex and drugs and rock and roll,' sang Ian Dury, 'that's all my body needs', laying the ground, probably in all innocence, for a later configuration of the 1960s as a decade of sexual selfishness and dangerous living. Over the last couple of decades sex and drugs and rock and roll have been demonized by politicians, journalists and other right-wing opinion-makers who have made the liberal ideals of the sixties into a scapegoat for the falling apart of the family in particular and society in general. But can sex and drugs and rock and roll really be held to blame for all the ills of contemporary society? It could be argued that the counterculture of the sixties, presented to us now as a package of sex, drugs and rock'n'roll, was, initially at least, spiritually rather than materialistically inclined, and embraced a communitarian rather than a selfishly individualistic ethos. Indeed it could be, and has been, argued that it was only post-1979 that the rot set in and things fell apart.

In this anthology of new short stories I have included a story by the late Laurie Colwin that is set in the early days of the counterculture, that short period in postwar American history when not only was it bliss to be alive, but to be young and stoned was very heaven. The people of that generation were inspired by visionaries and poets of earlier generations, by William Blake, by Wordsworth, by Shelley, and in the case of Ann Speizer, the protagonist of Laurie Colwin's story, by Gerard Manley Hopkins.

Laurie Colwin's 'The Achieve of, the Mastery of the

....

Thing', is a story written from a position of innocence and optimism.

It is not a story that could be written now.

How do contemporary writers reconfigure the past? What do sex, drugs and rock and roll mean to writers now, thirty years after what has come to be seen as their heyday? Not that anyone believes for a moment that Philip Larkin was speaking literally when he said sexual intercourse was invented in 1963; nor that people haven't been ingesting substances one way or another to alter their state of consciousness if not to blow their minds since the dim mists of prehistory. But how are they a part of our end-of-the-century days?

Not surprisingly, the power of the market place is a force that lurks behind many of these contemporary stories about sex and drugs and rock and roll. Sex, in stories such as Bonnie Greer's 'Stillness' and Ursule Molinaro's 'Amazons in the Night City', is shown as a purchasable commodity, as is rock and roll in Michael Carson's 'Postcards of the Hanging'. And Ivan Vladislavić's narrator in 'Autopsy' tracks Elvis through a new South Africa of international capital.

Back in the 1960s and '70s, in the days when Laurie Colwin's heroine, Mrs Speizer, was trying to find a dealer on the campus, drugs were part of the counterculture. To smoke dope was to challenge the status quo, to question the materialistic aspirations of the postwar boom years, to turn your back on respectability, responsibility and adulthood. It was to have fun, and to be funny. 'I was stoned and I missed it,' sang Dr Hook, at once mocking and celebrating the stoned person's inability to get anything together at all. He was able, then, to laugh at the idea of missing the chance of sex with a little cutie, of missing a man giving dollar bills away, of missing the whole of life itself. 'I was sto-o-o-oned and it rolled right by'. Nowadays drugs are not part of a counterculture. Whether the shift of drug-taking from a marginal to a central place within our culture can be laid at the door of the rampant consumerism of the 1980s, or the scientific and technological advances made over the last fifteen to twenty years in pharmaceutical laboratories; or whether you prefer to conjure with more nebulous concepts such as alienation, or late capitalism, the fact remains that, to use a contemporary turn of phrase, drugs'r'us. 'I'm not much of a user,' says Eddie, in Steve Aylett's story, 'Sampler'. 'We're all users, Eddie,' replies Kramer the basement chemist.

Where Laurie Colwin's story was cheerful and funny, these new stories are bleak and funny. The circumstances of drug-ingestion are considerably more dire and dangerous for Aylett's Eddie and for Janice Galloway's Alma in 'help' than they are for Laurie Colwin's Mrs Speizer, but the two contemporary drug-blasted characters are not unlike Mrs Speizer in their ironical perception of the world and their place in it.

Many of these stories, not just the druggy ones, are about characters who are touched in some way by death. Even the tough, single thirtysomethings of Nicholas Royle's story 'Trussed' are vulnerable; and I'm not sure we are quite meant to believe that Cherry Wilder's rock star hero James Raven escapes his date with death in 'Friends in Berlin'. Death lurks close by or in the interstices of the stories, in a way that it does not in the one story included here that was written nearly twenty years ago. It is striking that so many of the writers, responding to sex, drugs and rock and roll in the contemporary world, or looking backwards as Joyce Carol Oates does in 'A Woman is Born to Bleed', should find such food for thoughts of mortality. Is it that over the intervening years we have been forced to recognize the frailty and dustiness of flesh?

' . . . Death strikes their House,' sings John Cale in 'The Falklands Suite' (on *Words for the Dying*), his setting to music in 1989 of four gloomy poems by Dylan Thomas. With his bold rhythms and his rough voice, Cale transforms the gloominess of the poems into something altogether

. . . .

fiercer and more life-affirming. Perhaps this is what rock and roll is best at. It struck me, as the stories came in, that either they were being written from a position of pessimism, which accepts mortality and faces it with fierceness and bitter humour, or they were written from a position of optimism in the teeth of the experience of death and loss. Optimistic but not innocent: this describes Philip Hensher's 'A Chartist' and Diana Hendry's 'Just Breathing'. Both these stories celebrate the triumph of love over loss.

But although it is striking how many of these stories embrace, tangentially if not centrally, a bleak vision of the end of the millennium, there are of course exceptions: the delicate relationships of small-town South Africa threatened by a newspaper clipping of Elvis in Christopher Hope's 'Gone', or John Saul's new Europeans, in 'Honeymoon', who belong heart and soul to the commodity culture but are redeemed – perhaps – by sexual desire.

Exceptions too are the stories – by Lisa Tuttle and by Michèle Roberts – that play with earlier, literary representations of sex and bring a feminist consciousness to bear on their retellings. Just as sexual intercourse wasn't invented in 1963, so female desire wasn't invented by 1970s feminists. None the less feminism, which some might argue grew out of and partly in opposition to the sex, drugs and rock and roll revolution, made it easier for women fiction writers to express that desire. Michèle Roberts's 'A Bodice Rips: A Novel in Seven Chapters' refers to and draws on a similar position of optimism and innocence to that in Laurie Colwin's 'The Achieve of, the Mastery of the Thing'. This is partly to do with the optimism of childhood, a time when anything and everything is possible. Ann Speizer, despite being a professor's wife, is resolutely not grown up. In the stories by Lisa Tuttle and Michèle Roberts sexual desire lives in the imagination as well as in the body. In the imagination, too, anything and everything is possible; it lies outside the strictured demands of the market place.

A feminist voice is apparent, too, in Janice Galloway's

....

'help'. This story, I think, offers a quintessentially nineties view of sex and drugs and rock and roll, and thus provides an interesting contrast to Laurie Colwin's earlier story. 'help' is permeated with disillusion and despair and betrayal and madness; but it is also angry and engaged and suffused with an oblique wit.

As a phrase within the powerfully hegemonic language of contemporary journalism, 'sex and drugs and rock and roll has come to signify, or to sum up, either all that is good, or all that is bad, about the last thirty years. The reality of course is more complex. I think that these stories reflect that complexity, and show us that sex, and drugs, and rock and roll are powerful inspirations to writers tracing the rhythms of our living and dying in the closing days of the twentieth century.

Sarah LeFanu
Bristol, 1997

A Bodice Rips: A Novel in Seven Chapters

MICHÈLE ROBERTS

CHAPTER ONE: THE DIAMOND

There was no time to lose. Maria paused in the middle of the green and gold drawing-room, biting her lips and looking wildly around. At the same time she was listening for sounds from outside. She ran to one of the long windows and peered out, then ran back. Her movements were clumsy, as though she were not used to moving hurriedly, as though panic had robbed her of her normal grace acquired two years before at finishing school. She caught up her long dress of yellow satin in one hand, but even so it kept getting in the way.

At any moment Count Ferdinand would be here. Those who had experienced his justice called him Ferdinand the Terrible. His victims could expect no mercy. He was famous throughout Valsarnia and beyond for his ruthlessness. Even the Emperor, that feeble and ill old man who had appointed him Regent until the young heir should come of age, was in awe of Ferdinand.

Maria moved back towards the uncurtained window, to watch for the lights of a car gliding up the long hill through the blackness of the forest. She wondered what she should do.

Her fingers closed over the treasures in her palm that she had snatched up from her dressing-table and brought downstairs with her. A small wrought-iron key, dangling from a slender silver chain, and a diamond ring. She unclenched her fingers and glanced at the ring. She remembered Sylvester's expression as he had put the hoop of glittering stones into her hand half an hour earlier.

– This was my mother's, he had murmured: and now I am giving it to you. Maria's heart had missed a beat, then started thumping. For a moment she thought he was about to ask her to marry him. But then she came back to reality. Sylvester was leader of the rebels. His life was vowed to serving the cause. He had often told her he could never marry. A wife was a luxury and would get in the way. He needed to be free, not to be tied down. To be able to depart at any moment, wherever the needs of the struggle sped him next. Moved by his selflessness, Maria had blushed and felt ashamed of the desires she dared not name. She had accepted the diamond ring and had promised to sell it for him as he wished and get the money to him via one of his comrades.

The circle of jewels on her open palm winked in the candlelight and the firelight. Somehow it seemed to be a symbol of strength. She breathed deeply, gathered herself to stillness, a semblance of calm, and took the only possible decision. She flung the silver chain over her head, dropping the small black key out of sight below the décolletage of her evening dress, and thrust the diamond ring into the pocket of her petticoat.

The long beams of two powerful headlights swept across the window. Tyres crunched over gravel. Car doors slammed. Men's voices rang out in the courtyard. The dogs barked. The bell clanged at the main entrance. Count Ferdinand the Terrible had arrived.

Maria clasped her hands together and turned resolutely to face the drawing-room door as though it were a firing-squad.

CHAPTER TWO: CHILDHOOD
Maria was an orphan. Her mother had died giving birth to her and her father had been too griefstruck to marry again,

....

preferring, instead, to dedicate himself to his beloved only child. She rarely saw him, because he threw himself into his work. He was a corset manufacturer who made his fortune when he patented his new invention and sold it to all the women of Valsarnia. The Revolutionary Bust and Stomach Stiffener, known to its devotees as the Squeasy, used thin ribs of steel to replace the strips of whalebone previously employed in ladies' foundation garments. The steel wands were inserted both horizontally and vertically, to provide a lattice of total control. Another distinctive feature of this flesh-hugging machine was that it was covered not with the usual pink linen or buckram but in canvas of the chastest and severest white. Maria's father died a happy man, on his daughter's eighteenth birthday, and left her a wardrobe full of corsets, a factory and a warehouse full of more corsets, and a corset business to run.

CHAPTER THREE: THE FUNERAL

Maria's father was buried in the regimental chapel of the great church in town. He had worshipped there every week for all of his adult life. Sunday after Sunday, while the padre intoned his sermon and exhorted his congregation to become soldiers of God, Maria's father had gazed dreamily at the regimental banners hung along the nave, the marble monuments to valiant generals slain on the parade grounds in time of violence and upheaval, the crossed swords and bayonets that decorated the columns, and the tall stained-glass windows behind the high altar that depicted the heroic knights of the holy tradition: St Michael the Archangel, the devil-slayer, St George, the dragon-slayer, and the patron saint of Valsarnia, St Victor, the serpent-slayer. Completely covered from head to toe in heavy silvery armour they raised their mailed fists and waved their huge spears aloft. Under their spurred and booted feet they trampled the writhing and wriggling symbols of evil, the wily and scaly snake-monsters with lascivious faces. The saints' helmets

....

were wreathed with the lilies of purity. Their visors were pulled down.

It was here, one drowsy Sunday morning, that Maria's father had received the first glimmerings of his great idea. He went home for Sunday lunch, his imagination filled with images of stern goodness encased in armour-plating, and gave his daughter his customary Sunday kiss. She wriggled and squirmed, laughing, in his arms. Her softness filled him with unease, with a kind of distaste. The idea of the Revolutionary Bust and Stomach Stiffener was born.

Now the sable-draped coffin stood on a bier surrounded by tall candles. The regimental choir sang the martial hymns Maria's father had so loved. The old padre spoke of the battle of the soul, of the valour and cleanness and uprightness of the true knight of God. The mourners, mainly old soldiers, stared at Maria, so young and so beautiful, her face peeping out of her black fur-lined hood, her hands hidden in her black fur muff, her little feet encased in high-heeled black ankle boots.

Leaving the churchyard, Maria dropped a long black suede glove. Her tightly laced corset did not allow her to bend and pick it up. Sylvester, who had been lounging elegantly under the yew trees at the gate, on the lookout for possible recruits to the cause, picked up the glove, kissed it and returned it to her. Thus they became acquainted.

– How shall I ever live up to my father's memory? Maria asked Sylvester in desperation one day soon afterwards: when I feel so weak and powerless and alone?

Sylvester replied: you can support those fighting for a just cause, for an end to tyranny, for the overthrow of despotism!

Maria was fired up in a moment by his valour. She was converted rapidly to the rebels' cause. Sylvester swore her to secrecy, and they pricked their thumbs and mixed their blood as a symbol of their pact. The Confederates, as the band of revolutionaries was called, needed money, a safe haven. Maria delightedly supplied both, emptying her bank account and making her new friends free of her house. She

....

4

promised Sylvester, on pain of death, that she would never betray him and his comrades to the terrible Count Ferdinand, who was Commander-in-Chief of the army as well as Regent of the Kingdom, and who was known to throw his enemies into windowless underground cells for life, if, indeed, he did not simply have them beheaded in the city square. Maria was happy. Women could not, of course, be Confederates, but she was the next best thing. She was a Confederate's girlfriend. She was in love with Sylvester.

Her love made her so bold that she dared to offer him more than money, more than a hiding-place. She bent over him, one day, as he studied possible escape routes on the map spread out on the table in her dining-room, and murmured: take me, Sylvester! Take me!

Absorbed in his plans, he did not hear her whispered entreaty. She repeated her words more loudly. Sylvester sighed and looked up.

– Not now, darling, he reproached her: not just before the start of a campaign! I must save all my energies for the struggle!

He glanced at the clock on the mantelpiece.

– It's your turn to keep watch. Off you go.

Maria climbed the stairs to her room. She would have liked to have run, but her heavy steel-lined corset made free movement impossible. Blinking back her tears, she stood on guard by the casement, upright as one of the Imperial sentries, vigilant as one of the saintly knights in silvery armour depicted on the stained-glass windows of the regimental chapel. She peered through the uncurtained pane into the gathering dusk. Nothing stirred.

The telephone rang. Maria walked across to her little writing-table and picked up the receiver.

It was a woman's voice that spoke, deep and contralto.

– Tell Sylvester to fly. Count Ferdinand has been tipped off as to his whereabouts and is moving in through the forest. He is bound to search your house. Tell Sylvester to

....

hurry. Tell him I shall be waiting for him on the seashore, with the boat.

The voice was urgent, harsh. The woman rang off abruptly. Maria put the phone down. Then she picked it up again. The line had gone dead.

Maria opened her bedroom door with trembling hands. She clutched the banister of the staircase to steady herself. She had not expected discovery so soon. Something had gone wrong. Danger was very close. Count Ferdinand, she was certain, from what the voice on the phone had said, had been alerted to her part in the plot. She shuddered at the thought of him entering her house and questioning her. But if only she could get Sylvester away to safety, she knew that she could brave anything for his sake. She lifted her chin and walked downstairs very slowly, unable to hurry because of the tight lacing of her steel-lined stays.

In the green and gold drawing-room she told Sylvester about the phone message and showed him the entrance, hidden behind a panel of the wainscoting, to the secret passage which led out into the cave in the forest. A woodcutter, who was an ally of the Confederates, lived nearby, and would be on the ready for anyone issuing from the cave and giving the password. The password was Sylvester's code name: Far-Off.

Sylvester pressed his mother's diamond ring into Maria's hands, urging her to sell it for as much as possible and to send the money on to him via the woodcutter. Carla would do the rest.

– That wonderful Carla, he exclaimed: she's never let me down yet.

– Who's Carla? Maria asked.

But there was no time to waste in idle chatter. There was no time for tearful farewells, for fond embraces. Sylvester dived into the secret passage, and Maria locked the door after him and closed the concealing panel. She carried the key and the diamond ring out of the room with her, biting her lip.

....

She went slowly back up the stairs. The main thing was to stand firm, to keep the faith. She must fight the good fight, act normally, and pretend to be greatly surprised that anyone should accuse her of being mixed up in revolutionary politics.

First of all, therefore, she decided to change into evening dress, as she usually did at dinner-time. Her father had always liked her to dress for dinner and she had not yet broken herself of the habit. Besides, she had so many evening frocks it was a pity not to wear them. Accordingly, she rang for her maid and asked her to unlace her corset, which did up at the back with a steel string and fifty little steel hooks.

The maid struggled and panted. At last the steel cage was off. It fell, clanging, on to the floor. Maria's flesh leapt out.

She bathed hurriedly. Then it was time to put the corset back on. Now Maria's unflinching loyalty to her father suddenly wavered. She foresaw an evening of possible physical activity, in which she might be required to run up and down stairs several times, sending semaphore messages from windows or checking the telephone in her bedroom, or leading Count Ferdinand on a wild-goose chase away from the door to the secret passage. She would need to be able to move fast, as Sylvester did. Therefore she would not be able to wear her corset.

She bent her head in anguish.

– Forgive me, Father! she cried.

She threw the corset into the corner of the room. It seemed to her that all the warrior saints in the regimental chapel hung their heads in shame. She had abandoned their high ideals. She had betrayed their beautiful code of chivalry.

– Forgive me, Father! she moaned again.

Then she selected her favourite evening dress from the wardrobe and slipped it on. It buttoned up at the front, the little cloth-covered buttons concealed under a fold of material. Rather than steel cutting into her through canvas,

....

she now had the delicious sensation of thick, rich satin next to her skin, flowing over her soft flesh as smooth and cool as milk. She lifted the yellow folds in her hands and stroked them. Her petticoat was the merest wisp of gossamer swishing against her thighs. She put on her best amber and pearl tiara, hooked topaz rings into her ears, clasped on a few gold bracelets, picked up the diamond ring and the key from her dressing-table, and stepped into her gold evening slippers.

Then she ran downstairs.

It was such a marvellous experience that she ran back up and then ran down again. And then up again and then down again.

Then she stood in the drawing-room, her bosom heaving. She was panting and flushed. Her eyes sparkled with the unwonted exercise. Her mind raced. She was frightened for Sylvester, and determined to save him from the clutches of Count Ferdinand, but she was also preoccupied and puzzled by the mysterious woman's voice on the telephone. Who could she be? Did Sylvester have *two* benefactresses? Maria clasped her hands together in anguish. But it was too late for thoughts of jealousy. Ferdinand was in her house. Any moment he would be in the room, confronting her. She had the key and the diamond ring safely hidden on her person. All she had to do now was play her part. Stall him as long as possible. Give Sylvester time to get away.

Standing as erect as possible on the soft carpet of her drawing-room, listening to the firm, determined tread of the man ascending the stairs outside, she felt her cheeks flame and her mind whirl with images. The diamond ring and the key hidden inside her dress ... Sylvester creeping out of the secret tunnel into the cave ... her father's coffin draped in black ... the warrior saints with their stern mouths ... the woodcutter waiting in the dark forest outside the entrance to the cave.

She lifted her chin and trembled with fear. The door swung open and he strode in.

....

So *this*, Maria thought: was Count Ferdinand the Terrible.

CHAPTER FOUR: FERDINAND THE TERRIBLE

Authority emanated from him like a physical force. Maria knew she must not respond, must not give way. Yet her body suddenly felt pliant, as though simply by entering the room he had overpowered her. She forced herself to look at him steadily.

He was a tall, commanding figure dressed in the uniform of his élite crack corps of horsemen, the Dark Riders. He wore a black tunic, black breeches, and highly polished black riding boots. A long black cloak swept back over one shoulder and was fastened at the front with gold clasps in the form of lions. Gold braid edged his epaulettes and cuffs. A single gold stud shone on his high black collar. He carried a black cap, with a gold plume, in one hand.

His dark face, with its deepset black eyes and ironic mouth under a thin line of black moustache, was stern. He bowed to her and clicked his heels, and she felt sure he was mocking her.

– You know what I've come for, he said: Far-Off Sylvester. Where is he?

Maria gasped. If indeed he knew Sylvester's secret code name, the game was certainly up. She could hear the tramp of feet all over the house, as the Dark Riders searched high and low for the leader of the rebels. Play for time, she thought. This was not difficult. She found that she could not speak, so transfixed was she by terror.

She was face to face, after so long, with the most feared man in the kingdom, he who was spoken of only in whispers, he who had the ear of the dying Emperor and was acting Regent until the Emperor's young son should be of age to rule. Folk said that Ferdinand would never give up his power. Under cover of crushing the rebellion led by Sylvester, he would establish his dominion ever more firmly and force the rightful heir to give up all claim to the throne.

....

Looking at Ferdinand's haughty face, Maria could well believe it. Her voice, when at last she found it, was hoarse.

– Go away, Count. You are mistaken in your suspicions. I know nothing of anyone called Sylvester.

Ferdinand smiled at her grimly.

– You are a brave woman, but also a foolish one. We followed Sylvester all the way to your house, we saw him come in, and we know from your housekeeper, who opened the door to us just now, that there is a secret passage leading out of your drawing-room, to whose door you alone have the key. Your housekeeper, I fear, is not above a bribe.

He showed his teeth in a sardonic smile as he watched Maria turn white.

– Don't lie to me, he said: and don't try to play games with me. Else I shall be provoked into playing them with you.

Maria's armpits were wet with sweat. She forced herself to look straight back at him.

– What kind of games, Count?

The dark eyes, with something unfathomable as well as ironic in their depths, were fixed on hers. He put down his leather riding gloves, his whip, and his plumed cap on the side table against the wall by the door, and advanced towards her where she stood in the centre of the room. His movements were swift and decided. He had the bearing and gestures of a man habituated to command. His face was hard, but the mobile mouth relaxed as he looked at her.

Maria flinched as he approached, but she held her ground. She shivered suddenly, wishing she had thrown a stole over her arms and breast, for she was naked above the low-cut gold satin frock except for a band of gold tulle that encircled her shoulders. Her full long skirt swung out in a soft bell. She plunged her hands through the invisible slits cut in the sides of her gown, into the pockets of her petticoat. Her left hand touched the diamond ring hidden there. She looked at Ferdinand as haughtily as possible. Now that he was so close to her she could see the softness of his black eyelashes, of

....

his close-cropped black hair. She could see that his thin, fine face was a little careworn. His features were clear-cut. His mouth looked as though it could be cruel.

CHAPTER FIVE: A GAME OF HIDE AND SEEK

Ferdinand moved forward again. Maria's right hand flew out of her pocket and leapt to the silver chain which showed its glint at her neck and fell into the bosom of her gown. She took a step backwards. Ferdinand followed.

– Just give me the key to the door of the secret passage, he said: there's no need to be afraid of me. I shan't hurt you.

– I'm not afraid of you, Maria said, hating her trembling voice: even though your behaviour is outrageous, forcing your way in here like this.

His lips twisted.

– That is something, at least. I'm glad you are not afraid of me. As for forcing my way in, I am on the Emperor's business and I have the Emperor's signature on a search warrant to go through your house until I find the traitor Sylvester whom you are hiding. I should warn you that unless you cooperate with me I shall have you searched too. Now give me that key.

He reached out and put his hands on her arms. She jerked with shock. Her eyes flew to his. He moved his hands slowly and deliberately up her bare forearms, over her elbows, to her shoulders, grasping the swathe of gold tulle that encircled them. She kept very still under his touch. She felt the warmth of the contact, ten little points of fire burning through the tulle, two patches of fire that were his palms. He gripped her shoulders harder. His face was close to hers. The dark, intent face of a stranger who was treating her as though he knew her intimately, who had dared to take her by the arms and slide his hands slowly up to her shoulders in a threatening caress.

His voice was quiet.

– I know where you have hidden the key. Your gestures

....

have told me. Your body's too honest to lie. If you won't give it to me freely, of your own accord, I shall have to take it. Do you understand?

A wave of fear mixed with excitement rushed over her. She felt her face washed by blushes of red. She managed to speak.

– I don't know what you mean. I haven't got the key.

He shrugged. His hands moved to the front of her dress. He studied the concealing fold of satin that covered the bodice, then slid his fingers underneath it and found the little buttons. Taking his time, leisurely and deliberate in his movements, he began unbuttoning Maria's dress. One button slipped out of its buttonhole, then another. The top of the dress parted, began to gape open. Ferdinand's hands moved further down, closed around the third button, the fourth. They were little satin-covered knobs, of the same yellow as the dress. They opened easily; they fell under his thumb and slid out of their yellow holes. The dress was so designed that you could put it on and take it off yourself, quickly, without needing to call for someone to come and help you get in and out of it, to fasten and unfasten it at the back. Maria had chosen this dress precisely because it was not like a corset. To wear it she did not have to depend on anyone else.

Maria stood proud and still, with the air of an unwilling captive. Ferdinand was standing so close to her that she could see every line and flourish of the rampant gold lions engraved on the clasps of his black cloak. At the first touch of his fingers on her skin she had felt that she would faint. The shock of the touch brought with it a pleasure over which she had no control. His fingers went on making contact with her flesh. Cool and sure, they inserted themselves between cloth and her body. He was opening the panels of satin very slowly, letting the dress reveal her nakedness. The dress being unloosed, expertly parted inch by satin inch, allowed the warmth of the candles and the fire in the grate to move over her. She felt she glowed golden like them. Her heart

....

pounded. She could smell something hot and sweet, like the crushed petals of flowers.

The fingers working on the buttons, grazing her with caresses as they went, moving in and out between the dress and her skin, reached her waist at last. Maria breathed deeply. She shuddered as a wave of sweetness pushed through her. She tried to keep still but she was trembling. She needed to sit down.

Ferdinand paused. His face was faintly amused. Maria stared back at him. He lifted his hands and tugged at the two sides of the dress, pulling it off her shoulders so that it fell down around her waist, in crumpled gold satin folds.

She could not speak. He lifted the key, which was slung on the thin silver chain that dangled from round her neck to lie in the curved hollow between her breasts. The clasp of the chain had worked its way round to lie next to the key. Ferdinand lifted it away from her skin, using both hands, and opened it. He pulled the chain away from her neck, off her, and put chain and key into his breeches pocket.

CHAPTER SIX: THE HUNT GOES ON

Ferdinand lifted the fallen folds of the bodice of Maria's dress, pulled them up, covered her shoulders once more. He re-buttoned the yellow satin into place. He did it efficiently and swiftly, like a mother getting a child ready for school. Maria stood obediently in front of him. She ached and burned at each light, deft touch, as his fingers strayed across the slippery material covering her skin. Far too thin, the cloth, which clung then slid, as he made it move on her flesh and she could not stop herself from shuddering with pleasure.

She could not look at him. He fastened the top button. He took her hand and lifted it. She felt his lips touch it. She snatched it back as though he'd bitten her. His voice was gentle.

....

– Thank you. You made my task far less unpleasant than it might have been, and I am very grateful.

Maria watched him turn, go straight to the secret panel in the wainscoting, swing it open, unlock the door behind, and pull this open in turn. She thought: he knew where it was all along. How? And then she remembered the housekeeper, who had given in so easily to a bribe, and told all she knew.

– Sylvester is long gone, isn't he? Ferdinand said: he'll be at the other end by now, coming out into the cave. My men will be waiting for him there. We've got the woodcutter and we'll get Sylvester.

He frowned.

– Nevertheless, we'll search the tunnel. Just to make sure. And you and I will wait here, while the search is carried out.

He shouted, and two Dark Riders came running. They stooped, and entered the little door into the secret passage. It swallowed them up and they were gone.

Maria forced herself to raise her eyes and look at Ferdinand. His gaze was whimsical. He strolled back across the room and halted in front of her. Her lips buzzed and stung. Her knees felt weak and shook.

Ferdinand's tone was conversational and bland.

– And the diamond ring left to me by my mother that Sylvester stole from me? Where have you hidden that, may I ask? Are you going to tell me, or are you going to force me to look for that too?

Maria jumped. But before she could move a step his hands shot out and caught her. His breath was hot in her ear.

– Oh yes, Sylvester is my brother. Didn't you know? He wants to be Regent, and who can blame him? Unfortunately, it is I whom the Emperor has chosen, being the elder, to guard the interests of his heir, and see that he comes into his kingdom when the time arrives.

– You're lying, Maria panted: I don't believe you.

....

14

Struggling to get away, she caught her high-heeled shoe in a fold of her dress and tripped. He pulled her further off balance, so that she toppled into his arms, which closed around her and held her up. Once more his hands pushed her dress off her shoulders, but this time roughly. Holding her in a vice-like grip with one arm, he caressed her neck and shoulders, tugging down the swathe of tulle, while she tried uselessly to fight him and he laughed. His caresses were tender as silk. His hand ripped open the front of her dress, no wasting time on buttons, and stroked her breast, pinching the nipple gently until a moan escaped from Maria's lips. Then he pushed Maria's chin up, forcing her mouth against his, making her lips yield and open. She shook against him. Her insides churned. She tore her mouth away from his.

– No, she whispered: no, I haven't got the diamond ring. I don't know what you're talking about.

He lifted his head and looked at her. His eyes glittered, black and sardonic. His voice was harsh.

– Let us stop fencing. You have fought well but your fight is over. Sylvester was captured in the forest by my men, before I entered this house. We've got Carla too.

He paused. Maria was shivering. The very air between them seemed to quiver with menace. She felt dazed. Perhaps, she thought confusedly, this was what hunted animals experienced when cornered, face to face with the huntsman at last. The game was up.

He tightened his grip on her. She disdained to struggle and to give him the pleasure of knowing how easily he could overpower her. She lowered her eyes and bit her lip.

Ferdinand was regarding her grimly.

– I'm afraid your friends are less faithful than you, he said: the woodcutter betrayed you, just as your housekeeper did, and just as Sylvester did. Once he realized he was fairly caught he did not scruple to give me the the name I wanted. Offered the choice between life imprisonment and exile, Far-Off chose exile. And as part of the bargain he named

....

his second most important accomplice after Carla. You. You've supplied him with money and sanctuary, but all this time, I'm afraid, he's been using you. He has abandoned you without a care for your safety.

Maria heard these words in silence. It was the end. It was all over. Sometime, the shock and numbness would wear off and she would feel ... what? Sylvester had not been loyal to her. She had merely been his tool. He had cast her aside in order to save his own skin. Later on she would find out what she felt. At the moment she was aware only of being held in Ferdinand's powerful embrace, of his dark face close to hers.

She had the oddest sense that she had known all along that Sylvester was not to be trusted. That woman on the telephone. Carla. Of course, she must have been his lover all the time.

– But he's your brother, she exclaimed faintly: how can you send him into exile?

– Better exile than life imprisonment or death, Ferdinand said: just as it was better to capture him in the forest than here, and so implicate you. I wished to spare you.

– Why should you be generous to me? she whispered: when I have fought and resisted you at every turn, when I believed all the lies Sylvester told me about you?

His mocking smile was back.

– Perhaps because I wish to get back the diamond ring and keep it for myself, before I decide whom to give it to.

He moved rapidly, without warning. Still gripping her, he bent forwards and sideways. His hand picked up her skirts in bunched folds, plunged beneath them. Startled, Maria cried out. She felt his mouth gently bite her earlobe, before his voice spoke hotly into her ear.

– You've got it in a pocket somewhere. And I'm going to search you until I find it.

His hand scooped up layers of dress and petticoat, inserted itself between dress and skin. Maria twisted in his grip, her legs pressed tightly together, then forced apart by

....

his fingers which relentlessly explored between her knees and up, further up, while he supported her with one arm around her back, making her lean away from him while his hand dived repeatedly into her skirts, and she clutched and thrust at him and cried out, ohhhh, as he parted the lips of her pocket and was in, there, home, holding and stroking her diamond ring gently, repeatedly, endlessly, firmly, while she clenched her teeth trying not to cry out again but not able to stop herself: ohhhh. Life was certainly dangerous when you did not wear a corset. You were certainly not safe. You were not in control. *Anything* might happen.

CHAPTER SEVEN: THE KEY

The game was loosely based on the plot of *The Black Riders* by Violet Needham, which Maria had got out of the local children's library. She made up her own version of the story, which she preferred to the one in the book. She felt that hers was more true, that it contained all the bits underneath and in between, which Violet Needham did not spell out because she was writing for children, after all, who were not supposed to imagine such things.

Sometimes Maria played the heroine's role, and sometimes her cousin Nanda did. Whoever was the man had to be both Sylvester and Ferdinand, one after the other, and it did require a certain acting ability, to be capable of becoming both the perfidious villain and the dashing hero, and indeed to convey which was which. Maria was better at playing the man than Nanda was, but on the other hand she loved being the woman, and feeling all that delicious fear. Sometimes she thought it would be easier if she acted all by herself and played both parts, and lying in bed at night she could do this. But there was no denying the pleasure to be gained from doing it with someone else, especially someone like Nanda whom Maria could order around and who did what she was told, cracking her whip and stroking her moustache before ripping open Maria's dress.

They were ten at the time, and took their games seriously.

....

17

They rehearsed over and over, even though nobody would ever see the performance but themselves. The rehearsals were the best part, especially at the end, because they never let themselves get there. They went over and over it, the moment when Ferdinand caresses Maria so powerfully, and they knew that was the best moment, the one just before the end, when you can imagine the moment will never cease, that this exquisite painful explosive need will go on rising up and up like a rocket, they will never become bored with each other or experience sexual disappointment or wander off, they will remain in that state of heightened tension desiring each other madly with all their future ahead of them, a moment that doesn't have to end, a game that never has to be over because it can be repeated for ever. The game would always be there, and this present tense. It could be repeatedly rerun, like the cine film of their childhood. Maria was a child pornographer; shamelessly she corrupted her cousin Nanda and got her to join in. The game resurfaced regularly in Maria's memory at times of crisis in her adult life. Aged fifty-five and feeling restless and dissatisfied, she could look back and know what she missed.

Sampler

·······································

STEVE AYLETT

'Snake does not bite man; snake bites what man thinks'
— Vinson Brown

'You're all brain and headlights, Eddie. Your every move shows you're in love with your coat.'

'So?'

'So you look like a student — stagger outta here talking shit no one'll slam an eyelid, it's perfect. They'll think you're quoting Baudrillard — the tedium is the message.'

This from a bastard with hair like aerosol cheese. Head like a fire axe. Gob like a stick-on trick. One-way staring eyes. Transfixed by dogma, you'd assume. But here in the university basement Kramer had pushed beyond the theoretical and was testing weird shit on kids too poor to have a centre of gravity. The black hole of the philosophy department had swallowed a friend of mine. Now it ran around the night-time boiler room checking light levels and adjusting dials on what looked like an iron lung.

'This the isolation tank?'

'Think of it as a particle-accelerator — I ain't got all year to wait for you to come up. Just for the kick-off. You'll be testing a new drug every night, Eddie. Some roll-over with the halflives but I can adjust for it in the results, don't you worry.'

'Jo told you I'm not much of a user.'

'We're all users, Eddie,' laughed Kramer, checking the angle on one of the camcorders. 'You know the Victorian explorer James Lee discovered Malay 2 in the jungles of

·········

19

Sumatra – called it the Elixir of Life. Seeds out of a pod plant, boiled up. Said the stuff nixed the effect of any drug in your system, got you straight in a half-hour. Today we're so out of whack with chemicals inherent to modern life, if we dropped Malay 2 we'd get our first taste of what it is to be human.'

'Got a lot?'

'Nobody'll back a hunt for it, Eddie – too much money in the false war. Never came across any and I've got some fierce stuff, believe me.' He grinned, slotting a cassette into a recorder. 'American mainly. Them analogue laws have fired the imagination of bathtub chemists coast to coast – theoretical highs, illegal before they exist and a regular challenge.' He knelt and detached a grating from the wall, reached into the vent and dragged out a Samsonite case. 'A substance like speed taken like grass, or stuff like ayahuasca but with no detectable indole and a snack-time halflife. Really something to shoot for, isn't it?'

'I guess.'

He hefted the case on to a table and flipped the catch. 'You guess.' His laughter ricocheted round the basement like a bullet in a limo. 'I like that. Jo said you were a clown.'

'Where is Jo? Haven't seen her for a bit.'

'Around. We get started?' He took out a ghostlike baggy.

I had to remember Jo and that this was my amateur stab at a private investigation. I was hoping for a handle on the coming ordeal. Maybe I could forgo the tolling spars and booming refineries of hell and scare up a rosier revelation. But I was scared to pieces already. In Kramer's palm lay a weird seed. 'What's that and what's it doing here?'

'A kind of sea onion.'

'So small?'

'Only one layer, my friend. Fifth from the middle.'

'So specific?'

'Bet your life.'

'And the second half of the question?'

'Nothing. Until eaten by you, sunshine. Then you'll take

....

20

a square look at your wounded life and tong out the bullet. It's a tryptamine indole like psilocybin. Compound eye of the soul. You know your *Flatland*? Nicked from Hinton? Just as a spherical object intersecting a 2-D plane appears out of nowhere as a morphing 2-D circle, the intersecting of a 4-D hypersphere into our 3-D continuum appears as a morphing 3-D lens-form, like a flying saucer.'

'Or an old hat.'

'I know, Eddie,' Kramer laughed. 'But I'm paying you to listen to this, right? And keep mum about our proceedings here – walls have ears. Or they will if you take enough of these. Chugalug.'

I necked the stuff and washed it down.

'You're doing fine, Eddie,' Kramer said as I stripped and climbed into the sensory deprivation tank. I lay back and was floating in salt-dense water, feedback wires taped to my head. 'I like to think of an experiment as a mound of dough booted off a high cliff, Eddie – it tends to develop a shape and momentum of its own. That's the real joy of it, see?' And he slammed the hatch.

TRAD

I was hanging weightless in the pitch dark, Kramer's gear climbing the tree of my nervous system. Sensory input reduced to near-zero. No colour, no sound worth a damn. Nothing happening. The eighties all over.

Sudden, massive anxiety. I'd been tricked. This thing was a time machine. This was 1983, I was sure of it. Sterility. Nothing. Didn't anyone see how boring this was?

I breathed deep – gusts filled the universe as I tried to reason calmly. Dead phases in history always had an end. Once even the dimmest of my generation realized we were growing in a vacuum, the logical course would be to fill it out ourselves. So at the decade's end there'd be a bleed of colour composed of drugs, music and a weak stab at creativity.

Until then I'd just have to sit it out. Again.

....

Where did I get the idea the process would be accelerated? Rhomboids were turning in space – prisms dilating and shrinking as they thundered past in a wake of displaced molecules. The pinpoint pupils of a thousand stars stretched into lines of acceleration. Drawing slowly near was a massive rumbling something, an irony-intricate convolution, roiling endlessly into its centre. I shot into the paunch of a cloud and a gush of cellular fluorescence unveiled the heart of the thing – nodular beings darting back and forth across a havoc lattice. It was like finding a microchip in an oyster. Enamel things like fridge magnets sped around a schematic warren of supercharged synthetic.

I was on the surface with them, meeting one. I could only assume its face was the first of its kind. It was like a badly moulded trophy. Other marionettes barrelled over like rolling trashcans. There was nothing lifelike about them at all. I addressed them with all the calm of a cornered chef. 'You're scaring the shit out of me and you bloody know it!'

Here my meaning was translated into a visual datacloud which bulbed in space between us. My meaning was so basic and unrefined, however, that the datacloud consisted merely of my own head, screaming in terror. In reply, one enamel goblin manipulated this image, tugging at the head's jaw. Its action translated as: 'If both skull *and* teeth are made of bone, why bother with gums?'

'There's a reason.'

'Which is?'

'I *know* there's a reason.'

'Do insects bruise?'

I was hemmed in by grinning, rampaging technical trolls, a robotic wrecking-crew cracking up and reconfiguring with laughter. My head image was grasped, skin torn off like a hood – haywire quills riddled at last the neglected hemispheres of my brain. Mayhem by the numbers. Fierce carnivalia in a hectic paradise of blinding headaches and derision. They held aloft an alien relic of intensified experience. Its title was *Don't Take Your Eyelids So Seriously,*

....

Billy Jean and I was made to understand this was the 'Book of Life'.

'It *can't* be,' I said, resisting with every burnt fibre. 'Don't. Be. So. *Stupid*, man!'

Under the clanging stars they stood stock still to show me clearly that they were wearing check trousers and implicit in this act was the command that I should do the same and thus bear witness to the sacred dimensions. When I held fast they created a thoughtshape which made known that if I refused I would be placed inside a Charlie Chaplin movie and the resulting depression would mean the end of me. And as if to illustrate, the universe banged into a fixed, flat, black-and-white square in which a figure hung – Chaplin, surely, doing some dismal stunt and expecting adulation. 'OK, Eddie? You been screaming to beat the band in there.'

My hands shot up at Kramer's throat and he pulled back, hauling me out of the isolation tank. As he wrestled free and staggered, I saw the drug was still on line – the walls were like paper screens, the entire building a semi-transparent 3-D schematic. 'Whoa!' Kramer gasped. 'Jo said you had a temper.' From his mouth bulbed the ectoplasmic thoughtshape and it was Jo herself, saying: 'Kramer lies. A bastard like that'll go tilling through your innards with a hook to find something amusing.'

As Kramer moved I saw the fourth-dimensional part of the man receding from him like the ganglion behind an eye. This was the varicose root of his intentions and I glimpsed the shit-and-poison ugliness of it an instant before the drug cut out.

Back at the flat, I felt like the bug that awakes to find it's turned into a clerk. Sick, the clock snipping away at me. Lie in the dark till there's no hard feelings. Except I wasn't allowed that kind of time.

GRAIL

'Religion is the opium of the people, Eddie,' Kramer smiled, dumping grey powder into a blender and replacing the lid.

....

'And it's cheaper.' He flipped the switch and the contents blurred.

'What's this?'

'Ecclesiastical pharmacology. Pounded holy relic. Dried and sifted saint. Either it works or the Bible's shit, my friend.'

'The ashes of people?'

'Are dangerous to your health when prepared correctly. But don't worry your sticky little head about that. Skulked from a ransacked tomb with these dry beauties. Seb and Wolfgang in there. As a bridge I've buffered in 10,000 mg of piracetam and the pestle powder from these.' He held up what looked like a couple of chalk stubs.

'What are they?'

'The horns of an otherwise useless giraffe. Weird, eh?' But his voice indicated that he didn't think it weird at all.

I swallowed the mixture – it tasted like rust or herbal tea. 'How much active ingredient?'

'What I term a "recognition of the problem".'

'Which is?'

'A thousandth of a per cent of the solution.'

In the tank, watching the cohering shapes of the trip waft through the darkness. A panoramic glide over life's accidental parameters, heart fluttering in the updrafts. There was something in the stale stuff after all. A continent taking form.

A one-note recurrent heaven receded like astroturf. I'd thought it would broil and change but this was chronic. Statue people were fixed in it as though in quick-dry cement. Stuck out of the jigsaw edges were antique moralities, their justifications severed and flapping. Denizens merely glanced as if I were part of the landscape, an overhang of mild effrontery.

The weirdly cruise-controlled tour continued – all that had been denied in heaven was hoving into view. Convolute slang channels emptied into deep ocean. Suspicion was sumptuously tiding and receding. Polychrome components

....

drifted like dead sea-fruits. Molecules of invention flurried in jubilance, the air candied with unbound personality. The sea became a waterfall which tumbled and thundered relentlessly upon an infinite bruise – the soft fontanelle of god's mistakes. I added myself at once to its efforts, hurling downward – and like Alice descending the well I noticed diverting strata in the walls I was passing. Here was all the righteous indignation denied the devout, the romping rebellion repressed by the humble, the gene memory of sarcasm. Imagine the message I could take back with me. Four million years of concentrated scorn locked in the DNA of contemporary man. The fossil record alone must be stacked with tableaux of piss-taking neanderthals. Ancient put-downs long since forgotten. Think what we could learn from the coelacanth. I heard reverberations from the inner sanctum of hilarity. If this didn't constitute enlightenment I couldn't imagine what would.

It was like waking up before you hit the ground – I was about to plunge through god's skylight skull when the trip cut out. Tearing urgently at the feedback leads, I clambered out of the tank.

The room was all turbulent fiery red – Kramer was ponced up, transformed. Hooves like cloth irons, a black coat, a nose full of teeth, fluorescent eyes and a tangle of horns from here to the ceiling. This guy thought he was some kind of reindeer.

'Hat-rack antlers, eh?' I boomed, beefed up and pounding with heroic energy. 'The universe proceeds from my nostrils.'

Religion did two more things for me – it allowed me to rig up a satire-activated psychic snare anchored to Kramer's chakra points and, in blurring the boundary between fact and fiction, allowed me to believe satire could have an effect in the world. After what seemed like hours of eloquence, in which I scorched home the notion that he didn't know where his soul ended and his tailoring began, Kramer simply responded, 'You've a lot to learn Eddie – the stitches aren't out on your childhood.'

....

25

And he played back the video of my repartee, in which I merely sat like a furless rat, eyes hooded, whispering the word 'vengeance' in every language and dialect ever known to humanity.

GUTTER

I felt as dead as an airplant and the secret agenda I'd been guarding escaped me. Had someone I knew had an accident? 'You're deep enough in. We don't need the tank any more, Eddie. Lie on the stretcher here and I'll hook up the EEG.'

I lay staring at the basement ceiling.

'See this bug, Eddie? Nanotech – a thousand micromachines embedded in a silicon substrate. We're talking media memes, my friend, programme-specific neural adjusters in a chitin-coated intramuscular pill, or tabloid. Acts like a parasite forcing you to feed the disease. Hatches the royal eggs of hypocrisy in your skullcase. Renders conversation a grotesque carnival of rear-lit generalities, just the way you like it.'

'Have I taken it yet?'

'Has he taken it yet – I like that. Let's say you have and the next one's on me, eh?'

'How many can I take without risk?'

'None. But I'll give you some free advice if you have a bad time and live.'

'It's a deal.'

He put a carpenter's rivet gun to my arm and banged the trigger. 'Make a fist, Eddie.'

For a while I listened to the brain damage circling its place, the windblown public telephone of my chattering teeth. Black static was blizzarding, volatile and irrelevant. Then I was sideswiped into a commotion of whirlwind supposition and lazy equivalence, trying to get a fix on stability in a vortex of perpetually recoiling space. I found myself hungering for the wooden stone at the heart of the peach, a truth which didn't change from one moment to the next.

....

Then I was rawboned in emptiness, slowly formulating screams in the vacuum. Grey erosion under a gutless sky. Sat around me were dry dupes wired securely into a power-house of contradictions. The expedient distortions of the local bifocal morality made it near impossible to concentrate on a single object, but I homed in on one guy bound and gagged between binary apprehensions, receiving regular shocks in which he could only concur. I was embalmed in the man, seeing through his eyes, and before him a grey screen was flashing TAX SHOCK – BABY SHOCK – WAR SHOCK – ROYAL SHOCK and so on every few seconds. And though he reacted to each with a clench and moan, it was muscle deep. He didn't know he was only pretending.

I craned my neck up at an endless hierarchy of bullshit, gargoyled and stratified, runnelling with toxins. Sentient junk flowed around me like poison. Armed with nothing stronger than my innocence, I was filled to the marrow. Here knowledge was a hot potato passed on rather than downed and digested. An argument as thin as a mouse's belly skin was unassailable. Anyone who grew his own mind was diminished, voiceless and futile under lofty neglect, incinerative condescension and the derisive intimacy claimed by government, which I now perceived as an arti-ficially low, spike-frame ceiling an inch above us. Thinking here was like eating plastic and I was still trapped inside this guy and his concrete coffin suit.

Then a real shock went through me – I'd rolled off the stretcher on to the floor. The basement was blear, flat, doomed. I saw a beef skeleton walking through it. Kramer put a thermometer in my eye and measured my screams. 'Like your style, Eddie,' he said, then held up an inkblot card. 'What do you say this is?'

'A mirror?'

'Any feelings of paranoia?'

'Why? Who sent you? Are you recording this?'

'You know I am.'

....

'Don't stare at me,' I breathed in gusts of demented outrage. 'Don't *ever* look at me!'

'I'll sit over here, Eddie.'

Like that of a frog his face was fixedly sarcastic and masked whatever scheming transpired there. One minute you're thinking it's the cutest frog you ever saw, the next it's bitten your cheek and pulled you head first into the blood-foaming swamp. 'And no one to help you,' I announced in the smudgy video playback the following night, my image twitching like a NASA monkey. 'Just the screaming and the hollering and the burning knowledge that you could and should have avoided the entire situation. Meanwhile the Germans have sucked your underpants out the back of the dryer and created a clone out of your DNA, a clone which commits crimes for which the police put out a warrant for *your* arrest, while the underpants are fired into orbit from a circus cannon.'

Kramer watched without comment, his ghoulish equilibrium worse than any put-down.

'That's right!' shouted the madman on the screen, neck-cords straining with assertion. 'The insidious theme-parking of the drugscape in this nation is only a part of it! Expanding – yeah, right! The universe is made of erectile tissue and we're *headed* for the big bang, baby! We're going *nova*, baby!'

Kramer paused the machine mid-rant, my face a blurred gnash. 'Good work, Eddie – rope *that* off and charge admission, eh? Just a second now and I'll get tonight's drop.'

I watched him open a plastic ice-box, trying to keep the hunger and fascination from my face. The room was fizzing with psychostatic and the spinal joys of persecution mania. I noticed an EEG printout was still in the machine from the previous night, and took a look – instead of the scratched bandwidth of fluctuating brainwaves it bore a headline: DOPE TRIALS DEATH SHOCK. Reading that stuff could rot your brain. When I looked again, the sheet was blank and Kramer was calling me over.

'A mind's the most controlled substance there is, Eddie.'
He'd lifted a melon-sized something from the ice-box, its
detail blurred in cellophane.

SMALL GREYS

'We all know about Roswell 1947 and the little grey space
guys, but what the average joe doesn't suspect is that alien
neurochemistry is biocompatible with our own and, when
properly preserved, can be eaten like pistachio ice-cream.'

'Why all the talk, Kramer? Just gimme the stuff.'

'No, really – it was a tradition among the ancients that
the strength and wisdom of their fathers could be ingested
through cannibalism of the brain and other organs, and
studies of treated neuroplasm have provided confirmation.
Take a look at this beauty.' He had finished stripping away
the wrapping and on the table between us was a severed
grey domer with pursed lips, flick-knife ears and the dead
eyes of a shark. He used a cranial ridge as a slimline handle
to lift away the skullcap like a casserole lid. 'Forty-seven's
a top vintage, Eddie – tuck in.'

It tasted like pasta, or worse. Already sensing its slow but
fierce insinuation into myself, I spooned the lubricious grey
matter and watched the dead head. The room was blotting,
holes opening in the air. Bits of wall and the grinning
Kramer were dropping out like jigsaw pieces, a brittle façade
beyond which cascading protozoan and microbial life
bloomed into lagoons under an aching blue sky.

Field conditions here were so aggressively lethargic I
immediately surrendered, stretching an eyelid between two
angels to use as a hammock. Oases beclustered with sex
spores, trance lakes of slow automatic fish, heady heated
asphalt, fluttering octane clouds, ramparts, noon-blue apples,
gusts of thick air swirling with chemical particulates of
know-it-all elixir, each watery narcotic drench leaving me
as happy as a dog in a sidecar. Contracting red rubrics
cruised over, clicking into place on a reef of beautiform
coral. All framed by curlicues of languid abraxia. It was so

....

graphic, this nonstop everyplace, I forgot what I was waiting for, who I was meant to be. This went on for years, what with one thing and another.

Finally, when I was admiring a sundial in some pillared cloud temple, its triangular hand became the fin of an approaching hammerhead. The fin sliced the landscape like a knife through a movie screen, exposing a darkness I could never have imagined. I wandered through to explore this gloom and gradually recalled that this was Earth, the basement, Kramer. Determined to remember what I'd learnt in paradise I scrawled revelations with the urgency of a novice. The next day I awoke with a rubber forehead and the following distilled gospel:

1. Armadillos are simply dogs in chainmail.
2. Never roast a farmer. If you think they complain under normal circumstances, you don't know the half of it.
3. When a man drops his wife's dish, the universe opens for a moment like a lion's jaws.
4. Underwater, punch force is reduced.
5. Each sneeze frees a hundred lawyers.
6. At every action ask yourself, 'Why feel ineffectual when my very frustration advances the world cause?'
7. One thing is sure to hasten celebration – the death of a waiter.
8. Always remember the cat when shoving a bastard off balance.
9. At day's end, surrender gracefully your trousers.
10. My belch will shake down your monuments.

It was like a new age solve-all by some LA cadet who never worked a day in her life. Except that these were rules you could live by.

Well pleased, I tilted across a flat which was breeding meaning in corners. Stand-alone peptides drooled down the walls. In the bathroom, my reflection looked back at me as though from the belly of a wicker man. A bony scaffold and hubcap pupils were surmounted by a halo of resentment. It was Jo's look. She'd sit in a chair, shop-dummy white,

....

breathing through her bruise of a mouth, drugs echoing in the universe of her blood. At night she'd go out again – and come back worse. Then she didn't come back.

How long since I started in with Kramer? Four days? A year? Had he even paid me? What had I got? Nothing but the shabby notoriety of having stuck my oar into an adjacent dimension.

But I needed it. My soul was shrinking, depleted. Medulla brainlights burst around me like flak. I stumbled into the living-room and glugged down the contents of a lava lamp. A yawn monster swelled out of the wall and faded immediately.

BIG BLUES
'The universe works on a principle of cycles of improvement, my friend,' Kramer stated, standing between two smocked-up surgeons. 'Reincarnation shifts us upward through the species and finally the dozen or so human lives allotted us. We're not allowed to remember our past lives or the lessons learnt there – a system so patently stupid a number of souls suicide out of each and every incarnation as a protest.'

'Whatever it is, get on with it.'

'But here's the capper, Eddie – by the last incarnation a protester's retina becomes calibrated to contraband altitudes of despair and clarity.' He laughed amiably. 'I'll tell you, Eddie, there's a wound so deep that when knitted by scar tissue it bisects the subject. Maimed isolation, mate of mine – it's a quick and easy procedure.' A gas mask was clasped over my face. 'I've every faith in you, Eddie.'

I woke in the clenched centre of a scorpion headache. I was back at the flat, days or hours later. Crawling into the bathroom. Splashing water. In the mirror, a face bottle-blue with bruises. Black stitches around the eyes like the lashes of a rag doll. And they weren't my eyes.

The flat atomized into cinder drifts and dark dunes. From horizon to frying horizon, scissor insects laboured toward

....

annihilation. I saw with sulphurous clarity that the turning Earth was a turbine of evil, dumping for ever its payload of horrors.

But I observed this punishing panorama as though sat beneath the bone sky of another world. Contusions the size of galaxies were nothing to do with me, except that I might be hospitalized in a trance of disinterest. I was now all shell. I had attained a state of pure irony. Cold static howled through me. Everything had died unmourned.

Scorched beyond identity, I crawled out of the bathroom. While I was gone a swarm of fluorescents had assumed responsibility for filling the living-room. With the smell of burning hair and a bandwidth buzz, an oceanic face of rippling milk was swirling out of the wall. 'Jo.'

'Sweet of you to notice.'

'How'd you get in the wall?'

'Sometimes the needle sucks – Kramer had this theory about people being a drug which has the world under its influence. I'm here, there and everywhere.'

'Why'd you let it go so far? Do you know your face is melting like wax? You're as big as the whole place – everything's shot to hell. Can't handle it.'

'Are you finished – quite finished? For a start, think of the shit you wrote the other night – remember? Your ego hit the powerlines. A drug revelation's a philosophy that's been yanked too young from its mother's tit. And there's no contest between dignity and junk, lover – Kramer's experiment depends on it.'

'He'd need a control, though – someone who hasn't taken the stuff.'

Her eyes blinked, ripples spreading outwards. 'He's the control, you moron. Only a knife'd separate the half-shells of the bastard's dishonesty.'

And I thought I'd avoided all this in rejecting further education. I stood, resolved.

Jo's face broiled, shifting. 'What are you going to do?'

....

EVERYTHING

I popped the grille cover and stuck my arm inside – the case was there. At the table, I flipped the catches and started building a hit beneath the bare lightbulbs of the boiler room. Tryptamine, grail, memes and brain preserve, pressed into a dozen silicon substrate pills and loaded into the rivet gun. I had a headache like a white sky.

Noise and bluster at the door. I crammed myself in behind the boiler.

' . . . You'll be testing a new drug every night, Wally. Some roll-over with the halflives but I can adjust for it in the results, don't you worry.'

'You know I'm not much of a user.'

'We're all users, Wally . . .' Kramer's voice trailed away. He'd seen the case.

I stepped out. Standing hesitant by Kramer was an empty kid with a doorknob head. I levelled the rivet gun. 'Go.' He looked to Kramer for help, got none, and left in a hurry.

'You were meant to wake up tomorrow, Eddie,' Kramer said, tilling vaguely through the paraphernalia on the table. 'I would have been there to greet you.'

'I had help.'

'I trust you not to call the police, Eddie – I truly trust you. In these times of ours that's worth a great deal, more than you can know right now.'

Did he think I was too sick and out of it to see his game? He was right – he turned and threw a fistful of grail dust in my face. My faculties exploded like Chinese firecrackers. Imprisoned in the maze of my own ears, I shouted for release.

Then I was after him with the gun, up the stairs and pushing through students as blank as a form. But it was midnight and these were ghosts of failure. I was tolling like a cracked bell. Deep pathologies opened up along every hallway.

Kramer was out across the tyre-screech street, the city full of history smoke. A bus reared past me, alien portholes

. . . .

STEVE AYLETT

lit with spectators. Rain was blistering the streets. Kramer's
shadow rippled over ribs of rotting architecture. London
was sinking, and always was.

I cracked off a shot and hit a dog, which exploded with
a backfire. Two more shots whizzed past Kramer, another
hit a stoplight and stuck like gum. I kept plugging at the
retreating figure, and slowing. As I followed down an alley
I began sinking into the ground, which had turned to
sludge. I was wading, fell flat on my face.

'Life's a landscape of delay, Eddie,' Kramer said. He was
standing over me. 'You get this with your new eyes. Oh you
can never have too much surgery my friend. And the arcane
pharmaceuticals in bud behind those eyes – what indepen-
dence could compete? Shove it out and let it grow a coat,
Eddie. You'll have a charmed existence treading monastery
ways paved with peanut brittle and the mere inconvenience
of bleeding from the lugs till death steals the breeze from
your gob. Would I sell you a wooden lemon?'

A buzzing atom of objectivity would have shown it was
a crap argument, being based on the notion that freedom
was feasible. But I had in me religion's guilt, revelation's
wire and the media's consensual distortions, frauds which
needed feeding.

Kneeling on the wet ground, I raised the rivet gun to my
forehead. 'For what we are about to believe—'

The city went up in a psychic inferno, buildings swatted
into typhoon blurs. I was looking down on the proceedings
from atop a building – fluorescence eating across the map.
'We escaping up here?'

'No, boy, this here's the Canary Wharf tower, see?' He
turned me to look up the gradient of the pyramidal roof.
We were stood on the rain-lashed ledge beneath it. He
began dragging me through gale-force terror up the dark
slope, yelling. 'Forget what you've heard about Chartres and
masonic altars, Eddie – this pyramid's the endpoint of a
quantum-bore needle channelling earthline energies and

....
34

shite from the five directions! Fall on the sword and you inject the whole fucking world!'

We'd reached the summit, altitude turbulence thundering the structure. Rain runnelled down the incline. I held my hand before my face – I was glowing like a halogen lamp. Beyond, the city was ash beneath a meat sky.

Then I was clung in panic, torn by skywinds. This was really happening. What was I doing here? Kramer stood easy a way off strobing in the pinnacle light, admiring the horizon. 'Kramer! Too much!'

'Have I ever let you down, Eddie?'

'Yes! And my name's not Eddie!'

I slipped, slamming on to the roofpoint.

Heartbomb shock. Screams stretching in a biochemical supernova. I blurred down the centre well of the silver tower and hit the earth, blooming outwards like a depth charge – duped. My soul blushed across the planet and seeped into the pores. I was with Jo and others, a part of me in the world's every atom, here, there and everywhere. I was a drug, and I'd been injected.

It's hot and cold here, carnal red and cool green, stone dead and fizz-grid creative. Human beings tickle across the surface, but won't for long.

Amazons in the Night City

URSULE MOLINARO

I'm a sex therapist. A dominatrix. To my prude of a
mother & my Ivy-League sister I'm a slut. –Which is only
an anagram of their inhibited lust.– They want nothing to
do with me. We haven't spoken in years. My father, on the
contrary, stays in touch. He's kinda proud of what I've done
with my life. He says: I carry on the tradition of the hetaeras,
the best-educated women in ancient Greece, who enter-
tained the bigshots of their day with poetry & songs.

I consider what I do an artform. For instance, I use ostrich
feathers to tickle a chained-up man's genitals. It adds glamor
to the excitement, & looks gorgeous when the feathers are
white & the man is black, like Adonis, an elegant-boned
Watusi who freelances for me. He's very popular with my
clients.

Especially with the former army officer who now heads
a cosmetics outfit. He's one of my regulars. A man in his
late fifties, all skin & bones. He looks permanently dehydrated, as though he'd been left for dead in the desert he
was storming. No advertisement for the creams & lotions
his company manufactures.

He loves to put clamps on Adonis's balls & pinch &
beat & tweak them.

With the authority of an official from the Red Cross or
the United Nations I step between them & try to make him
stop. I'm dressed in black vinyl shorts & haltertop with
laced-up hip-high high-heeled vinyl boots.

All the while I insult him. Hissing or yelling or whispering ominously how abject how vile how unfair &

....

cruel he is. I also make sure that the clamps aren't on too
tight, or his pinches too painful, or that his aim isn't
too accurate. Adonis suffers beautifully, like an exhausted
gazelle that has been overtaken. His huge liquid eyes are
heart-breaking. He's a superb actor, type-cast for the part. &
of course he wants to please me. I'm his boss after all. His
stern mistress with whom he longs to have sex. –I'm also
the stern mistress of my dehydrated client. Ultimately it's
the imaginative power of my words that makes him climax.

Another regular is a chunky car salesman who's into pee.
Like a sheepish toddler he stands before me, naked but for
the giant diapers he had me put on him, waiting for me to
wag a mean mother finger, warning that if he wets himself
he'll get a spanking. Right away he wets them.

Usually he wants his spanking by hand, but sometimes
he prefers a hairbrush, or a high-heeled mule. That's up to
me to guess, or he'll get petulant.

On occasion he has me balance an ornate chamber pot
on his head, on top of his tight grey curls, as he sits on the
floor with his chunky legs stretched out before him like a
baby. I have to stand over him with my legs spread wide,
in front of a long mirror, so he can watch me pee.

At the sound of the tinkle in the pot he starts giggling.
Like a mischievous child he pushes against my legs. My aim
gets sloppy, & pee starts running down his cheeks his neck
into his hairy chest. When it hits his belly button he comes
in a gush of laughter.

Always exactly when his hour is up. It's impressive how
thrifty these executives are. How precisely they time themselves, even in their pleasure. Of course I'm equally aware
of the time. We understand each other. I'm as good at my
job as they are at theirs. I really like what I do. It's creatively
challenging.

That's what I'm telling the elderly woman I'm sitting
next to at Michael's midsummer birthday dinner in an old-
fashioned French restaurant that is poorly air-conditioned.
They set up our table along the copper-trimmed bar so we

could smoke. I don't care about smoking one way or the other, but Michael's elderly friend lit up as soon as she sat down & the waiter brought her an ashtray.

I stare at her age-freckled hand, which is holding the cigarette to her mouth. At the black nail polish on her extra-long fingernails. At the 2 huge rings, one of them a serpent coiled upon itself, on the index finger.

When I saw her teetering in on Michael's arm, with a racy haircut above that old bird face, all dressed in black leather, I made Michael put her next to me. I was sure she was an ancient former dominatrix. However, she tells me that: She used to work at the UN, hating every minute of it. She was wasting her life earning a living.

She says: I'm so lucky to find my work challenging.

Why didn't she find some other job? I ask. & quote a Hispanic drag-queen friend of mine who says about all my women friends: They're white & they have a pussy. What's their problem finding work?

She laughs: The salary was terrific. & she was just starting to write. She'd try to write at work when there was nothing to do, which was quite often, but the section head always came over & made her stop.

The man had a shoe fetish. She used to wear very high heels in those days. He'd sit across from her & stare at her shoes under her desk.

I put one foot on the dinner-table to show her the shoes I'm wearing. Also, to draw a little attention to myself in this company of writers, most of whom haven't met me yet. They gaze at my foot on the table & shrug back into their conversations.

But the old woman is nodding ecstatically. Exactly what *she* used to wear. She used to adore shoes like that. Now she can barely walk in flats. That's the one thing she regrets about being old.

Maybe, if she'd put her feet on top of her desk when her boss came to make her stop writing if she'd told him that she'd walk all over him with her stiletto heels unless he

....

gave whatever work there was to somebody else   he would have let her write a whole novel during office hours.

She shakes her racy haircut: He would have been terrified of what people might say.   –When she finally quit, he kept protesting like a stepped-on puppy: How could she! Such a secure job! Such long vacations!

My job leaves me plenty of time to write, I tell her: Besides giving me all kinds of subjects to write about. When I retire I plan to write full-time too.

She's smiling sweetly: Am I working on something now?

Yes. & I've finished & published a short book about the Marquis de Sade.

She has no use for the marquis. In her opinion he doesn't deserve the accolades he's getting from the currently young. –She once translated a letter he wrote to his wife from his cell in La Bastille, complaining about a missing button on a carelessly ironed shirt.   The man was a whiny self-lamenter who enjoyed hurting the women he persuaded to let him try out his perverted-peasant experiments. He was a miser who never paid what he'd initially promised to pay. He thought women deserved to be punished for being objects of sexual desire.

I object: That wasn't at all how the marquis felt about women. I wish I'd known him. We could have achieved great heights together with our combined imaginations. Like Sacher-Masoch with his Wanda.

She minds Sacher-Masoch less, even though he was just as controlling an ego-maniac as my marquis. But even as an animal rights advocate she can relate to the image of a Venus in furs, though now she can no longer conceive of wearing furs either. Torturing animals to deprive them of their rightful coats. But in those days she went through quite a few. A cab-driver once ordered her out of his cab after he asked her what kind of fur she was wearing, & she told him: Chimpanzee.

Was she naked under that coat? I ask: Was she wearing only black-seamed hose & stiletto heels?

....

Of course not. She was on her way to work.

I could go to work like that. & maybe she should have, too. That poor frustrated boss of hers probably undressed her in his mind every working day of the week. No wonder he couldn't bear to see her write. She was giving off all the wrong signals.

Not at all! She was trying to show that intellect needn't look dowdy.

That wasn't the way *he* saw it. I think she was cruel to him.

If she was he deserved it. That man was abject. Cringing towards his superiors & petty with his staff. –Besides, he had a dowdy wife who'd come to pick him up after work.

She would have done the dowdy wife a kindness if she'd let him play out his fantasy the way I let my clients play out theirs in my studio. He would have gone home a nicer husband. Even those who go in for power projections & torture games go home cleansed. Pain will do that for you. Pain is hard. It's direct. It's honest. It enables the sadists to go back to their bourgeois mush. Until the next time.

De Sade *was* bourgeois mush: she says.

We're between courses. She has taken off her dominatrix leather jacket & is sitting in a jungle-green sequined dominatrix blouse with tight long sleeves. She lights another cigarette & is gazing at me through the smoke. Or perhaps she's gazing into her fur-coated past.

Have I seen or read *The Balcony* by Jean Genet? she asks: She thinks I would find it a rich source of inspiration for my work.

My clients are my source of inspiration. I have developed an almost psychic sense for what each one wants. –For instance, if she were to make an appointment & come to my studio as a client although I rarely do women I'd know that she'd want a beautiful young slave like my Adonis, although maybe a little shorter & rougher/more visibly uneducated to treat her like his great Lady Bountiful alighting from misty heights. She'd start assuring

....

him that they're really equals: his beautiful body & her gorgeous brain or her gorgeous money. She feeds his belief that eventually she'll let him in. Eventually. Eventually. Until he gets tired of his blatant inferiority, & she gets hurt & acts surprised. –Isn't that her pattern?

She bursts out laughing. A laughter of recognition. Which means that I'm right.

Which I tell her. –I bet she's had many lovers. Maybe she still has ... Perhaps she'd like to meet my father ...

She raises a bejeweled hand: The last thing she needs is another old body in her bed.

I feel stung: My father is younger than she is.

Most people are these days. She thanks me for my kind intentions, but she's no longer interested in sex. The urge suddenly dropped away a number of years ago. It has been a great relief.

She makes sex sound like a disease.

It's a dependence, even if it feels like freedom at the time.

It's the seat of life: I say: I feel sorry for her. She's brain-dead in her pussy. What a shame.

I too take my jacket off. One of my breasts slips out of my high-neck black blouse, which is silk cut on a bias. She looks at my perfectly well-shaped breast resting next to her elbow on the table cloth as if it were somebody's used Kleenex. Then she says something in French to the waiter that sounds like: Oyster on the half-shell. Maybe she's ordering, but the waiter is laughing.

I wriggle my breast back inside my blouse & put my jacket back on, despite the old-fashioned heat in the place. I'm not giving up sex until I'm dead all the way: I tell her.

....

A Chartist

PHILIP HENSHER

There was no one upstairs at all. I went up three times in an hour, in case they had all knocked off for a tea break, which seemed unlikely, but there were just a lot of men with their shirts off wandering up and down. It was three in the morning in a club in Brixton.

You felt the lack of the dealers. The club was full of men dancing in a rather hopeful sort of way, bopping in a sixth-form manner rather than the usual, hips-out strut; there were occasional little pockets, islands of men who had obviously planned ahead and brought their own gear, men flailing and grinning, their jaws working. They seemed odd among the cheerily unsorted crowd.

The third time I went up there I bumped into Sean.

'What's up?' I said.

'Nothing,' he said. 'What are you after?'

'Some gear,' I said. 'There's nothing going on.'

'No,' he said. 'I was talking to the barman. He said they've been raided and they all got carted off by half eleven. No chance. Who are you with?'

'Some people I was at dinner with,' I said. 'They sent me up here to get them enough E for five.'

'With a side order of speed, I suppose. No chance.'

Sean was a half-friend of mine. I'd known him on and off for a year, I'd never been to his house and he'd never been to mine. I saw him in the same two places, in clubs, and at the first nights in galleries. Once or twice I'd been out for a drink with him. I thought he would, but now I knew he'd never be much more than a half-friend I sometimes had a drink with. He was quite a glamorous artist – the sort people talk about, though not the sort people buy, since his works were too absurd even to contemplate setting up. One man in North London had set one up, had bought a room-sized piece for a sum of money which, Sean said, had kept him going for a year and a half. There had been a gratifying stream of press coverage – some of which I'd written – and afterwards a complete lack of further commissions, or anything like that. Though a fair amount of interest from which anything might come, and a little bit of fame.

The joke of Sean was that I always pretended to be passionately obsessed with him. Friends of mine always referred to him as 'your lover' since he was very good-looking and I liked him. 'Saw your lover on the street the other day.' It wasn't true – I wasn't obsessed with him, though he was a nice man and at his best with his shirt off. He was famous for being monogamous, or almost so; though, as someone once remarked to me, sometimes it was hard to believe when you saw him in a club at five in the morning. I knew what I thought, and didn't say anything to anyone about it.

'Where's Joe?' I said. Joe was his partner.

'No idea,' he said. 'Haven't seen him for weeks.'

'Is he away?' I said. I shouted a bit over the noise and the thump as the first swathe of the number dissolved into accelerating beats, before the dance music cut back in.

'No,' he said. 'I don't think so. He moved out.'

'He moved out?'

'Yeah,' he said. 'It's a bummer.'

'Come on,' I said. 'Let's go and talk about it.'

The club has a room slightly insulated from the dancing-floor, so that the music comes out as a dull thud rather than the speakered shout that makes your ribs thud. People go there, it is said, to chill out; I never heard anyone use the expression, except in the same ironic way that they might say 'Had some well dodgy gear Sat'day'. So Sean and I went into this room without a proper name. There were

....

three bespectacled drag queens practising their low-level bitchery in a corner; one man who had overdone it was lying on his back on the floor, quite ignored, quite unaware that he had lost a shoe.

'I don't know what happened,' he said. 'It was my fault.'

'I'm sure it wasn't,' I said. 'Come on, tell me.'

We'd never slept with anyone else, Sean said. You know he was the first man I ever slept with. And he was late coming to terms with it, and he'd only ever had one other man before he met me, in York. Joe was a really shy man. He didn't look it; he was. He liked going to clubs, and to bars, but he would do anything to get out of going to a party. He hated going to dinner parties, he hated giving dinner parties. When he changed his job, he lost a lot of sleep just thinking about how he was going to get on with the people he was going to work with.

It was mad. He wasn't the most confident person in the world. No one would have thought he was. But he was easy to like. It was the combination of a man who went out all the time and one who was self-deprecating, shy, easily embarrassed by small difficulties. No one found him intimidating, or hard, or anything; everyone saw the little problems he had, and didn't talk about. People liked him.

The thing was, what people didn't see was that he'd turned this shyness into a kind of virtue. He didn't see any reason to try and get rid of it, though he'd rather not have been shy. He just thought that was the way things were and there was no altering any of it. That was really where the monogamy thing came into it. We'd decided that we weren't going to sleep with anyone else, we weren't going to pick up a boy at a club and say to each other, well, see you tomorrow. There's nothing wrong with that, I don't think. It used to be the way things were.

But he wasn't doing it because he thought it was a good idea. We decided that we wouldn't sleep with anyone else because he didn't believe he could pick someone else up. It was all because he wasn't confident enough. Of course he

....

could have done. People used to come on to him all the time here, when he was dancing, or whatever. Whenever I went off somewhere, when I came back there was always some really gorgeous boy grinding his arse against Joe's crotch, and him with this apologetic look on his face, as if he couldn't help it.

You'd think that would have persuaded someone that they could score as easily as anything. But it didn't. When I said this to Joe – I only ever said it to cheer him up, to make him think he wasn't as hopeless as he thought he was, I never said it to persuade him to go ahead and sleep around – he'd only ever say, 'Oh, the thing about this place is people are always playing weird games with each other. It doesn't mean anything.' He seemed to believe it. He really seemed to think that if he'd said to one of these boys who were coming on to him like that, 'All right, then, come home with me,' they'd have laughed at him for taking it seriously.

And it was the same everywhere. Once there was this guy who was coming on to him to this unbelievable extent at some dinner party – not just flirting, but, by the end of the evening, asking him for his phone number, and not believing him when he said, 'I don't think that would be a good idea.' He said that, and when we got home, he said to me, 'Oh, he was just saying that,' as if this man wasn't serious. I really had to persuade him that it was a bit more than that. Crazy. That was where the monogamy came from, not from wanting only me, or thinking not having every man on a dancefloor wasn't, in itself, a good idea. What really scared him was this idea that if we started saying, like everyone else, 'Oh, well, we can have it off with some Spaniard now and again without worrying about whether it's going to mess up our relationship,' then we'd set off and I'd score and he wouldn't be able to.

The weird thing was that I didn't particularly want to tap off with anyone else. I was just mad about Joe. I know it sounds completely unbelievable, but still, after seven years, he'd take his shirt off and I'd just be struck with lust. I just wanted to fuck him the whole time. Even when he was being a complete pain in the arse, I still wanted to fuck him. I fancied other people, of course I did, but I never wanted to get off with them particularly. And I never thought of myself as being particularly faithful. It was like monogamy had been forced on us by something outside, something outside our control. For him it was just the fear that there was no one else for him; for me it was this lust I couldn't control, just for him. We'd both rather have been without it. But there was nothing we could do about it, and it looked like such a good idea from outside, we never really talked about it; we never really complained about it. Maybe there was nothing to complain about. Probably there wasn't. You never know what holds people together, what that glue is.

About a year ago, I met this geezer. He was all right. He wasn't mad, or anything. I saw him around and we always talked. He was funny, and everything; a nice man. It wasn't that I ever missed him if he wasn't at a party, or down here, but when I saw him, I thought, oh, right, he's here, good, I'll talk to him in a bit. Joe met him and he thought about the same of him that I did, nice man, nice-looking, let's have him round to dinner sometime. And that was it. Of course, we never did have him round to dinner, just carried on bumping into him. You think the same thing about probably twenty people at any time in your life; you think, oh, must get him round, but there's no particular reason to.

Last November I was down here and bumped into him – I remember when it was, it was when there was that big storm. I'd been here since midnight, and when I came out at six I'd no idea anything had happened. There were all these trees just lying all over the place and I remember coming out and just looking at it. There was a car outside with its windscreen shattered – a roof tile had just gone straight through it. I'd met this man that night. It stuck in my mind.

....

'Do you mind if I talk to you?' a boy said to Sean and me. He had just come up.

'We're just talking to each other,' Sean said.

'Oh, I'm just looking for someone to share a cab to Trade,' the boy said. 'Are you going on there?'

'I don't think so,' I said. The boy was too skinny to be nice to.

'Only I've just come up for the night,' he said. 'I've never been here before. I was looking to see if I could get any E but there doesn't seem to be any about.'

'No,' I said. 'No one takes drugs here.'

'Get away,' he said. 'I know better than that.'

'Well, I've no idea where to get any,' Sean said. Then he leant forward and put his face right against the boy's. 'I'll tell you a secret. We're not clubbers. We're not queers, either. We're plainclothes policemen, and we're looking for poofs who take drugs.'

'Get away,' the boy said. He turned from us and went out of the room, looking for someone to share his taxi with. Sean rolled his eyes, and went on with what he was saying.

He was someone I sort of knew, this man I met. I used to meet him most weeks down here. Anyway, we danced a bit together, then I said, I'm knackered, come and have a sit down. We were both off our faces, and you know how everyone seems like your best friend then. So we were sitting here – Joe was away, I think – anyway, he certainly wasn't here. And I don't know why, but this man started telling me about what seemed like his main hobby.

'I like to know who's had who,' he said. I didn't know what he meant. 'I like to know who's slept with who.' I didn't understand why anyone would want to know something like that. Well, I did, I suppose. It's quite interesting when you hear that two people you know have just started sleeping together, or when you hear that two people you know used to sleep together ten years ago and now just bump into each other at parties and are just friendly with each other. So I can see that's quite interesting. But this

....

man had taken it a stage further than that. He'd actually drawn up a chart of who'd slept with who.

'Why are you telling me all this?' I said.

'Wait,' Sean said. 'There's more.'

He didn't have the chart with him, Sean went on, but he drew a little example of what it looked like, and explained how you got on to the chart. A name would be connected to another name by a line, which would lead on to someone else. The aim was to establish how many fucks you were from anyone else, anyone you hadn't actually fucked or would want to. He was quite proud of the fact that he was only three fucks away from Leonard Bernstein in one direction, and seven from Prince Charles in another.

Then he explained how you got on to the chart. He had a word for people who had got on to the chart. He called them chartists. It was a joke – at least he thought it was funny. I did, too. I'm talking as though I despised it from the start, but I definitely didn't. I thought it was a funny thing to do. I thought it sounded as if it was full of these kind of scandalous, glamorous people. I sort of wanted to be one.

I didn't stand a chance, though. You didn't get on it by fucking just one person. You had to be connected to two people. And I'd only ever fucked Joe in my life, so that was that. And he wouldn't get on the chart because he'd only ever fucked me and this man in York. So I laughed and said I'd like to see the chart some time and forgot about it.

About a week later I was in Soho and saw this man in a bar. I went up and said hi again to him. Like you do. And there was something the next day, something or other I thought he'd be going to. I asked him if he was going, and he said yes, and let's have a beer afterwards. And then I said, hey, bring your chart along, I'd like to see it. He looked at me in this weird way. 'I didn't know I'd told you,' he said. 'Well, you did,' I said. 'Last week. I remember, even if you don't.' He came along the next night and afterwards

....

we went out for a beer. I didn't think he'd have brought it, but he had.

I don't know really why I was interested. Most of the people I'd never heard of, apart from a few people we both knew, and a few people everyone's heard of, like Cary Grant or whoever. It was like this huge piece of paper – I remember being in the Café Pelican and everyone obviously thinking we were completely off our heads with this piece of paper twice the size of the tablecloth, and laughing like hyenas. We'd been laughing about who'd fucked who for about half an hour when I noticed this name. 'Who's that?' I said. 'Oh, it's just some bloke in York this friend of mine fucked and then told some friend of his who went up and fucked him too. It was about a year ago. He's quite a useful link.' 'I'll say,' I said. The thing was, this bloke in York was Joe's ex-boyfriend.

It wasn't really much of a coincidence, and it didn't mean anything. But anyway, I said Joe had gone out with this man, and things started getting interesting. 'We could get Joe on to it,' he said, 'if he's fucked him and you. But you're not on it.' 'No,' I said. 'I've never slept with anyone else.' 'You're joking,' he said. I wasn't. 'Is that true?' he said. 'I thought that was just your line. You've never had anyone else?' 'No,' I said. 'Not that I wouldn't mind.'

Till I said that I didn't know I thought it. It really annoyed me, in a way, that I couldn't be on the chart because I'd never slept with anyone. It doesn't sound now like much of a reason to shag someone else, because you want your name on a piece of paper. Maybe I always wanted that, to have my name on a piece of paper, to get noticed. To be history. Now I am history. That's funny. It isn't much of a reason. But you only need one.

'Just never had the opportunity?' he said. 'No,' I said.

That was the opportunity. The opportunity I needed to fuck up my life for good, get rid of someone I loved and who loved me for no reason at all. Well, you know the rest, or you can guess it. I went back with the man and fucked

....

49

him. No, I didn't even go back with the man; I never went to his place, and he never came to mine. We fucked in the alley behind a bar in Covent Garden. You know the one. Yes, you do.

Two days later, this packet came through the post. I opened it. It was a new chart; it was exactly the same as the old one, except now it had two new names on it, a new series of lines, drawing connections.

I opened the chart at breakfast. Joe wanted to see it.

He moved out about a fortnight later.

Sean stopped talking. He closed his eyes. The room seemed terribly small; the music thudding too close to me. I didn't know what to say.

'Why have you told me this?' I said.

'Because you didn't know it,' he said.

'Yes I did,' I said. It was almost true. 'I knew that I'd told you about the chart, and I remember having it off with you. It was only three months ago.'

'You didn't know what happened.'

I didn't know what to say. I could hardly bear to listen to him telling me a story about myself; I could hardly bear to listen to my own actions, and their consequences.

'I'm sorry,' I said. It was just a joke, the chart; it was an idle amusement, and it had never occurred to me that having a name on it, that having recorded someone's bland liaison, could in any way affect anyone else's life. For a bizarre moment, I stopped thinking about Sean, and Joe. I wondered about the other two hundred names on the chart, the two hundred chartists. I wondered what had happened in their lives because of what I had written on a piece of paper, and I wondered what that piece of paper had caused. 'I'd never have done it,' I said.

'You didn't do it,' he said, 'It was me, really.'

'What's the time?' I said.

'Four,' he said. 'It's going on late tonight.'

I took his hand in mine.

'I can't do anything to make it up,' I said. Perhaps I was

....

sincere. 'I would do anything to change things for you, but I can't.'

'No,' he said. 'The thing is, that this was always planted in things from the beginning. The way me and Joe would end was there from the start, because he wanted faithfulness for the wrong reasons, and I wanted faithfulness for the wrong reasons, I suppose. Maybe not.'

'I think fancying someone is a good reason for faithfulness,' I said. 'It's the only one – it's the only free one.'

'I'm thinking about going,' he said. 'Have you got money for a cab?'

I got out my wallet. I looked in it for twenty quid among the usual detritus of receipts and bills and notes of phone numbers. In there, among all this, was a little snap-fastened plastic sachet. I fished it out.

'Look,' I said. 'I'd forgotten about it.'

'What is it?'

There were two pills in the sachet. I had bought them last week; I hadn't got round to taking them. I had forgotten about them. They might be the only two pills left in the club; in the world. They would do for me; one now, one in four hours' time. They would.

'Do you want one?'

'Go on, then.'

So things were different. I took him in my arms. We danced till dawn. All that.

....

help

JANICE GALLOWAY

Lucille was singing 'Dream a Little Dream of Me' with Mama Cass and none of the notes were right. None of Cass's were particularly right either but it wasn't her fault. Not this time. It was the batteries. Lucille's man had made her a bunch of tape-loops, all her favourites, so she could play them round and round all day and she did; round and round till the music died on its feet, melting and running like something out of a horror movie. It hadn't got too far yet but Alma knew what was coming: the drag in the middle of lines that became a slur, a slide, then the voice from the crypt before you knew where you were. Lucille never seemed to mind. She never even seemed to notice. She just kept playing them. At least Mary-Lou had a Walkman.

Alma looked over and there she was, in the far corner of the room, the wee box under her arm fizzing and ticking, Mary-Lou lip-synching away with wires coming out her ears. *Bitch bitch bitchin bitch*. God knew what kind of music that was. *Bitch bitch bitch*, twisting the handles of that grey poly bag that hung on her wrist all day like a burst balloon, rocking like Grandma Walton. Alma cocked her head to one side, watching. The rocking and the words were totally different rhythms, probably neither of them the same as the music. Dianne was out so nobody was crying and listening to The Beatles; Roxanne had taken her acid house stuff somewhere else. And Rhonda wasn't there. Rhonda was never there when music was on, thank christ. Music made Rhonda difficult. Very difficult. There was nowhere you could go to miss it entirely though. Mama Cass dying, Mary-

Lou cursing and ticking like a bomb. Further down the corridor, the TV was shooting fuck out the day room and Victor was on the warpath. He'd been hanging about for ages since after tea-time, scowling at folk who weren't doing communal things, snorting or laughing in that forced way he did so you'd ask him what the joke was and he'd have the satisfaction of not telling you. Keeping an eye, he called it. Just making sure you girls aren't getting up to anything you shouldn't haha. Ha ha. Alma could see him from here, breezing through the ward door in his check shirt and footering with the cards on Roxanne's locker. He had on those tight jeans he wore a lot, the pair he really seemed to like. They had a whitish, threadbare bit to one side of the zip as though his cock was enormous, doing all that damage to innocent denim. Maybe that was what he liked about them. Alma let her eyes trace the length of the jean's leg, keep going.

What are you looking at? he said. He didn't shout but his voice carried. It was that kind of voice.

Alma looked up to see him not looking back, his eyes fixed on the inside of a big card with a duck on the front. A duck and the words CHEER UP! in neon pink. Cool as shit.

Don't know, said Alma; the label fell off.

Victor put the duck card down, picked up another one with a teddy bear in a nurse's hat. I don't know, he said: Ask a civil question and that's what you get. Cheeky cow. He put the bear down too and stuffed his hands down the back of Roxanne's pillows. Just as well I have such a rewarding job, he said. Turn that racket down, Lucille eh? Lucille kept on singing and Victor stuffed both his hands down the back of Roxanne's bed. Searching. Alma watched him, realized she hadn't seen Roxanne since tea-time. She hadn't missed her but she hadn't seen her either.

Where's Roxanne? Alma said.

Victor's cheek was on Roxanne's pillow now. Alma could hear his beard scraping against the starchy white cotton. He didn't answer.

....

53

Victor, she said.

Nothing.

She had another fit? Alma said.

Alma just mind your own business eh?

I never said anything. Just—

Aye I know. He pulled the top sheet back, hauled up the mattress and stared at the wire mesh over the frame.

I'm interested in Roxanne's wellbeing, Alma said. I'm just asking. You know, since this hospital supports the patients' charter and the right to know?

Alma kept looking at Victor. He looked at Lucille. Lucille, he yelled. I've told you once. Then he wiped his nose with the back of his hand, went back to his searching.

The handbook says just to ask the staff any time we have a question, Victor. So this is me doing it. Is Roxanne OK?

Victor moved very slowly. He took both slips off the pillows, dropped them on the floor, then just stood, staring down at them.

What are you looking for? Alma said. She tried to make it sound chirpy. If you tell me I might be able to help you.

Victor stopped halfway through pulling off the under-sheet, looked right into Alma's eyes.

Alma, he said. Just in case you ever want any wee favours from me. Shut. Up.

She's not got anything, Alma said. If she did have anything she'd not put it there. She's not daft, Victor.

Alma, he said. A voice that didn't want to say it again. Alma.

Alma looked round the ward. Mary-Lou wired to her wee box, Lucille changing her tape. Alma might as well have been in here on her own. Sometimes, if you tried really hard, you could get Victor to piss off. It took concerted forces though, a real team effort. She shrugged, went back to looking at her nails, the newspaper on the floor. PRINCESS TO HELP RAISE PROFILE OF SLIMMING DISEASE. Behind her back, Mary-Lou started *bitching* again, her bed creaking as she rocked harder.

....

Somebody ought to do something about that lassie, Victor said. He started opening Roxanne's locker drawers, forking his fingers through her letters, her pictures, her unwashed tights. She's fucking obscene.

Dianne was in the kitchen, two cups and a fag on the go. She handed Alma a striped mug without asking, cup full of something the colour of tar. Alma looked at it, swilled it about a bit to show interest but didn't drink it. Dianne knew fine. She leant back on the sink, eyes over the thick white rim of the mug.

See that Victor? Dianne said. She sucked the tea like it was a fag, never off her lower lip. I canny stick him. Drink your tea hen, do you good.

Alma smiled and kept the tea where it was. Dianne shook her head.

I've just been up Male and they canny stick him eithers. Sammy Manson says he left this poor old guy in a puddle of shit for an hour before he could be bothered changing him. She sucked again. An hour.

Any visitors, Dianne?

Miserable big bastard, she said. I hope he ends up in here.

Alma sighed.

He's no kids. No kids. And he's meant to be looking after folk. He hasny a fucking clue.

Alma looked at the kitchen door, raked it with her eyes. She didn't want to talk about Victor, what went on behind people's backs, children. Dianne knew.

He hasny though, she said. He shopped Roxanne for pinching towels. They're probably giving her ECT for being a bad girl.

Chance would be a fine thing, Alma said. Dianne laughed, stopped quickly, took three big drags of tea. Alma smiled.

Declan come and see you?

Dianne shook her head with her mouth full, surfaced. No the night. See he was round last night but he canny keep

....

paying the fares. It's no his fault. We haveny a car or anything, see. He'd be here all the time only we've no car. We'd be sick of him if he had his road. Only he couldny come the night.

No. Alma couldn't think the last time she'd seen Declan. Heard about him plenty but never seen him. Maybe she'd always been out or something. Maybe.

See your man didny come eithers. What's his name?

Gerry, said Alma. He's my boyfriend.

Gerry, Dianne said. He didny come. Or yer ma.

No, Alma said.

Never mind. She'll be tomorrow. It must be terrible for her eh? I'm saying it must be terrible for her but she'll come. Being your ma and everything. Mothers take it hard if there's anything wrong with their wee ones. Rhonda says—

Right, said Alma. It sounded as rude as hell but she didn't care. She wanted Dianne to stop talking, especially about Rhonda. Alma hadn't the stamina to hear the Rhonda story all over again. Not tonight. Thanks for the tea, Dianne, she said. She stood up.

Aye, Dianne said. Her eye caught the still-fullness of the cup in Alma's hand, raised her own in a kind of salute. Fling it away if you're no wanting it, then. You don't have to kid me on. I know what lassies are like. I've had four. Believe you me, I know.

Alma was gone.

Auburn water in the toilet bowl, auburn auburn. The water in the toilet bowl turned auburn. Dianne's insides must be that colour, Alma thought, watching the tea curl through the blue. All that tannin. Alma could see Dianne's face in the water as well, the walnut colour that came through her skin. Jesus. She imagined Victor coming in and finding this stained water not flushed away, thinking christ some-body's been peeing blood in here but he wouldn't. Alma knew fine he wouldn't. Not much got past Victor. He'd know it was tea and give the first harmless bugger he met

....

a row for being wasteful. You're supposed to get it out the machine: six cups a day. Alma thought about Victor getting out the patients information list, showing you the *Patients are requested not to take more than a daily allowance of* SIX CUPS part, saying, *It's not a bloody hotel in here.* He's right there, thought Alma, watching the tea-stains, the toilet bowl other than perfectly white, dental. It's not.

Outside in the corridor, the first trolleys were being loaded up along in the staff bay, that queerly cheery clinking of bottles that sounded like a pub the first time she heard it. The night shift were swapping notes. She better shift if she was going to find Michelle. The book was back in the ward but she could find Michelle first, bring her back for a blether or a cup of tea or something. Alma had found herself wanting to see Michelle more recently, especially at night. Nights were her worst times and talking to Michelle was soothing, somehow. After Dianne and Lucille, after Victor and every other bloody thing in this hospital, talking to Michelle was a kind of medicine. Fourteen. Michelle was fourteen, looked like an angel, never had a bad word. A-ward were in love with her. The first time Alma saw Michelle, that's where she was; in female psycho-geriatric drying Mrs Kidd's hair with the working hairdryer. Alma hadn't known Mrs Kidd's hair was that length. She hadn't even known her name. They all waited for her coming along there now, called her pet. And they ignored Geraldine. Geraldine was Michelle's minder. In the bath, the toilet, next to her at the refectory table, beside her bed till she fell asleep: Geraldine's job was to watch Michelle's every fucking move. Nobody knew why Michelle needed a minder. They didn't ask. Alma bet they suspected though. Alma suspected herself. She suspected there was something darker going on with Michelle and all those sharp wee metal bits inside the hairdryer than most folk thought but she didn't say. Nobody did. Or mibby it had something to do with drugs, the way she'd been so interested in the book. The book was on Alma's locker. Trocchi. Gerry had brought it in, said Alma should read it. Michelle saw it sitting on the locker-top and picked it up. My boyfriend's reading this, they'd said, both of them at once. And they'd laughed. And Alma had watched Michelle laughing and wanted to let her borrow the book. She'd read enough of the bloody thing now anyway. So Alma made up her mind: she'd find Michelle and loan her the thing tonight. Now. The problem was finding her. Alma walked the length of the corridor, checking. Michelle wasn't in any of the rooms. She wasn't in A. She wasn't in the towel press, at the coffee machine or the OT kitchen. The toilet block was straight ahead. Alma looked at the double doors, wondered if she and Geraldine were behind there somewhere, whether Geraldine watched the whole thing, what she did with her face. Inside, though, there were only geriatrics being toileted by two staff, the cubicle doors wedged open. But no one else. Back in the corridor, queues were lining up already at the tea machine, milking it; the sound of loose change making music in trouser pockets. There was only one place left.

The quiet room was at the end of the corridor. Staff put flowers in there to keep them nice, let OT use it now and again for poetry sessions but it was usually empty. And freezing. Alma had come here the day after admission and stayed put, writing letters to nobody and greeting. To an empty space. Nobody else had come in the whole time. Alma had been there every day so far, twenty days running. There had never been anyone else, at least not for long. She could imagine Michelle there, though, Geraldine sitting beside her bored out of her mind. Alma walked back the way she had come, moved into the ante-room corridor. She could hear nothing, see no bar of light along the bottom of the door. Alma pressed her cheek to the painted chipboard. Then stood back and turned the handle.

The first thing Alma saw was the window. The room was

....

freezing and the window was open, as far as the chain restraint would let it. The second was the piece of outside that showed in the space. It looked near: the dark above the chemical plant milky, the rest thick black. No stars, nothing else; just black. The third thing was someone else. Someone else was sitting in the far corner on one of the burst easy chairs. And it wasn't Michelle. The air around her wasn't the way the air was around Michelle. It was too still, too heavy. You didn't have to be able to see to know who that was. It was Rhonda.

Hello hen, Rhonda said. Like a door, something you didn't want opening.

Hello, Alma said. She wondered if Rhonda had had her medication yet, if she was in here hiding from it. Rhonda had bad nights. She had nights when the only thing you could do was keep out her way.

I'm just sitting, hen, Rhonda said. Don't put the light on eh? I'm not wanting the light on. I'm just sitting.

Alma nodded, said nothing. The time was up where it would have been possible to make a joke or something, say something that could get you out again fast. Now, it would just look made-up. It would look like what it was. Alma could think of nothing to say. There was nothing else to focus on but the figure in the chair, Rhonda's hair, her eye-sockets like inkwells, the curtain behind her head with the big faded patches from the sun. Pale stains like a disease that never got any better. The carpet was the same. Standing on it now felt like standing in the sea, not knowing what you were balanced on, what might be coming slow through the water to get you. She couldn't hear Rhonda's breathing but Rhonda could hear hers. She knew because she could hear her own. Like she'd been running.

You looking for some peace too, hen?

No. I'm fine, Alma said. Fine.

Oh? That creaking again, insinuating. Oh? Like she didn't believe a word. Like she knew Alma didn't either.

I'm just looking for Michelle.

....

That the wee lassie? The one that's cutting herself all the time?

Alma said nothing.

Looks like butter wouldny melt but they're watching her all the time, hen, the nurses. As if it'll make any difference. If she's made up her mind, watching her's no gonny help. Terrible eh? Must be terrible for her mother.

You've not seen her then? Alma said.

No. You'll no see her in here, Rhonda said. Too quiet.

Michelle's quiet, Alma said. There was a sudden flash of anger hearing Rhonda talk about Michelle as if she knew her, as if she had any right. Why wouldn't she be in here?

The place where Rhonda's eyes were glittered. No that kind of quiet, hen. She needs to be in with other folk. Rhonda drew on a fag in the dark, made the tip brighten her mouth, fade. If she's in with the rest, she's got something to do, something that makes her look fine. In here, there's just her. Just her and that big sumph Geraldine.

Alma heard the sound of exhaling, and something else, something breathy before she realized what it was. It was Rhonda laughing. Laurel and bloody Hardy, eh?

Alma was wanting out. Why didn't she move, just turn and shift?

She's no in here, hen. She's no likely to be. They'll no keep her here long in the hospital allthegether. She's up for a transfer. You wait and see.

Oh? said Alma. Oh?

I've seen her folks, Rhonda said. They've a bob or two, they've got money. They'll get their wee lassie like that away somewhere private as quick as buggery as soon as they see what it's like in here, who it's full of.

And she laughed again. That was when Alma smelt the drink. Sherry or something, something sweet.

Aye. Rhonda sighed, but you'll be all right, hen. You'll be fine.

She took a sip of something. Alma could hear the sound of the bottle. Rhonda swallowed and kept going.

....

You have to be desperate or know you're OK to come in here. Somewhere, no the now mibby but somewhere, you know you're OK. You know you're coming out the other side.

Alma said nothing, a dense kind of nothing. Her feet just wouldn't start walking.

See with you it's just the one. You can get over one. Even if you did it yourself.

Sorry? Alma said. Sorry?

Don't be like that, hen. Rhonda sounded weary, disappointed in her. Like Alma's mother. Don't kid on you don't know what I'm talking about because you do. You do. You don't have to be mealy-mouthed with me. It says on that thing in the office. I know what a termination is, hen. I know what you're in with.

Alma could feel her own heartbeat. She could hear it.

Termination, medical grounds and all that. Mental health it said. Did your boyfriend no want it?

It's nothing to do with you, Alma said. Or she wanted to say it. But nothing was coming out. There were words the size of billboards in her head and nothing was coming out of her mouth.

Things you do for them hen eh? He disny visit eithers, does he? He's buggered off. It's what they do hen. Mental health. *His* mental health. Rhonda laughed, scratching her head so you could hear her hair, a scrape like wire wool.

But you'll be OK. You can get over one. See I know. You can take advice from me because I know. I know.

Rhonda breathed out hard, so hard even at this distance Alma could taste a change, a sourness in her own mouth.

Seven miscarriages hen. Seven. They're treating me for the wrong thing allthegether. Schizophrenia. Schizophrenia my arse.

The silence that filled up the end of the sentences was solid, brittle. It was Rhonda that broke it, pressing closer still.

....

But I know how to get stuff. I know what I'm needing. And it's not their fucking tranquillizers.

Alma could see the shimmer of glass under the edge of the curtain, something still to come or finished maybe: a recent spill of it making a sheeny blot on the carpet near her own foot. Alma wondered who was bringing the stuff in for her, where Rhonda hid it.

I understand that all right.

This time she tipped too far, started keeling forward. Alma moved fast to catch her just before she tilted completely, slumped on to the floor. It was a good thing to do. Alma knew it was a good thing because Rhonda went softer, floppy against her hands. Cold as a corpse.

I'm all right hen, she said. She tried to look at Alma but Alma didn't want to look back. She kept her eyes on the carpet, pushing to get her up.

You're drunk, Alma said.

Rhonda laughed again, better this time. And you're a cheeky cow, she said.

I know, Alma said, Victor already told me.

Rhonda laughed till Alma sat her back in the chair, stood back. Look, you better get back through, she said. They'll catch you. You shouldny have bottles in here, Rhonda. They'll catch you.

Aye, Rhonda said. Aye. There was a long pause while Rhonda looked for her fag, failed to find it. Then she gave up and looked at Alma. You'll need to help me hen. I canny walk.

I'll get Dianne, Alma said. I'll get somebody OK?

Aye, Rhonda said. Fine. Fine.

As Alma left she heard Rhonda stage-whispering behind her back. That lassie hen, that Michelle. You help her hide her stuff. We're all in this world to help one another eh? You help her get what she needs. Kidding on butter wouldny melt eh? Laughing.

Laughing that wasn't laughing at all.

Alma ran.

....

*

Dianne was watching telly in the dayroom and now there was nothing but Jeremy Paxman. She put the sound off on her way past, leaving Big Terry still staring up, none the wiser. Alma watched Dianne go into the end room just to make sure, then went back through. Past the laundry store, the towels with SOUTHCROSS GENERAL written on them, past the dayroom and the dining-room there was nothing. Nothing but a night-nurse whose name she didn't know, holding up a wee cup full of pills, smiling. Alma's night dose. Not diothepin, not protriptyline, not lorazepam. Not tranylcypromine either. She couldn't remember what the new thing was but it was new. Improved. And they were sure it would start working soon. Alma realized she'd spent the whole evening looking forward to finding Michelle, giving her the book, feeling useful for something and there was no time left. She heard the TV being switched off, Terry starting his shouting. It was time to go to bed.

Alma had been lying listening to Mary-Lou's bag creasing and uncreasing for what felt like half an hour before she knew for sure. She wasn't going to sleep. It wasn't just her either, the ward was worse. Rhonda moaning and snoring, Dianne telling folk to be quiet in a too-loud voice, then Lucille. Lucille was always bad at the ends of days too but tonight was particular. She had her tape machine under the covers, pressing fast forward buttons, playing tiny wee bits over and over. The introduction and first verse of 'Blue Velvet', then 'Dream a Little Dream' again. She played it twice through before Elizabeth came through to check and found what she was doing, took the machine away. Bastards, Lucille said. Bastards. She'd be writing to her MP they were a shower of murdering bastards, then the crying. Alma stuck it the way everybody else did till the whining started, eerie and soft. Then Alma lay in bed and shook. She lay in bed shaking, wondering if it was the new stuff, withdrawal from the old stuff, just Lucille. She needed to see Gerry. She

....

needed to stop thinking about Rhonda. Her head was full of stuff she could do nothing about. Lucille whined. Alma lay in bed shaking and told herself it was OK, Gerry would come. Rhonda was wrong because Rhonda was bitter, Rhonda had been here too long and the bastards ought to transfer her somewhere safer, send her for counselling or something. Alma didn't want to think about Rhonda's weans, what might be wrong with her. She wanted to think about tomorrow, finding Michelle, Gerry coming. What Gerry would say if he came. Come out of this fucking place and get some decent drugs down you; not that stuff. Roxanne told Alma if he kept taking E he'd forget how to have erections and he wouldn't care. Roxanne, Victor raking about down her bed and giving nothing away. Roxanne with a fag glued to her lip all the time because she read somewhere it was sexy, it was making a comeback for women. And so was breast cancer, thought Alma, but it didn't make her laugh. Alma lay in bed shaking and wondered how much longer. Nobody had said this could happen if you got rid of your baby. Fetus, Roxanne said, FETUS not a fucking baby. The shaking was getting worse. Gerry said she'd be OK in a wee while. She'd be OK quicker if she'd take an E, there was nothing to be scared of, nothing at all. Maybe he was right. Maybe she was taking the wrong drugs, ones you couldn't look cool popping at his fucking club. Gerry telling her she shouldn't be filling her body with contraceptives, not with they kind of drugs, Alma, doctor drugs, they're not the kind young people should be having anything to do with. E now, E was going to set us free, boys and girls together. But things happen when you stop taking contraceptives. Not things. This. This. This. The shaking had developed a crying component now, crying that wouldn't stop. Maybe that was normal at this stage too but they didn't tell you that either. They didn't tell you fucking anything and that was all he could say. E is going to set us free. She didn't want fucking E. Roxanne did. She read the same bloody magazines as Gerry. Gerry and Roxanne ought to

. . . .

get together, she thought, but that didn't make her laugh
either. She wanted out of here. She wanted to see Michelle.
Lucille was still whining, like a kitten; quieter and worse.
And reminding her of something. That train whistle kind of
noise at the end of a song. The Railroad runs through the
middle of the house. Her grandad's song. Alma, the name
he picked for her. What he could make of this if he knew.
The tears were terrible, though. The veins in her nose felt
like potato tubers and she thought she would stop breathing
altogether. There was too much stuff in her head to think
straight. So she got up, Alma got up. Her legs were not
good but she walked. She blew her nose and held a hanky
up so they wouldn't think she was making an exhibition of
herself and she walked down the corridor. Alma wasn't too
proud to know some things. And Alma knew something.
She needed help.

The lights hurt. Full on and yellow. After a moment, she
could see trails on the lino from folk cleaning late, then the
door; sea-green with Sellotape marks on it from notices that
had fallen off. Timetables to see the psychiatrist. Old bits
of Sellotape. Watching her hand going out, the slowness of
it, till she thought she could stand it, till she thought she
would be able to speak. Nothing happened. Someone
laughed behind the door, a click and tapping sounds, low
talking. There were two people in there, drinking tea. Alma
watched her hand. It just hung there in front of the door.
It was shaking too. And it had to stop. Alma knew it had
to stop before she let it knock again: there was a question
of dignity here. Alma waited, crunched her fist tight and
raised it level, hit it against the door. Nothing happened.
She did it again. Someone in a green pinny answered. Not
a nurse. It was the auxiliary.

What are you doing out your bed? she said.

I can't sleep, Alma said. I need to talk to whoever's on,
please. A nurse. I want something to help me sleep.

You get to your bed and stop annoying the staff now, the

....

auxiliary said. You've had your medicine. I saw you. Away you go and lie down.

I can't sleep, said Alma. I'd like something. Please.

Elizabeth was there behind her, skinny and dark hair.

You again, Alma. What's she wanting?

The auxiliary kept her eyes on Alma as she spoke. She's not allowed on the corridor, is she?

No. Elizabeth opened the door further. Look, you'll need to get back to bed Alma. You're not allowed on the corridor after lights out. Away back.

I can't sleep in there.

Oh, she said. Really? She rolled her eyes at the auxiliary. And why not? Why can't you get to sleep, Alma? The auxiliary walked away, tutting, and Elizabeth turned back, looked her in the eye, pulling a face. Let's hear it.

It's too noisy and I can't sleep. I need to sleep.

You could hear it from here. Lucille rolling like surf, chewing up Mama Cass to something hellish.

Too noisy is it?

Too noisy. Alma was aware of trying to look her back in the eyes, managing but not being very good at it somehow, not feeling OK.

Look, just get back to bed and try this time. Try. You're not trying to sleep if you're out here. And you're not meant to be here either. No slippers on or nothing. Get yourself back to bed and just try to sleep like everybody else. It's the same for everybody.

I am trying, Alma said. I'm trying to sleep. I want something to help me sleep. The tips of her toes were turning blue, nails needing cut. The corridor wasn't warm any more.

She's cheeky, the auxiliary said.

Look, Elizabeth said. It's not noisy. It's not as noisy as you think it is. On you go and try.

I want to see the doctor, Alma said.

Elizabeth sighed. Get off the corridor.

No, Alma said. I want you to get the doctor. I want the

....

doctor to know I'm asking for something. I want to ask the doctor.

There isn't any doctor. Elizabeth looked scared somehow, wrong-footed. She looked very young. I'd need to phone.

Alma looked directly at Elizabeth. Her knuckles were hurting. Do that please. I'd like you to do that.

The auxilary tutted for a good minute or so while Elizabeth stared right back at Alma. Alma didn't shift. All right, Elizabeth said eventually. All right. If you say so. But I won't do it till you're off this corridor. You abide by the rules like everybody else.

Alma's throat was sore. She heard what they did. Humouring folk, not doing stuff they said. As soon as your back was turned they thought you'd forget. That was why they were so keen on turned backs, not noticing. Alma knew fine. And she knew something else. She knew she needed to hear that call. She needed to stay here, listen to the numbers being dialled, hear the words Elizabeth used to the call-doctor to know. Just to know. To check she wasn't miscalled or just not spoken about at all, overlooked out of. Out of something. Spite wasn't the right word. But whatever it was had to be pushed against, weathered. Alma thought if she didn't last through this, make herself heard over the top of other people at least this time, she'd never manage it ever again. She could be in here for ever, in and out these places like Rhonda if she couldn't do this and do it now. This was the most important thing she'd ever had to do. And she was seeing it through. She had to. Now.

I'm not moving, Alma said. I want to stay here till you've made the call. Please.

Elizabeth looked like somebody had insulted her, called her something terrible. Her chin squared up, mouth angled down. The auxiliary came up pushing her brush, green apron emerging from the light end of the corridor.

I heard her, nurse. I heard that.

Elizabeth did nothing. Alma looked at her, trying to make her eyes different.

....

I heard her. Threatening behaviour.

It's all right, Elizabeth said. She was pink. I've got the thing under control.

I heard her, though. I'll put in a report if you want.

It's OK. If that's what she wants, she can get it. Right, Jean.

Jean. It was the first time Alma had heard the auxiliary's name. Jean.

Right, Jean. You stay here and you don't move.

Elizabeth looked, aggressively solicitous, at Alma, touched her arm with a stiff arm. Stay here for your own safety, please. With Jean. Elizabeth looked at Jean then, made big eye contact. You're in charge then. While I'm away you keep an eye OK.

I'll watch her, Jean said. I'll make sure she disny do anything don't you worry.

I'll be right back. Elizabeth walked looking back over her shoulder, jaw tight. You're all right? Pantomime whisper for the auxiliary, her comrade, as she reached the staff door.

Jean nodded, grim as a frog, turned back to Alma. Alma heard the door close further up the corridor. She and Jean were alone. Jean seemed to like the fact, took a weird enjoyment in it. Alma could feel it. Alma looked at Jean, her hair dark purple with white roots, the black lines round her eyes. Alma looked at the black lines, at how they flaked into the skin, the creases beneath Jean's lower lids. One eye looked sore, inflamed or something. Her top lip was swollen. Alma reckoned Jean would be seventy if she was a day. She reckoned Jean shouldn't be working in a fucking hospital. Jean looked back at Alma, heavy-lidded. You're no shy, she said. Staring at folk. That's ignorant. She leaned on the brush, teasing. Pure ignorant.

Alma looked at Jean. It felt terrifying, dangerous. But necessary somehow. Jean's eyes were not well eyes. Maybe she had glaucoma.

See what you don't grasp, Jean said eventually, what you

....

don't seem to understand is you're sick. You're a sick person.

Alma kept looking at the black rims, their wear and tear.

People don't get in here unless they're sick. You're sick. A sick person. You understand me?

Alma said nothing.

You've to do what the nurses and doctors tell you because you're here to be helped. No to be cheeky.

Jean looked Alma up and down, shook her head.

There's no point talking to you, is there? What's your name? No point.

Alma said nothing.

Jean looked at Alma steadily, pissed off. I know what it is anyway. Alma. It's Alma. How come you've got that name? Alma?

Alma said nothing. The wee crucifix round Jean's neck flashed as she moved.

Alma bloody Cogan. She killed herself.

Neither of them said anything else till Elizabeth came back, flushed. The doctor was coming, she said. She'd be here in five minutes. She was having to leave somebody who was very sick on another ward but she was coming. In five minutes. Now get back to bed.

Alma said thank you twice. It mattered to be very, very polite. Then she turned and walked back to bed.

Alma lay listening to Rhonda snoring for what felt like a very long time but the doctor came. It's not as noisy as you think it is, she said after Alma told her what she needed, what was wrong. She had talked to Elizabeth but that was to be expected. She prescribed something and left without telling Alma her name. And that didn't matter either. Elizabeth came back then, told Lucille to shut up and left. Alma waited some more. It was Victor who came. Victor with three red things in a plastic cup, water. Alma had never been so pleased to see anyone in her life.

You being a nuisance? he said.

....

Yes, said Alma. I hope so.

He put on the bedside light though he didn't need to. The light from the corridor was clear enough. But he put it on. Alma held a bunch of tissues up to her nose out of vanity and watched him pick up her bedside book. Michelle's book.

What's the book then, Alma?

He put the sleeping pills down, held it up to his face like he couldn't see properly.

Trocchi. That how you say it? Trocchi.

I don't know, said Alma. My boyfriend gave it to me to read. It's his, not mine.

Trocchi, Victor said again. I've heard of him. He's the one that wrote books about heroin and stuff. He's as cool as shit the now, Alma. Aye that's him. Subversive, it says. He smiled at the blurb, put the book back down. Subversive. I read about him in *Loaded*. Put his wife on the game or something to get the money eh? Subversive, he said again. Cool as shit. He smiled.

Alma looked at Victor. She looked hard. Victor picked up the tub of pills.

You're not looking too impressed. He laughed.

No, said Alma. No.

Oh? he said. You not reckon he's up to much? He thought he was cheering her up. Maybe he was. How not eh?

Alma looked at Victor, almost smiled. If he was that bloody subversive, she said, her eyes level; if he was that bloody subversive, Victor, how come he didn't earn the dough by letting punters shove it up *his* arse, eh? That seems more subversive to me.

Victor raised his eyebrows, kidding on he was shocked.

You've a terrible attitude problem, young lady, he said. But he was still smiling. So, after a fashion, was Alma. He leant closer, ready.

What is it? she said.

Tamazepam, he said. Folk are paying for this in Paisley and here's you getting it for free. Right?

....

Alma nodded, her eyes shut.

OK, here we go, he said. He tipped the cup into her mouth, gave her the water. Alma swallowed and opened her eyes. Victor was still there, looking pleased.

All right for you, he said. I'll be up all night. New admit high as a kite on steroids and a set of transfer papers to fill in. You rest up here in bed while you can, Alma. Don't worry about us taxpayers. You just have a nice rest.

He gave Lucille her tape machine back on the way out, made her promise not to play it. Lucille started crying again as the slow wipe of Victor's shoes shifted away, past Roxanne's empty bed and into the corridor. And Alma knew she would sleep. She could feel it already. Rhonda turned, laughed in her dreams and Lucille started playing with the fast-forward buttons all over again. Soon, if she waited long enough; soon, when the drugs kicked in, she'd feel nothing at all.

Honeymoon

JOHN SAUL

We were in a tearoom in Copenhagen; it was a December afternoon, out of the drizzle. Celeste went to the counter to order chocolate. Orders for drinks were made at the counter, then brought by uniformed waitresses in white and green.

It was our honeymoon.

Yes, we had. Had already slept together, to answer the once preying question. In one year, including bursts of cohabitation, two hundred times? Three? How is this to be counted, am I talking nonsense?

My wife looked good between the waitresses; among the many generations, heights, coats, jackets, in line at the counter; looked attractive, even if the only sight of her was blond locks and her long purple coat falling straight downwards. But I could see her Flemish, van Eyck face in the mirror over the counter, concentrating on Danish coins. *Cherubic*, people say of her. I visualized her face in other situations; in the hotel room. I daydreamed about the bed-spread, the dishevelled sheets. The view of rooftops, the bells. We were in a city of embassies, high ceilings, mysteries.

Celeste sat down with a cake. It looked good.

Tony, she said. This city has *flair*.

I gave her a look which said: If that cake is something to go by, it has.

She offered me a forkful, big and flakey.

Which is why we must go back to the store with the glass. What was that street called?

I told her that I didn't know.

....

72

Anyway you're looking good, she said. The cold gives you colour.

Thanks, Suze.

(I call her Suze.)

The store with the glass set out on tables, the blue and orange and yellow, you know? What was that street? On on on ... you have the map. Was it *Grønnegade*? Tony, this is a *city* of glass. It's built on iridium, I read about it at the hotel – which is where we'll go back to after the store. This is just an interlude to our fucking.

I nodded. Everything is an interlude to that, I said confirmingly. Babe.

I spoke with authority. I was on my way to becoming a doctor.

And we wanted our honeymoon to go exactly as it should.

As a honeymoon should in the very late twentieth century, said Celeste.

Celeste had written something called the 21st Century Handbook. I am supposed to help her update it.

We had a spherical bowl of blue glass. It could be filled with water and used as a vase. Celeste took the bedspread and covered her head. She gazed.

We have no house, she said. But I see you in our apartment. To all effects you are already Dr Stern, soon with letters letters letters after your name. You are up at your desk late at night, your papers spread beneath a lamp. Your treatise is almost finished. Your first professional appointment awaits you. Whatever you turn to works. But is it enough? When you have your career; me; your children ... my attentive ears, my sex. Is that enough? Will you want more?

The Glyptotek museum was ninety-five per cent staircases.

No one will need to come here, my wife declared.

Need? I queried.

....

73

The art gallery is the warehouse; you come here to inspect the merchandise.

I will?

I mean people can. But mostly they won't want to.

What are you talking about? I said. Do you say this in writing?

Rooms 17–19 temporarily closed, a sign stated in English and Danish. We continued up the old brown staircase.

I mean the entire contents of the place can be bought per CD-Rom, said Celeste. Transporting its fortunate owner on an armchair journey up and down the stairs. Stopping on the mezzanines. Even looking across these little balconies. Whether the pictures are actually on view, on loan, or gone up in smoke, you can view the whole collection. Or in a shorter, cheaper version, the masterpieces. That's all I'm saying.

I stopped opposite a painting by Renoir. A woman in black was walking. Other women were watching her.

Not an acknowledged masterpiece, said Celeste. Even Renoir barely makes the Handbook.

But look, I said.

Her black dress glinted like fish scales. She was the most confident being on earth.

Renoir, Celeste shrugged. A very minor artist. All but his most familiar work will disappear.

You can't see yourself, Tony. But I tell you, your hair always gets so tousled.

I stopped staring at the spiralling spokes of rafters, so dark, varnished, on the newly whitened ceiling. Celeste pulled across the dresser with the mirror so I could see my own face.

You look French sometimes. With your hair so black. *Français. Tu es mon collaborateur.*

French? I said. *French?* I looked and felt like a young beast. Unshaven.

Is it sexy to be French? I asked her.

....

Celeste pulled a face to say she had no idea.
We lay back down.
OK, she said. Talk dirty to me.

I delivered my criticism of the Handbook. The Handbook made omissions. It was exclusively for the middle class. Why did it not, for example, have a chapter on how to find a job in a tough world? And what if everything broke down? What if one day the technological world exploded *paff!* in your face? What do you do?

But the Handbook, Celeste tells me, is solely for people who will buy the Handbook. There is no point in it offering advice to the poor, the old, the disabled.

Under 'Dealing with Violence' it will now say: *Get tough*.

The restaurant closed at two in the morning. The champagne bottle had been emptied, dripped dry and removed. As had the cups, the plates, the glasses. On the starched white tablecloth were just our hands, the unused ashtray and a candle down to a stub. The skiffle trio had packed and left; chairs were stacked. We buttoned up each other's coats. Outside the streets were cold and empty; the night trams ran only skeleton services at stupendous intervals. Even the lights in the quartet of Amalienborg Palaces were out. We walked through more rain, huddled together. It was our honeymoon. The hotel porter glanced up and went back to his book. We sat in the lift as it clanked to our floor. The lights of the corridor stabbed our eyes. We found the door, the key, the lock. We somehow undressed and flopped into bed.

I am a dinosaur, said my wife. *Down!* comes the iridium, she said plunging an icy hand on my stomach. *Down* in a cold hail, a meteor. Oh no! we dinosaurs do cry. Oh no. This will be the end of us. On it plunges for days and days, first radiant in the night, and then!

What? I said drowsily. What plunges?

The ancient meteor.

....

And then?

The dust flies up. Our heavy heads turn this way and that, lolling. We are bewildered. What is day and what is night? we ask. Some of us do.

I know, Suze. It is a grey murk.

Yes, a grey murk. It covers the sea in a great blanket. The plankton sighs, and ceases. I struggle to the shore . . .

Celeste lay full length on top of me.

. . . I am amphibious.

Oh babe.

I'm not moving until you go on.

On with what?

This is the last great dinosaur die-off. *Down!* comes the iridium. Sparkling rocks with starry sprinkles plunge *kerplatch!* into the ferny swamp – one day to become Copenhagen, become glass in the shops in Copenhagen. You must tell the story. You: must: tell: the: story.

You: are: drunk.

Get on with it. Or: no greater wrath than of woman scorned.

Right, I said hurriedly. Well, on land anxious creatures forage in the fog, stampeding uselessly in all directions.

Ah! Yes.

Until their crimped, cramped-up bodies writhe in the metallic dust and dark, totally zonked in the great tiredness.

But not so, Tony.

The great, great tiredness. All sleep, without exception.

No no, not so. One dinosaur, me, will make one last try to preserve the species.

Surely not tonight.

Tonight. Now tonight.

Tonight, I murmured.

Do you not say I have achingly beautiful breasts?

I do. You do have.

Look, you sonofabitch.

Did you say sonofabitch?

Sonofabitch! You're not going to get out of this.

. . . .

76

But.
Now feel my hand on you.
Babe, I'm dead.
If it takes all night.
Babe.
Tony. If it takes all night, the better for it.

Late in the day we made our public appearances. We looked at glass, shoes, kitchen furniture and American sofas; and, briefly, bookshelves. We were checking the shelves for the 21st Century Handbook (ed. Missinne, Celeste); but not even the British bookshop in Badstuestrade stocked it. We consoled ourselves with a café over the street, a place walled with mirrors and run by waitresses who wore starched aprons going down to their ankles. I took a pastry and waited for coffee. I had nothing in mind but these and the sight of Celeste enjoying a good midday meal under gravy. I asked myself whether these aprons had flair.

If it's not in that shop, said my wife, it's not in Copenhagen.

Paradoxically, she had an entry on books and bookshops. Both were unique resources, she reminded me, which would at the same time become scarcer and scarcer. I remembered the Handbook word for word. The Internet would have a category, *Literature*, to which all previously published fiction would be relegated and which, like the Glyptotek, would see almost no new additions.

Though there would be a new small corner, *Stories*, my wife told me. But while creative minds raced rampant across the Internet, this corner too would stay a narrow domain.

I saw my coffee coming in the mirrors.

It would? I prompted. A domain?

The province of the realistically told tale. With apparently real people, in real space and time. And stories having to fit a certain length. Like on the radio, like films made for TV. But I don't say this directly in the book. This is, hm, an analysis.

....

Ah.

(Ah, I was thinking, so this is the sort of thing people actually say on their honeymoons.)

The coffee was good, strong but creamy.

Celeste continued. Later, she said, the creative minds themselves would become expelled to some remote corner of the net, marginalized. Whatever did not provide regular financial—

This is the future? I interrupted.

I'm not saying this is how it should be, said Celeste defensively. This is how it is becoming. But I want to tell you something . . .

She wiped her mouth on her serviette, steadily round her cherubic lips.

I want you.

Suze, darling.

Because you do these things. *Tu fais des trucs.* I just want to tell you, Tony. I like how you fuck. I even love the way you lick off your spoon.

I lick my spoon?

Like you just did. You sort of turn it upside down and you lick it.

I'm losing the thread.

So lose it.

(Next, I was certain, she'd start teasing me under the table.)

I downed my spoon.

Let's concentrate on the Handbook, I said sternly. You leave a lot out, but you deal with some weighty stuff as well. You're saying art and literature, as we know them, are to run aground. What of history?

Celeste duly started below the table.

History is big, she said. Big, big.

Suze. Let's concentrate, OK? History.

OK. History is . . . a big chunk of something people don't know but think they ought to.

I nodded. Looking in the wall of mirrors, I understood

. . . .

suddenly: it was the unusual way these aprons fell straight from the hips. They had flair.

Since they think they ought to, people'll make quite an effort to retain historical information, Celeste continued. But once it's in their heads they won't know what to do with it. So, mm, there'll be an educational drive for us to connect the past to the present. The more sophisticated electronic systems, darling, will present us as part of one enormous whole; try to make history cosy for us. Are you following? Or just mirror-gazing?

Following, I assured her.

Anyway, she said. *Screw history*, they'll say in the end though.

Screw history? I said gingerly. And philosophy?

Forget it.

But I sensed wind coming back in my sails.

Love and marriage?

Oh boy.

Oh boy what?

Are you going to get it tonight.

Sex?

I quote. *Sex is the drive safeguarding our existence.* So why knock it?

Why, for that matter, marry me, Suze?

To possess you. I like to possess. It's a matter of desire, period.

But to possess?

Is for ever, like marriage.

I digested this idea staring at the rafters. More rain beat on the roof. It was thick but distant, a muffled beating.

Celeste put her lips to my ear.

Tell me I'm your bitch.

I will. You're my sexy bitch.

You're going to fuck me.

I'm going to fuck you. You're going to fuck with your man.

....

Now you're getting there. And I'm going to ride you.

I want you to ride me.

I tell you, Tony, she said breaking above a whisper, you won't be able to get up from this bed till you come.

Babe. You're going to come all over me with your juice.

Tell me, I love dirty talk.

You said in your book.

It's twenty-first century sex.

Already.

Anyone who hasn't talked dirty should start straight away, said Celeste. Without hesitation. Honeymoon or no honeymoon.

I looked into her eyes. She cupped her hand round my neck.

Sex is a miracle, she once told me. This doesn't get said in the book though.

So roll me, she says now. Fuck me.

It takes two, babe.

She's kissing me. The rain falls harder.

OK, babe, she says. OK.

Stillness

BONNIE GREER

December 11th

Why did I come to Europe? First, because Lucy brought
me on vacation. Europe is easy pickings for somebody
like me, so I decided to stay. The day I decided to stay, I
met a woman in the hotel tea-room. She was the age I like
– that sixties generation thing – and anyway she kept staring
at me. I could tell she had money. So I pretended that I
didn't have any to pay my check. I told her that my money
was upstairs with my mom and she was asleep, so the lady,
Marianne, paid. That entitled her to get friendly. She asked
me if this was my first time in London. I'd got her by then,
so I started checking out my 'target'.

I always like to zero in on something a woman has about
her. Something that can turn me on. It makes my work
easier. I liked her lower lip. I could tell that she sucked it
when she got excited. I could excite her.

When I told Lucy that I was going out for the night, she
tried to beat me up. But I'm twenty-two and in good shape.
Lucy is forty-five and she eats too many Dunkin' Donuts.
She almost broke her hands. She called me all kinds of
'black so-and-so's', but I know Lucy. Before long she was
begging me to fuck her, so I did. I don't mind a duty-fuck
now and then. But time is money, so I made it quick.

She started fawning all over me, emptying the pounds out
of her Chanel handbag, waving her credit cards. I took
everything. Why not? She took my youth.

I got a room on Baker Street, next to Sherlock Holmes's
place. OK, I know he doesn't exist, but sometimes I come

home at night and think I see him in his deerstalker, checking me out. Wondering what I do. If Sherlock Holmes would bring out some of his coke, I'd tell him whatever he wanted to know. Maybe he'd like a sample of my work. Fucking Sherlock Holmes! Deep.

That's how I used to think then. But that was before Caroline came to my door. I shouldn't have kissed her. I never kissed them.

December 12th

When I was a kid, we had five television sets. They were on all the time, night and day. I used to sit in a corner of my room, the one farthest from the door, and just be still. Then I could hear the prairie out beyond our town. The prairie is still. In my corner I could organize the stillness.

I was a smart kid. I was proud of that. I got myself out of that house, to New York City, college, all on my own. It was hard, but I kept my stillness around me. Other people noticed it, too. I liked that.

I shouldn't have kissed her. I kept it together until I kissed her. It broke my stillness. Now I have to get it back.

December 13th

It's colder in Edinburgh than it is in London. I don't know why the Brits keep their places so cold. Maybe that's why they drink so much, to stay warm. It's warmer outside than it is in this room.

I was walking down Princes Street today. I found this restaurant where they serve real American pancakes. With maple syrup, too. I had two helpings.

The kids do smack up here. Forget that stupid-ass movie *Trainspotting*, nothing's more boring than a smackhead, face it. When I lived on the Lower East Side, I used to watch those smackheads try to walk down the street. It was the only laugh I had around there. They would walk like they were sleep-walking, then stop ... and sway. You could rob

....

them blind, take their clothes, but a junkie only cares about junk. They're stupid, they get on my nerves.

Lucy told me not to laugh at them. Lucy had a soft heart for the weirdest things. She'd cry if she'd heard somebody's dog died. But she stepped over anybody in a cardboard box with their hand out just like they were garbage. Weird old Lucy.

December 14th

I did an E last night for the first time in months. I had to get out of this room. I walked into a club and a guy was selling them, so I bought one. I needed it for the music in that place. This bald guy was jumping around and singing out of tune. He was pierced all over his body. He stuck out his tongue and his tongue was pierced. OK, I surrender, I don't understand the Brits.

The E makes the world look nice. It makes it look what the sixties must have been like. 'Strawberry Fields Forever'. 'Penny Lane'. OK, there was a war, assassinations, Nixon, but it was the last time you could really be young. You could be yourself. You could be ahead of it then, instead of it being ahead of you. I like that time.

Lucy said that I should call myself 'Flower Child', because I looked like the sixties. Since she lived through it, I guess she knew what she was talking about. That's what I call myself, 'Flower Child'. You can make lots of money as a Flower Child.

The day I decided to work with Lucy, I went to church. I don't know why. I didn't go to Mass. I just sat there. It's quiet in church.

That's how Caroline was. Like a church.

December 15th

I got high again today, but that's OK, because I know what I'm doing. Anyway, grass to me is liking smoking a cigarette – it's better than a cigarette – I hate smokers. I did this joint and then went back to Princes Street. They have these

....

streets in Edinburgh that you have to climb. They call them 'the Wynds'. Mr Hyde in *Dr Jekyll and Mr Hyde* used to run up and down these Wynds. I pretended to be Mr Hyde and followed this guy in a kilt. I wanted to let him get high up enough so that I could see what he had on underneath. But he moved too fast.

December 16th

There's this Indian guy at the store on the corner where I buy my food. He looks like some kind of swami, then he says 'Cheerio' like the rest of the people up here. My parents would say I shouldn't think like that – 'So he's Indian, so what? Do all Indians sound like Peter Sellers did in the sixties? We raised you better than that.' Yeah, my parents marched with King, only they got five television sets out of it, and they fight like that 'peace/love' stuff never happened. They had me as some kind of symbol of 'black and white together', but my father talks about the ghetto like the people there aren't human, and my mother keeps dyeing her hair this nasty blond. And me? I know lots of ways to make a person come. For cash.

'We shall overcome'.

The landlady asked for the rent today. I made up this lie about my parents coming from America. She bought it. The heat came up like magic. Cheap bitch.

December 17th

I had a good night's sleep for the first time in days.

There is frost on the windows. It's like Kansas up here in Edinburgh, with all the cold and the snow. When I was a kid, I'd sneak my dad's Chrysler and ride as far out of town as I could, out to the prairie. You could hear yourself out there. Stillness.

I told Caroline about the prairie the first time we met. I never meet them the first time at my place, but I liked her voice. When I opened the door, she just stood there. She was small, with a really nice suit and shoes on, and she had

....

white gloves in her hand. Her hair was too long. But I liked that. Her hair was my target, my turn-on.

She asked me if she could smoke. I hate that, but I said yes to her. She asked me if I did couples. Frankly, I prefer ladies, but if she was there, I'd be OK. She asked me my age. I said nineteen. You got to be younger these days to make any real money. At that first meeting, we went to dinner together. She took me to her club. When we walked in, everybody looked at us. I used to make sure that people looked at me. I don't do that any more. I don't want them to look at me now.

What did they see? *I* saw a blow job here, a fist fuck there, it was in their eyes. I could've made lots of money that night, but I was with Caroline. I was glad to be with her.

She told me about her upbringing in some mansion, and I told her about myself. I told her the truth. I wanted to. We had lots of champagne. Then she asked me, because I am half black and half white, if I knew where I belonged. 'Sure,' I said, 'right here,' trying to be cool. But I didn't mean it. Caroline knew it. She just smiled. She was like the Madonna in church, the one with her eyes down, smiling at the angels at her feet.

Later, while we were having coffee in the drawing-room, she told me about this guy who was coming into town who she hadn't seen for a long time. I was to pretend to be her child. That was the gig. I was too high on champagne to say anything. Anyway, I would have done anything for her.

When we got outside, she asked me to kiss her. I never kiss them, but I kissed her. She touched my breasts. I usually don't have any feeling there, but that time I did.

December 20th

I picked this girl up at a club and we stayed at her place, this really big apartment in the middle of Edinburgh. She said her parents were in Paris for Christmas. We could see

....

Edinburgh Castle from her place. I could hear the cannon that goes off at noon better there. I really liked that.

The kid said she was seventeen, but I think she was fifteen. We just did drugs and danced around, and she kept telling me about being seventeen. Young people don't have any morals these days.

When I got back, the landlady was in my room. She said she'd been trying to fix the heater. I let her lie because I owe her money. I guess I'm going to have to give her what she's looking for and soon, or I'll be in the street. I think she likes being tied up.

I spent the night eating some poppadams the Indian grocer gave me. He's a nice guy.

It took me until I was twenty to be able to light a match. I think it was because I was afraid of burning myself up and everything around me. I've always wanted to burn things up.

I wanted to set fire to Nestor, too, the guy Caroline hadn't seen in all those years. Nestor was this West Indian diplomat. A guy who sat up real straight, and wore a very expensive suit. Like my dad. He looked like my dad. Since I had this thing about my dad, being with Nestor was a lot easier than I'd planned.

Nestor was really upset after she'd told him about me being his kid. He kept on explaining why he had to leave her all those years ago. Why he had to betray their dreams, blah blah blah blah.

I kept sitting there thinking, there they were, the whole sixties laid out in front of me. All that stuff they promised each other then, all that stuff they marched for. And in the end, they'd both gone back to their corners. Hope I die before I get old.

We finally went back to Caroline's house. She lived in what the Brits call a terrace. Something called Royal Crescent. There was a full moon out, and the light on the white columns made it look like *Gone with the Wind*. I hate *Gone with the Wind*.

....

But I liked the inside of her place. It was quiet and beautiful, like Caroline was. Stillness.

Caroline made more drinks. Then in the middle of drinking one of them, she started to cry. I was really drunk by then. I just wanted to undress her, kiss her all over, hold her, bring back that quiet inside her.

Nestor was crying, too. I was glad about that. I guess he was crying for what he'd lost. I wanted to tell him the truth, that I wasn't his daughter, get him out of there so I could be alone with Caroline, but I was on duty. After a long time they went crying into her bedroom. They were in there for too long. I looked around her place to have something to do. I saw these pictures on her mantelpiece of her real family, her husband and her sons. They were really upper-class.

They were in there for a long time. I kept wondering what was he doing to her? What was she doing to him?

I was really upset by then. I stole something. I took this small silver box on Caroline's mantelpiece. It had this half-human, half-beast, carved in silver on the top of it, chasing a silver girl through a silver forest. I put it in my pocket.

Then I saw my face in the mirror over the mantelpiece. I didn't know it was me.

As I was staring in that mirror, Caroline and Nestor came out of the room. Her face was red. Nestor had no expression. She paid me extra and said goodnight.

I didn't want to go. I didn't want to leave her. I wanted to tell Nestor the truth. Stop the whole game. But I had to stay a professional.

So instead, I went and picked up this kid. Back at my place I made him take a bath. The minute he got clean, he stopped being cool.

I gave him some cab money and threw him out. I needed some peace and quiet. I stayed in the next day. The day after that I was on my way to one of my regulars when I saw Caroline and Nestor's faces plastered all over the front page. The paper said that Caroline had shot Nestor and

....

87

then killed herself. The paper said the police were looking for 'a tall, mixed-race youth of indeterminate sex'.

December 23rd
I sent a Christmas card to my parents, and one to Lucy. I didn't tell them where I was.

December 24th
Bus stations are not great places. First there are families slobbering all over each other, and then the drunks slobbering all over themselves.

I'm on my way up to this village in the Highlands. My landlady told me about it. She said that's where she was from. She said she hated it. She said she had to get out. She said it had 'this great suffocating stillness'.

Trussed

. . . .

NICHOLAS ROYLE

1.

It was Caroline who told me that once past thirty-five, there's no way you will meet any more people who could come to mean something to you. Thirty-five is arbitrary, of course: just because it was thirty-five for Caroline, doesn't mean it'll be thirty-five for you or me. It might be thirty-six or forty, but it's around that age. The reason Caroline formulated this theory was she'd just (barely) survived a run of disastrous relationships and really thought she'd found the right guy in Graham whom she met at a dinner party in the week following her thirty-sixth birthday. Pleasant, considerate, he was even talented and apparently trustworthy, but he turned out to be worse for her than any of them and she ditched him. The mutual friend who had invited them both to his dinner party forwarded an e-mail which allowed Caroline to discover that Graham had done a bulk mailing to all his friends saying that Caroline had got rid of him because 'he didn't go with her furniture'. Underneath which he'd added: 'Fuck the middle classes.'

'He's more middle-class than I am,' Caroline said to me. 'And to think I trusted him.'

Just before Christmas, something happened that made me wonder about Caroline's theory.

Since I only work part-time, I have plenty of spare time to myself. When it comes round to Christmas and I have a sack-load of cards to post, rather than spend a small fortune on stamps, I hand-deliver any that are within reach of my

. . . .

Tube pass. Being a part-time worker, I welcome the saving this represents.

Judging by some of the cards I receive year after year from names that become increasingly hard to decipher (or do they just mean less to me with the passing of time?), everyone operates the same rules as I do with regard to Christmas cards. Which is this: I continue to send cards to certain people year in year out, whether or not I've heard from them in the intervening twelve months. They may not have sent me a card in recent memory. They may never have sent me a card. But it becomes a point of honour. I imagine them opening their card from me and smiling a sly little smile, thinking to themselves: So he's still out there, still sending cards.

One of the people I always send a card to is Chloë. I make a point of including the umlaut on her card because I remember how she was always a stickler for it. Chloë lives in an art deco block of flats on a busy road in WC1. I arrived there on a chill, bright afternoon in the first week of December. I looked down the ranks of names by the bell-pushes and found Chloë's. I pressed the buzzer and waited for a reply, but none came. I pressed again, then waited a couple of minutes before trying a third time. There was still no answer. This was not especially surprising; no doubt she was at work.

There was no general letter box for the building, and the glass doors could not be opened from the outside. Nor could a card be slipped between the gap between the doors, as a brass plate covered the join from the top to the bottom. I stepped back on to the pavement, the traffic roaring by just inches behind me. I wondered how agreeable it might be to live so close to such a large volume of cars, buses, lorries and motorcycle couriers. This is the price you pay for living in town.

Possibly at this point I should have withdrawn and added Chloë's card to the pile that required posting, but it seemed silly to be this close and not be able to find a way to gain

....

entrance. I noticed an elderly man in a thick overcoat and knotted scarf approaching the doors from the inside. I quickly ran up the steps and smiled at the man as he crossed the threshold. He didn't return the smile but he did hold the door open for me. Once inside, I pulled back the concertina doors to the lift. I rode the antique lift to the top floor and walked down the shiny linoleumed corridor to the door to Chloë's flat.

I hesitated, unsure whether to knock or simply slip the card through the letter box. Affixed to the door there was a small brass plaque bearing Chloë's name, which I found quite charming. An indication of a strong personality. Chloë Thomson lives here, whether you like it or not. She's even got her name on her door.

I first got to know Chloë when we were students living in the same halls of residence. Most of the male students considered her unapproachable simply because she was so beautiful. There was something about her manner as well that discouraged close contact. But that was fine with me, since I wasn't immediately sexually attracted to her and the slight distance allowed us to get on as friends.

Instead of either knocking or posting the card, I squatted, bending my legs at the knees, and gently pushed open the flap. I was suddenly glad I had neither knocked nor roughly pushed the card through.

Chloë was trussed up in a sheet or a straitjacket and was hanging upside down from the ceiling by a rope attached to a substantial-looking hook. She was in the main room which was located at the end of a narrow hallway. Other doors stood half open off the hallway. Chloë's body swung lightly from side to side. All I could hear was the faint creaking of the rope as it swung against the hook. I laid Chloë's card on the mat for a moment as I contorted my body to try to read the expression on her face.

I heard a sound from behind me. With care I swiftly reinverted my body so that I was crouching on my toes on the doormat.

....

One of the doors behind me, on the opposite side of the corridor, was being unlocked from the inside. Tumblers retracting, bolts rumbling through their housings, chain rattling back. I didn't wait. Only at the end of the corridor did I remember, flushed with adrenalin and feelings of guilt, the card which I had left lying on the mat. It was too late now. I saw a figure emerge from the flat opposite Chloë's and turn to lock the door. I could have hidden and waited, then gone back to have another look, but I don't mind admitting the whole episode had spooked me. I didn't know whether what I had witnessed was sex or torture or both, whether Chloë was alone or accompanied by someone I had not been able to see, and until I knew that, I didn't know how to feel about it.

That evening the telephone rang.

'Hello. Guess who this is.' It was Chloë, sounding eerily bright and cheerful.

'Well, well,' I stalled. 'Long time no hear. How are you?'

'Great.' I remembered then, she always said things were 'great' when I'd first known her. She said they were 'great' when they clearly weren't. When they were anything but. And she always said it in that automatic, falsely cheerful manner. 'Great.'

'Good,' I said.

'Thank you for your card.'

'You got it then?'

'Of course.' She didn't make any reference to where she had presumably found it, though I'd worked out what I would say if necessary: that I had given the card to someone who was entering the building, asking them if they wouldn't mind delivering it. 'Of course I got it,' she added. There was a moment's silence and suddenly I felt certain she knew I had been there and had seen her. I didn't know what to say.

'So how's life?' Chloë asked, which I hadn't been expecting.

'Fine. OK. How about yourself?' I added.

....

'Oh, this and that.'

I sensed another pause. Pauses in conversations with women like Chloë worry me. I sought to head the pause off at the pass by babbling. 'You must be terribly busy. We all are, these days, aren't we? Seems impossible ever to stop for breath, never mind find the time to get together, have a drink, talk about old times. You know . . .'

I was appalled at myself.

'I'll get my diary,' Chloë said.

What had I done? Before my visit to Chloë's building, I might have quite fancied meeting up for a drink. Now, I felt anxious. I didn't want to get mixed up in anything unpleasant.

We agreed a lunchtime the following week.

I got to wondering why I had continued to send Chloë a card, and was forced to admit the possibility that it was because I saw her as a potential partner, as long as she and I both remained single. There was nothing to be gained by jumping to conclusions: either Chloë was a would-be Houdini getting in some training, or I could be about to find myself needing an escape route of my own.

2.

I suppose I should have known better than to accept an invitation to go out for a drink with a man who downloads pictures from alt.sex.fetish.amputee. And who admits it to a female colleague just as he's opening the refrigerator to get the milk to make her a cup of tea.

Patrick opened the giant fridge door and took out a TetraPak pint of milk that had already been opened. I tried not to think about the other contents of the fridge, though I had presumably seen some of them on previous visits to the mortuary. He poured the milk into the china mug – his concession to delicacy – and because of the inexpertly opened carton, a trickle of milk ran down the outside of the mug on to the stainless steel table. It was funny that Patrick spent his working hours cutting open bodies, yet

. . . .

was no more skilled than the rest of us when it came to opening a pint of milk. I watched him squeeze the teabag with an unidentified instrument, then remove it and pass me the mug with the handle pointing towards me. He was polite: I'd give him that. Some men didn't even get above zero on politeness. In which case, they would never get above zero with me.

Of course, I was assuming Patrick was interested in me. That he fancied me. I never make such assumptions rashly. The cups of tea, the shy little smiles, the bouquets he gave me to take home on the Tube. The looks other people gave me when they saw the purple ribbon. Flowers were flowers to me then: my flat needed brightening up. I'm on the top floor of an art deco block facing front, with the gardens at the rear, so if I want flowers I have to fetch them myself.

To be honest, I could have done without the trips to the morgue, but the ash cash came in handy. Some doctors choose not to do it. Others, in the case of our hospital, lack enthusiasm for the subterranean corridors, the dripping pipes, the condensation on the distempered walls. You just have to check the body, make sure there's nothing suspicious and sign a form. There's not much to it. But on my first visit the combined effects of the hike through the sweaty underground corridors and the sudden chill in the morgue itself made me feel slightly faint. Plus the sight of Patrick surrounded by several gurneyed bodies and one lying right there on the table, chest splayed.

He offered me a hot drink and suggested I sit down. It became a feature of subsequent visits: we'd sit and chat while the body I'd come down to check lay waiting. Patrick seemed completely unaffected by the banal juxtaposition of life and death and I contrived to appear blasé in order not to give offence. He asked me about life on the wards, questioned me about internal affairs, so that I formed an impression of him leading a hermetic existence down here in the bowels of the hospital. I wondered if he were fright-

....

ened to come up and mingle with the rest of the staff and the patients. Did he worry that he would somehow taint them by his mere presence? I doubt it.

In his late thirties or early forties with thin sandy hair and somewhat old-fashioned imitation horn-rims, Patrick wore a grey coat not unlike a village grocer's. There were unpleasant stains on it. I tried not to think of Patrick as a lower form of life just because he worked in the morgue; there is a tendency among doctors to think like this. The mortuary attendants are rarely great socializers, not known for their interpersonal skills, and you can understand why. Patrick was also an only child. Our conversations covered some diverse areas after a while. I examined my motives for continuing to go down there after it became clear that Patrick was attracted to me.

I was not short of the attentions of men. There were one or two half-hearted suitors stumbling about the foothills of possible courtships. Had I been especially interested in either of them, I would have given some encouragement where appropriate. At the hospital there was another doctor, a senior registrar like me although in a completely different department, who had asked me out a couple of times. Had he pressed just a little harder, showed a tiny bit more resolve, we could have been a few months into some kind of relationship. But he, like the fellow outside work, seemed weak. Possibly they were even a little frightened of me, which is silly really, when you know me. I'm a pussy cat. I rather like to be dominated.

Patrick, too, was shy. Some of his shyness I put down to the difference in our status and Patrick's acute sense of that. Some of it was natural reserve, not unexpected in a man with his social contacts. He wasn't the sort of man who needed an address book. Lots of name-tags, not many telephone numbers. But his very persistence in the face of such odds charmed me. I could see him trying to reach me, slowly over a period of months. The sound of his voice on the phone – 'Would you like to come down and do a part two?'

....

– brightened up the odd afternoon. As I said, I could use the ash cash, and at £33 for a once-over and a signature, it was easy money.

Even his gaffe, when he boasted about downloading pictures of double amputees, failed to put me off. Mainly because it came only a couple of minutes after I saw his eyes blaze with life for the first time since I had been going down there. Just as I was preparing to sit down, my heel slipped in something wet on the floor, causing me to teeter spectacularly for a moment, bent double in front of Patrick. I know from seeing myself in the mirror how much of my cleavage would have been revealed to Patrick at that moment. In fact, I knew from the look on his face just how much was revealed. Pretty much everything. My life used to be punctuated with promises to myself that I would visit Rigby & Peller and get measured up for a fitted bra, but I never quite got round to it, and most of my bras had been ill-fitting since I put on a bit of weight after giving up smoking to celebrate getting my first house job.

Patrick looked away, but I had seen the flare of excitement in his eyes, confirming my suspicions. The body I had gone down to check was that of an amputee and I think Patrick was only searching for a way out of his embarrassment when he joked about my balance being worse than hers, and then sought to make amends by talking about the pictures you could download from the Internet.

It was just a couple of days later, when I was next down in the morgue doing a part two, that Patrick asked me if I would go for a drink with him after work – a real drink out in the real world. Yes, I said, why not.

In the pub we sat in a far corner, away from other drinkers. Patrick had never told me anything about his domestic situation, past or present, and I never asked. Looking down at my hands, which were folded on the table in front of me, he told me I was a beautiful woman. A very beautiful woman. In an attempt to cover his nerves, he immediately raised his pint glass. I took his other hand in mine and

....

squeezed it. Awkwardly he swallowed a mouthful of beer, spilling a thin trickle out of the corner of his mouth, and set his glass down. I caught his left knee between my two legs beneath the table and pressed them together. Then I released his leg, swept a beer mat on to the floor and bent down to pick it up. I did this as slowly as I could, even checking for myself that he had a good view, and when I returned to an upright position he was flushed and smiling.

We took a cab to my flat and, for the next seven hours, had sex, made love, whatever – virtually non-stop. In the early hours of the morning, returning from a visit to the kitchen for more orange juice, I teased him about his references to the amputee pictures and clasped my hands behind my back, dropping to my knees on the bedside rug. He leapt out of bed, his engorged cock bouncing comically, and fucked me right there on the rug. I played along by not using my hands. My faked helplessness clearly excited him more than anything.

It was not long before we were experimenting with bondage – ties and dressing-gown cords and leather belts. Patrick was curious about the hook in the living-room ceiling. The flat's previous owner had had it inserted into the steel joist when he needed to get his piano in through the window, so the estate agent had told me. For the next three weeks we slept together four or five nights a week, invariably at my flat. We were always either having sex or going to work shortly after having had sex; half the time I was light-headed and completely scatty. I wasn't in love, I knew that, but I was in lust. I caught myself wondering once or twice if what we were doing was wise, given ... well, everything. But I swept these thoughts aside. Looking back now, I realize there was an undercurrent of anxiety which I wouldn't acknowledge at the time. I gently resisted Patrick's moves to tie me more and more tightly each time, but I never resisted them firmly enough. I gave off all the wrong signals and he perceived nothing but encouragement.

....

NICHOLAS ROYLE

When he produced a length of sturdy rope I grew agitated.

'I don't think so,' I said when he pointed to the hook in the ceiling.

He dropped the rope and unzipped his fly, taking out his cock, and began to masturbate. I could never watch him doing this without wanting to do it for him, so I knelt down in front of him and took him in my mouth. He bent down and pulled my top up over my head then slipped the straps of my bra off my shoulders. I reached back and undid the catch. He placed his warm palm over my left breast and gently squeezed the nipple. I continued with long strokes up and down, up and down. Reaching round with one arm – Patrick had developed some muscles down in the morgue – he picked me up and laid me on the bed.

After we had both come, we lay side by side, looking out of the bedroom, across the landing, at the hook in the living-room ceiling.

'Please,' he urged one final time and I just shrugged.

The boyish excitement he displayed as he trussed me up was endearing.

'Trust me,' he said.

He was careful tying the rope to the hook and only let go of me once he was sure it was going to take my weight.

Maybe it was being upside down that completed the change in the way I saw things. Patrick sat in the corner of the room masturbating while I swung gently from side to side unable to move my arms or legs, a double amputee. He just watched and wanked, which I decided was not on. I wasn't happy. I no longer did trust him.

So later, after Patrick had let me down and I had said I wanted to spend the night alone, and I found the Christmas card on the mat in the corridor, I called Ben and we chatted. He asked me out for a drink and I thought I could probably do with a reality check, so I accepted.

....

3.

The incident with the hook changed everything. Chloë told me she didn't want me to come to the flat any more. She sounded as if she meant it. I thought she might cry, but she didn't. At least, not on the phone.

Nor did she want to do any more part twos, she said.

I tried to talk to her, but she wouldn't discuss it.

Most of the ash cash now went to a senior reg in A&E, a rosy-cheeked rugger type called Bryan Demeter. I didn't offer to make him any tea and the part twos were ticked off and signed for as fast as the undertakers could wheel them away.

I took up smoking. I heard that Chloë applied for a consultant's job in Aberdeen. I tried to contact her but she was always in a meeting. I could have gone upstairs to look for her myself, but I didn't. The nearest I got was the first staircase. There was a door at the foot of the stairs to which I had a key. It led out to the bottom of an interior well in the great old building, with blue sky at the top. I went there for a cigarette, as smoking was forbidden in the mortuary. I craned my neck and stared at the upper floors. Somewhere up there was Chloë. I wondered sometimes if I would ever see her again.

About sixty feet up was a swathe of safety netting stretching right across the well. I noticed a bird that had got its feet entangled in the netting and been unable to escape. It had died there, starved of food and water, hanging upside down by its feet.

I dropped my cigarette on the ground and extinguished it with my toe, then locked the door behind me and went back down to my bodies. Among them was the body of a young woman who had been brought down from A&E that morning. Bryan Demeter had done the part one and told me about her; I don't know what made him think I would be interested. Her name was Caroline and she had been viciously beaten about the head with one of her own Philippe Starck dining-chairs. Scrawled across her dressing-

....

table mirror in red lipstick were the words 'Fuck the middle classes'. Detectives found the lipstick at the rented flat of her boyfriend, Graham. He went quietly, apparently.

The Story of No

....

LISA TUTTLE

At first sight I thought I knew him and felt my blood heat, my muscles loosen, the breath evaporate from my lungs.

The imprint of his touch rose like stigmata on my skin, and the memory of his tongue hungry in my mouth aroused a need I hadn't admitted to myself for a long time, a desire for the forbidden.

'What is it?' asked my husband. Startled, I looked across the restaurant table at the well-known face and remembered who and where I was: a wife in her forties staying in an elegant, expensive English country house hotel with her husband, the vacation our anniversary present to each other. 'See someone you know?'

'No.' For that was in another country, and besides . . . 'He wouldn't be that young, if it was who I thought. He was that age *then*.' The man I remembered would be my age still and maybe would still find me attractive. That young man couldn't be much past twenty. If he looked at me, he'd see someone old enough to be his mother, someone not worth noticing, sexually invisible. He turned his head, and his clear green gaze fell on me with a shock like cold water, and he smiled.

'You're blushing,' said my husband with interest. 'Was he an old boyfriend?'

'No. Oh, no. Just someone I met once in Houston. Do you want to taste my salmon mousse?'

Once. A single night. Yet the memory of it was with me always. Many a dull or sleepless night I had pulled it out to comfort myself. I had used it so often it had come to seem like a story I'd read somewhere, and not something that had really happened to me. As a fantasy, I'd even shared it with my husband some nights in bed. But it was real – or had been, once.

I first saw him in a Montrose bar, drinking by himself. He had a tumble of black curls surrounding a long, clean-shaven face, with a sensuous mouth and startling green eyes. Only the overlarge, slightly crooked nose kept him from beauty, but his was a striking face and mine were not the only eyes drawn to stare at it. Nor was it only his face that attracted. He had a physical presence as disturbing as some rare perfume. His was not an outstanding body – nobody would have picked him to model for a centerfold – but it was long and slim and wiry. My husband, handsome, tall, and well-muscled, was certainly more attractive by objective standards, but I wasn't thinking of my husband as I admired the fit of the stranger's jeans.

I took a seat and ordered a drink. I wasn't looking for trouble. I hadn't been planning adultery. I was content, I thought, to look and not touch. I liked the way his lips curled around a cigarette and his eyes narrowed against the smoke. I liked his slender fingers, and the way he moved, shifting his weight or rolling the stiffness out of his neck and shoulders as unselfconsciously as an animal.

I gazed for a time at his intriguing, less-than-classical profile, then shifted my stare, let it fall in a caress on his shoulders, his back, down to the ass which so nicely filled his tight, faded jeans. He turned his head lazily toward me as if he'd felt, and liked, my touch. I moved my eyes back up his body to meet his eyes, and I didn't smile. He was the first to look away. Then I did smile, but only to myself.

Someone else, a man, approached him, cigarette in hand, and he gave him a light and responded to his conversational ventures absently, his attention hooked by me. I could feel his senses straining in my direction even when his back was turned, his eyes fixed elsewhere, his ears assaulted by the blandishments of the cigarette smoker – who eventually

....

gave up and took his need to someone else. Which was when my prey turned around and looked at me again.

I had to hide a smile of triumph. That I retained the ability to make a man desire me was reassuring. I had been feeling mired in marriage, as if my wedding ring had conferred invisibility, and his look sent a surge of well-being through me. As he straightened, flexing his shoulders and the muscles of his long back before moving away from the bar with an easy, loose-jointed motion, I imagined him naked and aroused and felt a tightening of my internal muscles.

He bought me a drink and then I bought him one. We sat and looked at each other. There were few words, none of importance. The conversation that mattered was conducted between our bodies, in minute shifts in posture and attitude, in the crossing and uncrossing of my legs as I leaned toward him and then back, in the way he stroked his own face with his long, slender fingers. He never touched me. I think he didn't dare. I tried to make it easy for him, resting my hand on the tabletop near his, moving my legs beneath the table. With every move I made I aroused myself more until finally, quite breathless and unthinking with desire, I reached out my hand beneath the table and put it on his denimed thigh.

The pupils of his strange green eyes widened, and I smiled. He put his warm hand on top of mine and squeezed.

'Can we go to your place?' he asked, his voice very low.

Confronted with reality, I lost my smile. What was I playing at? I pulled my hand away and stood up. He followed me so quickly that he nearly overturned the table.

'No,' I said, but he followed me out of the dim, air-conditioned bar, into the parking lot. The hot, tropical night embraced us like a sweaty lover. Someone, in a book I'd once read, had compared the smell of Houston to the aroma of a woman, sexually aroused and none too clean. I drew a deep breath; spilled beer, gasoline, car exhaust, cooking fumes, perfume, after-shave, rotting vegetation, garbage,

....

LISA TUTTLE

and, beneath it all, a briny tang that might have been a breeze wafted in from the Gulf of Mexico.

He was right behind me, following, and as I turned to tell him off, somehow instead I fell against him. And then we were clutching each other, breast to breast, mouth to mouth, kissing greedily. The need I felt when he first touched me, the intensity with which it rushed all through me was so powerful I thought I would faint. Then, slowly, resting in his embrace, I came back to myself, back to him. I had never known anything as sensually beautiful as his mouth; the soft, warm lips that parted against mine, dryness opening into wetness, a moist cave where the sly, clever animal that was his tongue lived and came out to nuzzle and suck at me greedily. His breath was smoky and dark, tasting of desirable sins, of whiskey and sugar and cigarettes.

His hands, long-fingered, strong and clever, moved over my body as we kissed, at first shy, but then, as I clung to him fiercely, making no attempt to push him off, becoming bolder. He was quickly impatient with the barriers of my clothes, which were little enough: a cotton blouse, a short summer skirt and underwear, my legs bare, naked feet strapped into leather sandals. One of his hands, which had returned again and again to cup and trace lazy patterns of arousal on my bound and covered breasts, now began swiftly and without fumbling to unbutton my blouse, while his other hand, behind me, was pushing up my skirt and tugging at the elastic of my panties. In a matter of minutes, maybe seconds, he could have me stripped naked.

I wanted nothing better than to be naked in his capable hands, but not here, in public, surrounded by strangers – was he crazy? 'No,' I gasped and pushed him off and pulled away, struggling to refasten my buttons.

He reached for me again, and I slapped at his hands. He looked stricken. 'I want you. Don't you . . .?'

I laughed. 'Not here, be reasonable!' There were people all around us, getting in and out of cars, overflow customers from the bar and people from the neighborhood out for a breath of air, drinking beer from six-packs purchased at the convenience store across the street. This parking lot and the whole street was like a fair or a carnival, an impromptu, open-air party to celebrate summer in the city. I waved a hand to indicate the crowd passion had temporarily hidden from us, and as if I'd waved away smoke we both saw, at the same time, a man and woman locked in a fervent embrace just yards away from us. As I stared, I realized that the woman had one hand inside the front of the man's trousers.

My stranger grinned at me, a wide, white, wolfish smile. He put his hands on my hips and pulled me tightly to him. His erection felt enormous. His breath hot in my ear, he whispered, 'Nobody's going to notice. Nobody'll care.'

It was true nobody else seemed to notice the passionate couple, or, if they did, they politely pretended not to see. Other people had their own concerns; why should they care? Nor would it have been different if the lovers had been of the same sex. The Montrose was the most Bohemian and most sexually tolerant area of Houston, which was why I had chosen it for my escape that night. It provided a place where I could temporarily forget who and where I was and become a stranger, pretending I was a free woman at large in San Francisco, New Orleans or Paris.

The smoky, spicy, sweaty smell of this other stranger, his body's heat and solid mass against me, the hands that caressed my hips and thighs and breasts, all wore away at my hesitation, as did his low voice, telling me a story:

'I was at a rock concert one time, thousands of people packed in close together, all standing up to see better, and moving, kind of dancing in place because there wasn't room to do anything else. I was with this girl ... she had on a really short skirt, like yours, and one time when she dropped her purse and bent over to pick it up I saw she wasn't wearing any underpants. So ... I got her to stand in front of me, and I unzipped, and slipped it in, and slowly, easily, pumped away. Nobody knew what we were doing. Even

....

when we both came nobody noticed, because everybody was yelling and hopping around.' He had pushed up my skirt at the back again and now snagged the elastic of my underpants – soaking wet by now – and began to ease them down.

'No.'

Half of me wanted him to ignore my refusal, not to stop, to take me there among the crowds, even to be seen by disapproving, envious strangers – the other half of me was horrified. What if somebody who knew me came by, somebody I worked with, or one of my neighbors? So I said no again more fiercely, and when I pulled away he let me go.

'You're driving me crazy.'

'What do you think you're doing to me?'

'Nothing, compared to what I'd like to do.'

We stared at each other, hot and itchy with frustration. I grabbed his hand. 'We'll find somewhere not so public. Come on.'

I had nowhere in mind except to get away from the crowds. We walked away from the laughter and talk, away from the blare of amplified music and the bright blur of neon signs toward the quieter streets where there were no bars or all-night service stations, no massage parlors or convenience stores; quieter streets lined with trees where the buildings housed beauty parlors and dentists, small businesses that closed up at nightfall. On one such half-deserted street he pulled me suddenly into the embrasure of a darkened antique shop and pushed me up against the wall.

'No.' I whispered the word, soft as a caress. I wasn't even sure he heard. His hands were swift and urgent. My blouse was unbuttoned, my bra undone, my breasts out, nipples teased and kneaded to an aching stiffness. I surrendered, undone, melting, and then quite suddenly I saw myself from the outside: some slut, half undressed in a public place with a stranger, letting a stranger do that to her – I woke up with a sickening shock. That couldn't be me. I'd always been

....

a good girl even; before I married I'd only had two steady boyfriends; I'd never picked up strange men. Now that I was a married woman this sort of behavior was unthinkable. Sex was something that happened at home, in bed, not in a shop doorway.

I tensed and fought off his hands. I twisted to one side and struggled to push him away, but he pinned my wrists together effortlessly, one-handed, and stared at me, a faint smile twitching his lips.

'No,' I said weakly, not meaning it. I suddenly wanted more than anything to be overpowered, to be made to do what I wanted to do, to have the guilt taken away. He gazed into my eyes and read there what I wanted as he rolled an erect nipple between thumb and forefinger. I felt fixed by his gaze, unable to fight. I stood very still, quivering. He let go my hands and tugged my skirt up to my waist.

'Take off your pants and spread your legs,' he said.

I felt dizzy with desire. 'No,' I whispered. I didn't mean I didn't want to, and I didn't mean I did. By my word I meant a different kind of yes; meant make me do it, do it to me, I'm helpless now.

His eyes were unwavering on mine, but for a moment I was afraid he wouldn't understand. Then he said, 'Try and stop me.' He tugged at the waistband of my panties, and then gently peeled them down my legs. When they reached my ankles, I stepped out of them and stood passively, my sex exposed to his view.

A little sigh of pleasure escaped his lips as he looked at me. Then he became stern again. 'Up against the wall and spread your legs.'

I swallowed hard, then found my voice and the only word I had left. 'No.'

He laughed. 'No? No? What does that mean? Your body's saying something else.' He slipped his hand between my legs. I gasped and quivered as he found my wetness. 'Your body doesn't lie. Your body says yes.' His touch was as soft as his voice, delicate and perfectly judged. I moaned and

....

closed my eyes, unable to watch him watching me as he stroked my clitoris. I let him continue until his touch was too teasing, his fingering too delicate for my much harsher desire, and then I reached down to push his hand harder against me and his fingers inside me. He gasped as if he were the one penetrated, and I cried out with pleasure, a loud and violent 'No!'

The wall was hard against my back. My thighs ached with strain as I rode his hand, the clever, stranger's fingers that knew me better, it seemed, than I knew myself, knowing just how to stroke and to probe together, knowing when a teasing gentleness should become more brutal. All this time he watched me, watched my face contort and read my desire as he murmured obscenities and endearments, commands and compliments alternating with a purpose like the hard – soft touch of his hand.

And then his other hand was on my ass, fingers probing the crack, and I moaned as he began to work me with both hands, back and front, and I cried out for more, still more.

Without taking his hands away, hardly faltering, he went down on his knees and began tonguing my clitoris, breathing hard with his own excitement. The warm, wet touch of his mouth was gentle, exact, and excruciating, and it was more than I could bear. Like lightning, white-hot, jagged, and intense, the orgasm flashed as I cried and yelled and clutched his curly head. 'No,' I cried, and 'No' again, as if I must, in my last, desperate moments of pleasure, deny the force of that pleasure, or the reality of it – as if that word would keep it from being real to anyone but me.

Later, but still too soon, while I was rocked in the after-glow, unwilling to be disturbed, he caught my hand and carried it to his crotch, pressed it against the hard, warm bulge of his cock.

'No.'

I have often wondered what I meant by that. Never in my life before that night had I said no meaning yes, but

that night no was my word, my only word, and he had
seemed to understand.

I pulled my hand away. 'No.'

Maybe I'd forgotten how to say yes. Maybe I wanted him
to force me. Maybe I'd just had enough and wanted to send
him away. Maybe, my own desire sated, I simply wasn't
interested in his. Later, when I wanted more, I couldn't
believe I'd meant I'd had enough then. I didn't want to
believe I'd been selfish enough to send him away unsatisfied
simply because my own immediate need had been met.
Most of the time I preferred to believe that when I said no
at the end I still meant yes, and that it was his understanding
that failed him, and me.

Whatever I might have meant, whatever I'd wanted it to
mean, he heard me say no, and took me at my word and
left, and I made no effort to call him back.

I never saw him again, although there were nights when
I went looking, and there has scarcely been a night since
then that I haven't thought of him and longed for another
chance.

After dinner, my husband and I took coffee in the large,
yet cozy library, seated on one of the couches upholstered
in leather as soft and supple as living skin, near the fire
crackling in the hearth. We didn't talk to any of the other
guests – we were being more English than the English on
that trip – but we didn't have much to say to each other.
Maybe we'd been married too long, maybe we were
inhibited by the company. Certainly I was memory-haunted,
aroused by the presence of the young man who looked so
much like my long-ago stranger. Guilt made me uneasy in
my husband's company, made me flinch when he touched
me. My eyes kept sneaking across to him, and I pretended
it was the books in the floor-to-ceiling bookcases that
interested me. I felt him watching me, too, usually just as I
looked away, but occasionally our glances would intersect,
meeting for one highly charged instant before we both

....

hastily looked away. Was it possible that this boy found me as desirable as had his look-alike of nearly twenty years ago? I hoped my husband wouldn't notice, but maybe it wouldn't be such a bad thing for him to know that another man wanted me.

It grew late, and we left the library, passed through the great hall, and mounted the grand staircase, our feet silent on the thick, pile carpet. I gazed up at the Pre-Raphaelite beauties who adorned the brilliant stained-glass windows but hardly saw them through my memories of warm, sensuous lips, long, clever fingers, and the cock I had never known.

I undressed slowly and dreamily in our luxurious room. I was down to the black silk teddy he'd surprised me with on Valentine's Day when my husband came up behind me and pulled me to him, his hands on my breasts, his breath warm in my ear. I could feel his erection, and I was as aroused as he was, but by the memory of someone else.

Guilt, or something else, made me whisper, 'No.'

He kissed me gently on my neck, and I moved my silk-clad bottom teasingly. His hands tightened on my breasts while his lips sought out the pulse in my neck. Caught up by rising excitement, again guilt mingled with desire and I breathed, 'No,' and he let go.

I remained rooted to the spot for a few moments in astonished disappointment, feeling the chill of his departure, hearing him sigh as he got into bed.

But what else could I expect?

No had never meant yes in our shared vocabulary. I had never wanted it to until now, just this moment, when I longed for a little telepathy.

Tingling with frustration, I peeled off my useless sexy underwear and climbed naked into bed.

'Goodnight, my darling,' he said, and the chaste kiss he gave me forestalled my chance of letting him know, with my mouth on his, how I really felt. Of course I could have done something more obvious, or simply told him in words,

....

but I couldn't think of the right words. I was in a mood to be taken, not to take, so all I could do was lie there wide awake, sulking about being misunderstood and horny, while he fell asleep with insulting ease. Surely, if he'd *really* wanted me he wouldn't have been able to sleep. Surely, if he'd really wanted me, he would not have walked away.

Time in darkness alone passes slowly. I thought again about that long-ago night and imagined I hadn't said no, but yes. Or that he had ignored my token protest, had pushed me against the wall and taken me, willingly against my will. Pleasure without guilt; I didn't want to, I couldn't help it, he made me . . . The game I had to play if I were to remain a happily married woman. Finally I got up. I thought I'd seen a copy of *The Story of O* on the bookshelves downstairs. With a little help from my hand, it might help me to sleep. I wrapped a silk kimono around my nakedness and left my sleeping husband.

The great house was silent, although not dark. Electric lights in the form of candles burned on the walls of the hallways, illuminating all the closed bedroom doors. I imagined all the other guests paired in pleasure except the solitary stranger, who might be lying awake now, as horny as I was, and for the same reason. I wished I knew which was his door.

In the library the fire still burned, casting enough light to show me that someone was there before me.

He must have had the same reason as I did for coming here. As I entered the room he turned in surprise from the bookcase, a book in one hand. He wore a short, flimsy robe, tied with a sash. Under it, I knew, he was naked.

We stared at each other without speaking for what seemed a long time. There aren't many times in life that you get a second chance. I knew I'd never forgive myself if I didn't take this one. I closed the door firmly behind me and walked into the room. When I was only a few feet away from him, standing in the full glow of the fire, I stopped, untied my kimono, and shrugged it off, enjoying the sen-

. . . .

sation as it slithered silkily down my naked body and settled on the floor, enjoying also the gleam of his eyes as he stared at me without speaking.

He made no voluntary motion, but I saw the rising of his heavy cock, and the blood-flushed, rounded head parted the silken curtain of his dressing-gown, roused by my nakedness. I had never seen it before, and it was bigger and more solid than any of my fantasies.

I smiled and licked my lips. A few steps more, and I sank to my knees before him.

'No,' he said. He caught me by the shoulders and raised me up. 'I'm going to fuck you – the way I should have done years ago. You won't get away from me this time.'

I was stunned. It wasn't possible that this was the same young man I'd picked up in a bar almost twenty years before – he wasn't old enough, and he spoke with an English accent. But if he wasn't the same man, how did he *know?*

His hands were on me, rougher than I remembered, and greedier as he felt and fondled my nakedness. Then he pulled me hard against him, the silk of his robe like the cool fall of water against my skin. His warm, firm cock butted at my sex, and he kissed me. How I could remember such a thing with any certainty after so long a time, I don't know, but his lips felt like the same lips, and his mouth tasted still of desirable sins: of whiskey and sugar and, very faintly, cigarettes. I nearly swooned with pleasure as his tongue moved in my mouth and his hands, gripping my hips, moved to caress and explore my buttocks and finally between my legs.

He laughed, finding me so wet and ready for his probing fingers. 'You're hot, aren't you? Can't pretend you don't want me.'

'No,' I murmured into his mouth, agreeing. I wanted him, now, hard, fast, slow, any way at all.

Without letting go of me, his mouth fastened firmly, devouringly, on mine, his cock prodding me, he walked me backward and pushed me down on my back on the very

....

same leather couch where I'd sat drinking coffee with my husband a few hours earlier.

The shock of memory, of sudden guilt, made me struggle up and exclaim, 'No . . . I can't . . .'

'Oh, yes you can.'

'No.' I said it reluctantly as I struggled to rise, sorry that he wasn't stopping me, outraged that I wasn't stopping myself. But my freedom was an illusion. As soon as I had regained my feet he caught me in his arms and picked me up with a strength I had not known he possessed. Ignoring my feeble efforts to escape, he turned me around and pushed me down, face first on the couch. It was warm and solid, both yielding and supporting, covered in leather so fine that I had the sensation of having been pressed down on top of some other person. Before I could even catch my breath he was lifting me by the ass, a cheek in each hand, and then I felt his lips on my labia, his hot, clever tongue raking my clitoris.

All protest, all urge to flight, rushed out of me in a low moan of pleasure. He drew his head away with a low laugh. 'Yes, you'd like that, wouldn't you? Let me do anything but fuck you . . . But that's what I'm going to do, and nothing you say can stop me.'

I said nothing. I didn't think about what I wanted, or what was right. I lay still and let him position me for his pleasure. I was lying nearly flat, face down on the broad leather-cushioned couch, my legs dangling over the edge. He lifted my ass and parted my legs and the head of his cock nudged at the slick lips of my cunt. I couldn't see him anyway, this stranger my lover behind me, so I closed my eyes and gave myself up to physical sensation.

He was very big and greedy in his lust. Although I was very wet and willing, he spared me no tenderness but thrust himself inside me hard and fast, using his hands to part the cheeks of my ass at the same time, as if he wanted to split me in two. Even as I welcomed and wanted this penetration,

. . . .

at the same time the sensation of being forced was strong, and I cried out, half fainting with the shock of it.

'No . . . oh, no . . .'

He laughed and thrust again, this time burying himself to the hilt in me. Withdrawing slightly, he thrust again. 'No?' With each thrust he repeated the word which came out sometimes as a croon, sometimes as a gasp, and I echoed him.

'No . . . no . . . no . . .'

Our denials came closer and closer together as he found a hard, driving rhythm that satisfied both of us. I lost all sense of place and time and even of self as he drove into me and drove himself, and me, finally, over the brink into a fierce, all-consuming orgasm, with a final shout in which our two voices mingled.

A little while later I felt him withdraw. I made a small sound of protest but no move, too exhausted and happy where I was, sprawled facedown and legs spread on the couch. Until I heard the door to the library open.

Annoyed that he could leave me this way, I opened my eyes and raised my head just as the lights came on. There in the doorway, coolly surveying me and my lover, was my husband.

He looked at me, lying naked and flushed, and then at the man, also naked, his still-rampant penis glistening with our mingled juices. It was very quiet. And then, shockingly, he smiled.

'Happy anniversary, darling,' he said. 'I hope you enjoyed yourself?'

I began to push myself up, my mind whirling.

'Oh, no,' he said. 'Stay there, please. Or shall I ask our friend to hold you down?'

My erstwhile lover was beside me at once, his hands on my shoulders firmly keeping me from changing my position.

'I certainly hope you enjoyed yourself, because now it's my turn,' my husband continued. There was a note in his voice that I had not heard in a very long time, and I suddenly realized that he had set this up, a sexual game of a sort I had never imagined he would want to play, an unexpected anniversary gift for both of us, and suddenly I felt more excited than I would have thought possible.

'You've been a naughty girl,' said my husband. 'So I've asked our friend to stay . . . I'm going to have to punish you first, before we can kiss and make up.'

I began an ineffective struggle to get away, but the stranger had no trouble restraining me. 'No,' I whimpered. 'Please. No.'

Autopsy

· ·

IVAN VLADISLAVIĆ

Um.

Basically, I was seated at the Potato Kitchen in Hillbrow partaking (excuse me) of a potato. Nothing very exciting had happened to me as yet: I was therefore dissatisfied and alert. Then the King Himself came out of Estoril Books, shrugged His scapular girdle, and turned left. It was the King, no doubt about it, I would know His sinuous gait anywhere. Even in a mob.

It was supper-time, Friday, 15 May 1992. Scored upon my memory like a groove in wax. I lift the stylus, meaning to plunge it precisely into the vein, but the mechanism does not have nerves of steel: the device hums and haws before it begins to speak. (The speakers, the vocal cords, the voicebox, the woofers, the tweeters, the *loud* speakers.) So much for memory, swaddled in the velvety folds of the brain and secured in the cabinet of the skull.

My potato was large and carved into quarters, like a colony or a thief. It had been microwaved and bathed in letcho with sausage and bacon. Also embrocated with garlic butter (R0.88 extra) and poulticed with grated cheddar as yellow as straw (R1.80 extra). Moreover, encapsulated in white polystyrene.

I was holding a white plastic fork in my left hand. I was stirring, with the white plastic teaspoon in my right hand, the black coffee in a white polystyrene cup.

The slip from the cash register lay on the table folded into a fan. It documented this moment in time, choice of

· · · · · · · · ·

menu-item and price including VAT (15.05.92/letch R9.57/
chee R1.80/coff R1.90/garl butt R0.88).

Although it was chilly, I had chosen a table on the pavement so that I could be part of the vibrant street life of
Johannesburg's most cosmopolitan suburb. A cold front
deep-frozen in the south Atlantic was at that very moment
crossing the mud-banks of the Vaal. The street-children
squatting at the kerb looked preternaturally cold and hungry
with their gluey noses and methylated lips.

One of the little beggars was an Indian. Apartheid is
dead.

I found myself in the new improved South Africa, seated
upon an orange plastic chair, stackable, but not stacked at
this juncture. It was one of four chairs – two orange, two
umber – drawn up to a round white plastic table with a
hole through its middle, specially engineered to admit the
shaft of the beach umbrella, which shaft was also white,
while the umbrella itself was composed of alternating seg-
ments of that colour and Coca-Cola red. My legs were
crossed, right over left. The toe of my right shoe was tapping
out against a leg of the table the homesickening heartbeat
of 'O mein Papa' throbbing from the gills of a passing Ford
Laser.

The King chose that very moment to exit Estoril Books
with a rolled magazine under His arm. He paused before
the buffet of cut-price paperbacks on two trestle-tables. He
examined cracked spines and dog-ears. He scanned the pro-
motional literature.

A saddening scenario presented itself: every book will
change your life.

Bundling Himself up in His diet, He turned left, took
eight sinuous steps, choreographing heel, toe, knee and hip
by turns, all His own work, and turned left again into the
polyunsaturated interior of Tropical Fast Foods. He was a
natural. He passed under the neon sign: a green coconut
palm inclined against an orange sunset while the sun sank

....

like an embolus into a sea of lymph. Las Vegas Motel –
Color TV – 5 mi. from Damascus – Next exit.

Adventure beckoned.

I had consumed no more than 25 per cent of my meal –
let's say R3.00's worth – and hadn't so much as sipped the
coffee, but I rose as one man, dragged on my trench coat
and hurried inside to pay the bill. My white plastic knife
remained jutting from the steaming potato like a disposable
Excalibur.

'*Danke schön*,' I said, in order to ingratiate myself with
the Potato Woman of Düsseldorf.

'*Fünfzig, fünfzehn*,' she replied, dishing change into my
palm, and banged the drawer of the cash register with her
chest.

Los!

On my way into the night I skirted five children squabbling over my leftovers: three-quarters of a potato (75 per
cent), divisible by five only with basic arithmetic.

I sauntered across Pretoria Street, dodged a midnight-
blue BMW with one headlight, cursed silently. In the few
short minutes that had passed since the sighting, a grain of
doubt had jammed in the treads of my logic, and now I
paused on the threshold of Tropical Fast Foods, in the
shadow of the electric tree, suddenly off balance. Where am
I? Or rather: Where was I? Hollywood Boulevard? Dar es
Salaam? Dakar? The Botanical Gardens in Durban?

Oh.

The man I had taken for the King was leaning against
the counter with His back to me, gulping the fat air down.
Blue denim jacket with tattered cuffs; digital watch, water-
resistant to 100 metres (333 feet); track-suit pants, black
with a white stripe; blue tackies (sneakers), scuffed; white
socks stuck with blackjacks.

The Griller assembled a yiro (R9.50). He pinched shav-
ings of mutton from an aluminium scoop with a pair of
tongs and heaped them on a halo of unleavened pitta
bread. He piled sliced onions and sprinkled the unique

....

combination of tropical seasonings. I turned aside to the poker machine and dropped a rand in the slot.

The machine dealt me a losing hand.

Meanwhile, the spitted mutton turned at 2 r.p.m., like a stack of rare seven-singles in a jukebox. A skewered onion wept on top of the pile. Where the Griller's blade had pared, the meat's pink juices ran, spat against the cauterizing elements, which glowed like red neon, and congealed upon the turntable.

I drew the Jack of Diamonds *and* the King of Hearts.

The man I had taken for the King turned to the Manager and spoke inaudibly from the right side of His mouth. There was no mistaking the aerodynamic profile, the airbrushed quiff as sleek as a fender, black with a blue highlight, the wraparound shades like a chrome-plated bumper, the Velcro sideburns, the tender lips.

The Manager amplified the whispered request for more salt.

The Griller obliged.

I kept the Jack *and* the King, against my better judgement.

The Manager cupped a paper bag under a stainless-steel funnel and tipped a basketful of chips (fries) down it. He dashed salt and pepper, shook the bag, and handed it to the King. The King throttled the bag and squirted tomato sauce (ketchup) down its throat like advertising.

The Griller finished assembling a yiro (R9.50). He rolled it expertly in greaseproof paper and serviette (napkin), slipped it into a packet and handed it to the Manager, who passed it to the King. The King took the yiro in His left hand. With His right hand He produced a large green note (bill), which the Manager held up to the light before clamping it in the register.

A flash of snow-white under the frayed cuff when the King reached for His change. Not a card up His sleeve but a clue: sunburst catsuit, doubling as thermal underwear.

The King dropped the coins into a money belt concealed under His belly. He took up the (fries). He swivelled

....

IVAN VLADISLAVIĆ

sinuously and tenderly. Anatomical detail: sinews and
tendons rotated the ball of the femur in the lubricious socket
of the hip. (Nope.) Of the pelvic girdle? (Yep.) He slid on
to an orange plastic stool. His buttocks, sheathed in white
silk within and black polyester without, chubbed over the
edge.

He pushed the shades up on to His forehead. He took
out a pair of reading-glasses with tear-drop rims of silver
wire, breathed on the lenses (uhuh), buffed them on His
thigh and put them on.

Now I might have hurried over, saying: 'Excuse me. I
couldn't help noticing.'

Instead, I looked away.

In the screen of the poker machine His reflection unrolled
not one magazine but four: the February issue of *Musclemag
International (The Body-Building Bible)*, the April issue of
Stern, the Special Collector's issue of *Der Kartoffelbauer*
(March) and the November 1991 issue of *Guns & Ammo*.
He spread them on the counter, chose the *Stern*, rolled the
other three into a baton and stuffed them into a pocket.

He opened the magazine to the feature on Steffi Graf
and flattened it with His left forearm. With His right hand
He peeled back the greaseproof paper and with His left He
raised the yiro. His Kingly lips mumbled the meat as if it
were a microphone.

The menu said it was lamb, but it was mutton.

A full-page photograph showed Steffi Graf serving an
ace. It captured her racket smashing the page number (22)
off the top left-hand corner of the page and the sole of her
tennis shoe squashing the date (April) into the clay. It captured the hem of her skirt floating around her hips like a
hula hoop. The King gazed at her thighs, especially the
deep-etched edge of the biceps femoris, but also at her
wrists, with their eight euphonious bones – scaphoid, semi-
lunar, cuneiform, pisiform, trapezium, trapezoid, unciform,
os magnum – enclasped by fragrant sweat-bands, and her
moisturized elbows scented with wintergreen.

....

Er.

Then He gazed at the talkative walls. The muscle in His
mandible throbbed, the tip of His tongue simonized the
curve of His lips with mutton fat. He spoke with a full
mouth, He pronounced the lost opportunities under His
breath: Hamburger R4.95 – Debrecziner R6.50 – Frank-
furter & Chips – R6.95.

He chewed. He swallowed.

Eating made Him sweat. He was fat, He needed to lose
some weight. He'd lost (six and a half pounds) in the fifteen
years since His last public appearance, but still He was fat.
An eight o'clock shadow fell over His jaw, He needed to
shave. He needed to floss, there was a caraway seed lodged
against the gum between canine and incisor, maxilla, right,
there was mutton between molars. He needed to shampoo,
His hair bore the tooth-marks of the comb like the grooves
of a 78.

He ate, it made Him sweat. A bead of sweat fell like a
silver sequin from the end of His nose and vanished into
a wet polka dot on His double-jointed knee. He swabbed
His brow with the (napkin). He licked His fingers and wiped
them on His pants. He got up and walked out.

Wearing His shades on His forehead and His reading-
glasses on His nose, He glided over the greasy (sidewalk).

I hurried after Him, pausing momentarily to pluck: the
Stern, which He had left open on the counter, the corners
of the pages impregnated with His seasoned saliva; the
(napkin) bearing the impress of His brow; and the sequin.
(I have these relics still.)

He took eight sinuous steps and turned left into the Plus
Pharmacy Centre and Medicine Depot. He padded down
the aisle, between the Supradyn-N and the Lucozade (on the
one hand) and the Joymag Acusoles: Every Step in Comfort
(on the other), to the counter marked Prescriptions/Voor-
skrifte.

The Pharmacist was a bottle-blonde. She was neither cur-
vaceous nor bubbly, wore a white coat, bore less than a

....

passing resemblance to Jayne Mansfield. The King spoke to her out of the left side of His mouth. He proffered an American Express traveller's cheque and a passport.

Two other customers were browsing: a man in a blue gown, a woman in a tuxedo. She shooed them out and closed the door in my face. There was a poster Sellotaped to the glass: Find out about drug abuse inside. Under cover of studying the small print I was able to gaze into the interior.

The King pulled a royal-blue pillowslip embroidered with golden musical notation and silver lightning bolts out of the front of His pants. He swept from the laden shelves into His bag nineteen bottles of Borstol linctus, sixteen bottles of Milk of Magnesia, twenty-two plastic tubs brimming with multi-vitamin capsules (100s), fifty-seven tubes of grape-flavoured Lip-Ice, three bottles of Oil of Olay, four aerosol cans of hair lacquer, twelve Slimslabs, three boxes of Doctor McKenzie's Veinoids, five bottles of Eno, twenty-five tubes of Deep Heat, a king-size bottle of Bioplus, five hot-water bottles with teddy-bear covers, an alarm clock, six tubs of Radium leather and suede dye with handy applicators, a jar of beestings and a box of Grandpa Headache Powders.

The Pharmacist tagged along, jabbing a calculator.

He signed the cheque.

I rootled in a bombproof (trash can).

He took eleven sinuous steps.

The Pharmacist held the door open for Him, and shut it behind Him when He had passed, breathing in His garlicky slipstream.

He found Himself once more upon the (sidewalk) among the hurly-burly of ordinary folk.

I might have made an approach with right hand extended: 'Long time no see.'

Instead, I hid my face.

He breathed. He took off the reading-glasses, He pulled down the shades. He settled His bag of tricks on His left shoulder. He turned right.

....

The King moved on foot through the Grey Area.

Now He took five hundred and seventy-one sinuous steps and turned right again. Attaboy.

Window-shopping:

He passed Checkers. He passed the hawkers of hubbard squashes. He passed Fontana: Hot Roast Chickens. He passed the Hare Krishnas dishing out vegetable curry to the non-racial poor on paper plates. He passed the International Poker Club: Members Only, and the Ambassador Liquor Store: Free Ice. He passed the Lichee Inn: Chinese Take-aways. He gave a poor girl a dime. He passed the hawkers of deodorant and sticking-plaster. He passed the Hillcity Pharmacy, Wimpy: The Home of the Hamburger, and Summit Fruiters. He shifted the bag of tricks to His right shoulder. He passed Hillbrow Pharmacy Extension (a.k.a. Farmácia/Pharmacie). He passed the hawkers of wooden springboks and soapstone elephants. He dropped His Diner's Club card in a hobo's hat. He passed the Café Three Sisters, Norma Jean, Look and Listen, Terry's Deli, The Golden Egg, Le Poulet Chicken Grill, Gringo's Fast Food, Bella Napoli and Continental Confectioners: Baking by Marco. He passed the hawkers of block-mounted repro-ductions of James Dean with his eyes smouldering and Marilyn Monroe with her skirt flying. Late, both of them. He passed the Shoe Hospital: Save Our Soles. He passed the hawkers of block-mounted reproductions of Himself with the white fringes of His red cowboy shirt swishing, and the black fringes of His blue hairstyle dangling, and the grey shadows of the fringes of His black eyelashes fluttering. Himself as a Young Man. His name was printed on His shirt, over the alveoli of His left lung.

He felt sad to be a reproductive system.

Sniffing, He turned right into the Wurstbude.

'*Guten Abend,*' He said. '*Wie geht's*?'

'*So lala,*' said the Sausage Man of Stuttgart.

The King extracted a pickled cucumber as fat and green as His opposable thumb from the jar on the counter. '*Ich*

....

möchte eine Currywurst,' He said, sucking on the cuke, *'mit Senf, bitte.'*

(R4.70.)

He held His breath as the wurst went down the stainless-steel chute. One flick of the lever and the blades fell: the wurst spilled out in cross-sections two-fifths of an inch thick.

'Fünfundzwanzig ... dreissig, sieben, zehn,' the Sausage Man said.

'Ich bin ein Johannesburger,' the King replied. *'Auf Wiedersehen.'*

At the barrel-table outside He ate the lopped sausage expertly with a brace of toothpicks, in the time-honoured manner. He broke the bread and mopped the sauce. He dusted away the crumbs.

Momentarily satiated, shaded, the King moved once more through the Grey Area; once more He moved sinuously; once more He appreciated the cosmopolitan atmosphere. (We both did.)

Now He took two hundred and seventy-five steps (Squash and Fitness Health World, Tommy's 24-Hour Superette, Bunny Chow, Bengal Tiger Coffee Bar and Restaurant, hawkers of baobab sap and the mortal remains of baboons, Econ-o-Wash, Magnum Supermarket, Jungle Inn Restaurant, Quality Butchery: Hindquarters packed and labelled) and turned right.

He stopped. He parked the bag of tricks. He hitched down the track-suit pants with His left hand and unzipped the catsuit with His right. He reached into the vent and abstracted a dick.

I was too far away, propped against a fireplug like a gumshoe, to determine whether this organ had charisma. But I was close enough to hear a musical fountain of urine against a prefabricated bollard and to see afterwards on the flagstones a puddle shaped like a blackbird.

He moved. He took one hundred and one steps (Faces Health and Beauty: Body Massage, American Kitchen-City,

....

Hair Extensions International) and turned left into the dim interior of Willy's Bar.

The fascia of Willy's Bar was patched with the gobblede-gook of the previous tenant's plastic signage: Julius Caesar's Restaurant and Cocktail Bar, upside down and backwards.

Willy's Bar was licensed to sell wine, malt and spirits, right of admission reserved.

The King and I felt like blacks, because of the way He walked. Everyone else felt like whites. Nevertheless, Apartheid was dead.

I ordered a Black Label and went to the john.

The King sat at the counter. He put on His spectacles and fossicked about in the bag of tricks. He swallowed a handful of pills. He swallowed a Bioplus on the rocks and chased it with a Jim Beam.

He had a fuzzy moustache of curry powder on His upper lip. It affected me. I hid my face behind the *Star* (City Late) so that I wouldn't feel spare.

We watched the weather report together. The cold front was on our doorstep, they said. The King was dissatisfied. I thought He might draw a handgun, but He did not. He just took a powder and pulled a mouth.

I read the Smalls.

Spare is another word for lonesome.

We watched *Agenda*: the ANC's economic policy.

Ah.

While a party spokesman was explaining the difference between property and theft, the strains of 'Abide with Me' drifted in through the batwing doors.

A far-away look stole over the King's features. He gulped His drink, slapped a greenback on the counter and went out.

I followed after, lugging the depleted bag of tricks and the change (R3.50).

O Thou who changest not, abide with me, the Golden City Gospel Singers beseeched Him. In a moment He had

....

insinuated Himself into their circle, between the blonde with the tambourine and the brunette with the pamphlets.

A chilly wind blew over the ridge from the Civic Theater. It picked up a tang of Dettol from the City Shelter and Purity from the Florence Nightingale Nursing Home. It swept sour curls of sweat and burnt porridge out of the Fort and wrapped them in dry leaves from the gutters. Tissue-paper and handbills tumbled over the flagstones. The wind coughed into the microphone.

Ills have no weight, and tears no bitterness.

The King opened His mouth. Then He gaped, as if He'd forgotten the words, and shut it again. He would not reveal Himself.

I wept. I wept in His stead. For what right had I to weep on my own behalf? To weep for the insufferable bitterness of being dead for ever and the ineffable sweetness of being born again?

The hymn came to a sticky end. A siren bawled on Hospital Hill. The brunette pressed a pamphlet into my hand: Boozers are Loozers.

I seized His arm and felt a surprisingly firm brachio-radialis through the cloth. He shrugged me off – a sequin shot from His cuff and ricocheted into the darkness – but the damage had been done: no sooner had I touched Him, than He began to vanish.

I was moved to call out, 'The King! The King!' The brunette embraced me and cried, 'Amen!' Two hours later I still had the imprint of her hair-clip on my temple.

While I was being mobbed, someone walked off with the bag of tricks.

Laughter: involuntary contractions of the facial muscles, saline secretions of the lachrymal ducts, contortions of the labia.

Vanishing-point: a crooked smile, a folderol of philtrum, nothing.

I hunted high and low for the King, in karaoke bars,

....

escort agencies, drugstores, ice-cream parlors and soda foun-
tains, but found no trace of Him.

I have a feeling in my bones – patellae, to be precise –
that He is still out there.

Appendix
The very next morning I saw Steve Biko coming out of the
Juicy Lucy at the Norwood Hypermarket. I followed him to
the hardware department, where he gave me the slip.

The Achieve of, the Mastery of the Thing

LAURIE COLWIN

Once upon a time, I was Professor Thorne Speizer's stoned wife, and what a time that was. My drug of choice was plain, old-fashioned marijuana – these were the early days when that was what an ordinary person could get. By the time drugs got more interesting, I felt too old to change. I stood four-square behind reefer except when a little opiated hash came along, which was not often.

Thorne was an assistant professor when I first met him. I took his Introduction to Modern European History – a class I was compelled to take and he was forced to teach. Thorne was twenty-seven and rather a young Turk. I was twenty-one and rather a young pothead. I sat in the back of the class and contemplated how I could get my hands on Thorne and freak him out. I liked the idea that I might bring a little mayhem into the life of a real adult. Thorne was older and had a job. That made him a real citizen in my eyes. He also had an extremely pleasing shape, a beautiful smile, and thick brown hair. His manner in class was absolutely professional and rather condescending. Both of these attitudes gave me the shivers.

I employed the tricks childish adolescents use to make the substitute math teacher in high school nervous. I stared at his fly. Then I stared at him in a wide-eyed, moronic way. At a point of desperation when I felt he would never notice me, I considered drooling. I smiled in what I hoped was a promising and tempting fashion.

It turned out that Thorne was not so hard to get. He was only waiting for me to stop being his student and then he pounced on me. I was high during our courtship so I did not actually notice when things got out of hand. I was looking for a little fun. Thorne wanted to get married. I felt, one lazy afternoon when a little high-quality grass had unexpectedly come my way, that a person without ambitions or goals should do something besides smoke marijuana, and marriage was certainly something to do. Furthermore, I was truly crazy about Thorne.

I got wrecked on my wedding day. I stood in front of the mirror in my wedding dress and stared intently at my stick of grass. You should not smoke this on this day of days, I said to myself, lighting up. Surely if you are going to take this serious step, I said, inhaling deeply, you ought to do it straight.

You may well imagine how hard it was for an innocent college girl to score in those dark times. You had to run into some pretty creepy types to get what you wanted. These types preferred heavier substances such as smack and goofballs. How very puzzled they were at the sight of a college girl in her loafers and loden coat. For a while they thought I was a narc. After they got used to me they urged me to stick out my arm and smack up with them, but I declined. The channels through which you found these types were so complicated that by the time you got to them you forgot exactly how you got to them in the first place, and after a while they died or disappeared or got busted and you were then left to some jerky college boy who sold speed at exam time as well as some sort of homegrown swill that gave you a little buzz and a headache.

Of course I did not tell Thorne that I used this mild but illegal hallucinogen. He would have been horrified, I believed. I liked believing that. It made me feel very free. Thorne would take care of the worrying and I would get high. I smoked when he was out of the room, or out of the house. I smoked in the car, in the bathroom, in the attic, in

the woods. I thanked God that Thorne, like most privileged
children, had allergies and for a good half of the year was
incapable of detecting smoke in the house. And of course,
he never noticed that I was stoned since I had been stoned
constantly since the day we met.

Thorne took me away to a pastoral men's college where
there were sure to be no drugs, I felt. That was an emblem
of how far gone I was about him – that I could be dragged
off to such an environment. However, a brief scan of the
campus turned up a number of goofy stares, moronic giggles,
and out-of-it grins. It did not take me long to locate my
fellow head.

In those days professors were being encouraged to relate
meaningfully to their students. I did my relating by telephone. Meaningful conversations took place, as follows:

'Hello, Kenny. Am I calling too early?'

'Wow, no, hey Mrs Speizer.'

'Say, Kenny. Can't you just call me Ann.' I was only
three years older than Kenny but being married to a faculty
member automatically made one a different species.

'Hey,' said Kenny. 'I'll call you Mrs Ann.'

'Listen, Kenny. Is it possible to see you today on a matter
of business?'

'Rightaway, Mrs Ann. I'll meet you at six in front of the
Shop-Up.'

That's how it was done in those days. You met your
connection in an inconspicuous place – like the supermarket,
and he dropped a nickel bag – generally all these boys sold
– on top of your groceries and you slipped him the money.
Things were tough all right. Furthermore, the adminis-
trations of these colleges were obsessed by the notion that
boys and girls might be sleeping together. Presumably the
boys would have had to sleep with the drab girls from
the girls' college ten miles away which had a strict curfew.
Or they would be forced to hurl themselves at the campus
wives who were of two varieties: ruddy, cheerful mothers of
three with master's degrees, private incomes, foreign cars,

and ten-year marriages. Then there were older wives with gray hair, grown sons, old mink coats, and station wagons. These women drank too much sherry at parties and became very, very still. Both kinds of wife played tennis, and their houses smelled evocatively of a substance my ultimate connection, Lionel Browning, would call 'Wasp must.' Both of these kings of wives felt that students were animals; and they didn't like me very much either.

I was quite a sight. I was twenty-three and I wore little pink glasses. I wore blue jeans, polished boots, and men's shirts. For evening wear I wore extremely short skirts, anticipating the fashion by two or three years. I drove the car too fast, was not pregnant, and liked to listen to the Top 40. Faculty wives looked at me with fear – the fear that I knew something they did not know. When they had been my age they had already produced little Amanda or Jonathan and were about to start little Jeremy or Rachel. They wore what grown-up women wore, and they gave bridge and tea parties. These women lived a life in which drugs were what you gave your child in the form of orange-flavored aspirin so they did not, for example, go rooting around the campus looking for someone off of whom to score.

The older wives said to Thorne, whom they adored: 'Gracious, Thorne, don't Ann's legs get cold in those little skirts? Goodness, Thorne, I saw Ann *racing* around in the car with the radio on *so* loud.' These women hadn't seen anyone like me before, but years later after a few campus riots they would see a much more virulent and hostile form of me in large numbers. From my vantage point between the world of students and the world of faculty it was plain to see how much professors hated students who, since they had not yet passed through the heavy gates of adulthood, were considered feckless, stupid, with no right to anything.

It was assumed that Thorne was married to a hot ticket, but no one was sure what sort. This pleased Thorne – he did not mind having a flashy wife, and since I never

....

misbehaved I caused him no pain, but I looked as if I were the sort to misbehave and this secretly pleased him. My image on campus however was not my overriding concern. I was mostly looking for decent grass.

Connecting on the college campus of the day was troublesome. Everyone was paranoid. I was lucky that I did not have to add money to my worries – I had a tiny bit of inheritance, just enough to keep me happy. I was a good customer when I could find a supplier, mostly some volelike and furtive-looking boy. Those blithe young things who spent their high school days blowing dope in suburban movie houses had not yet appeared on campus – how happy we would all be to see them! One's connection was apt to flunk out or drop out, and once in a while they would graduate. As a result, I was passed hand to hand by a number of unsavory boys. For example, the disgusting Steve, who whined and sniffled and sold very inferior dope. Eventually Steve was thrown out of school and I was taken over by another unpleasant boy by the name of Lester Katz. He carried for Lionel Browning, and Lionel Browning was the real thing.

Lionel, who allowed himself to be called Linnie by those close to him, had laid low for his first three years at college. In his senior year he expanded from a self-supplier to a purveyor of the finest grass to only the finest heads – by that time there were enough to make such a sideline profitable. Lionel's daddy was an executive in a large company that had branches abroad. Lionel had grown up in Colombia, Hong Kong and Barbados, three places known for fine cannabis. He was a shadowy figure at college. He lived off campus and was not often seen except by my husband, Thorne, whose favorite student he was. I had never seen him – he sent Lester to bring me my dope, with messages such as: 'Mr Browning hopes you will enjoy this sampling.' It killed Lester that he called Lionel 'Mr Browning.' He said it killed Lionel that Professor Speizer's wife was such a head. When he said that, I looked into his beady little

....

eyes and it seemed a very good idea for me to go and check out this Lionel Browning who very well might have it in mind to blackmail me. Or maybe he was the uncool sort – the sort who might sidle up to his favorite professor and say: 'That dope I laid on your wife sure is choice.' Lionel lived off campus in a frame house. Only very advanced students lived off campus. On-campus rooms were very plush – suites with fireplaces and leaded glass windows. But the off-campus fellows considered themselves above the ordinary muck of college life. These boys were either taking drugs or getting laid or were serious scholars who could not stand the sight of their fellow boy in such quantities.

Lionel lived on the top floor and as I mounted the stairs – I had, of course, made an appointment – I expected that he would be a slightly superior edition of the runty, unattractive boys who sold dope. This was not the case at all. He looked, in fact, rather like me. He was blond, tall but small-boned, and he wore blue jeans, loafers with tassels, a white shirt and a blue sweater – almost the replica of what I was wearing. He smiled a nice, crooked smile, offered me a joint, and I knew at once that I had found what I was looking for.

Lionel did not fool around. He got bricks – big *Survey of English Literature*-size bricks of marijuana that came wrapped in black plastic and taped with black tape. Underneath this wrapping was a rectangular cake of moist, golden greenish brown grass – a beautiful sight. It was always a pleasure to help Linnie clean this attractive stuff. We spread newspapers on the floor and strained it through a coarse sieve. The dregs of this Linnie would sell to what he called the lower forms of life.

The lower forms included almost everyone on campus. The higher forms included people he liked. His own family, he said, was a species of mineral-like vegetation that grew on lunar soil. There were four children, all blond, each with a nickname: Leopold (Leafy), Lionel (Linnie), Mary Louise

....

(Mally), and Barbara (Bumpy or Bumps). His family drove Linnie crazy, and the thought of their jolly family outings and jolly family traditions caused him to stay high as often as possible, which was pretty often.

In matters of dope, it depends on who gets to you first. I was gotten to in Paris, the summer before I went off to college. I looked up the nice sons of some friends of my parents, and they turned me on. I had been sent to practice French and to have a broadening cultural experience. I learned to say, among other things: 'Yes, this African kif is quite heavenly. Do you have more? How much more? How much will you charge me per matchbox?'

The nice boys I looked up had just come back from Spain. They were giant heads and they had giant quantities. These boys were happy to get their mitts on such a receptive blank slate as me. Pot, they told me, was one of the great aids to mental entertainment. It produced unusual thoughts and brilliant insights. It freed the mind to be natural – the natural mind being totally open to the hilarious absurdities of things. It mixed the senses and gave flavor to music. All in all, well worth getting into. We would get stoned and go to the movies or listen to jazz or hang around talking for what may have been minutes and may have been hours. This was more fun than I ever imagined, so my shock when I went off to college and discovered my fellow head was profound. My fellow head was sullen, alienated, mute when high, inexpressive and no fun at all. Until I met Lionel, I smoked alone.

Lionel was my natural other. Stoned we were four eyes and one mind. We were simply made to get high together – we felt exactly the same way about dope. We liked to light up and perambulate around the mental landscape seeing what we could see. We often liked to glom on to the 'Jill and Bill Show' – that was what we called one of the campus's married couples, Jill and Bill Benson. Jill and Bill lived off campus, baked their own bread, made their own jam and candles and knitted sweaters for each other.

....

Both of them were extremely rich and were fond of giving parties at which dreadful homemade hors d'oeuvres and cheap wine were served. Linnie and I made up a Broadway musical for them to star in. It was called *Simple on My Trust Fund*. We worked mostly on the opening scene. Jill and Bill are in the kitchen of their horrid apartment. Jill is knitting. Bill is stirring a pot of jam. A group of ordinary students walks by the open window. 'Jill and Bill,' they say. 'How is it that you two live such a groovy, cool, and close-to-the-earth life?'

Jill and Bill walk to center stage, holding hands. 'Simple,' each coos. 'On my trust fund.' And the chorus breaks into the lovely refrain. Once in the coffee shop Jill confessed to Linnie that she only had 'a tiny little trust fund.' This phrase was easily worked into the 'Jill and Bill Show'.

Jill and Bill, however, appeared to be having something of a hard time. They were seen squabbling. Jill was seen in tears at the Shop-Up. They looked unhappy. Jill went off skiing by herself. I had very little patience with Jill and Bill. I felt that with all that money they ought to buy some machine-made sweaters and serve store-bought jam. Furthermore, I felt it was slumming of them to live in such a crummy apartment when the countryside was teeming with enchanting rural properties. The idea of a country house became a rallying cry – the answer to all of Jill and Bill's trouble.

Linnie mused on Jill and Bill. What could be their problem? he wondered, rolling a colossal joint.

'They're both small and dark,' I said. Linnie lit up and passed the joint to me. I took a life-affirming hit. 'Maybe at night they realize what they look like and in the morning they're too depressed to relate to each other. What do you think?'

'I think Jill and Bill are a form of matted plant fiber,' said Linnie. 'I think they get into bed and realize that more than any other single thing, they resemble that stuff those braided doormats are made of. This clearly has a debilitating

....

effect on them. This must be what's wrong. What do you think, Mrs Ann?'

'A country house,' I said. 'They must buy a lovely country house before it's too late.'

That was the beginning of 'Ask Mrs Ann', a routine in which Linnie and I would invent some horrible circumstance for Jill and Bill. Either of us could be Mrs Ann. It didn't matter which. One of us would say, for instance: 'Answer this one, Mrs Ann. Jill and Bill have just had a baby. This baby is a Negro baby, which is odd since neither Jill nor Bill is Negro. Naturally, this causes a bit of confusion. They simply cannot fathom how it happened. At any rate, this baby has webbed feet and tiny flippers. Jill finds this attractive. Bill less so. Meanwhile Jill has bought a sheep and a loom. It is her girlish dream to spin wool from her own sheep, but the sheep has gone berserk and bitten Bill. In the ensuing mêlée the loom has collapsed, dislocating Jill's shoulder. Meanwhile, Bill, who has had to have forty stitches in his thigh as the result of violent sheep bite, has gone into the hospital for a simple tonsillectomy and finds to his amazement that his left arm has been amputated – he is left-handed as you recall. Jill feels they ought to sue, but to Bill's shock, he finds that he has signed a consent to an amputation. How can this have happened? He simply can't fathom it. But there is relief in all this, if only for Jill. Jill, whose maiden name is Michaelson, suffers from a rare disorder called "Michaelson's Syndrome", which affects all members of her family. This syndrome causes the brain to turn very slowly into something resembling pureed spinach. By the time she is thirty she will remember nothing of these unhappy events, for she will have devolved to a rather primitive, excrement-throwing stage. Whatever should they do?'

All that was required of Mrs Ann was the rallying cry: a country house! Many hours were spent trying to find new awful tidings for Jill and Bill, and as those familiar with the effects of marijuana know, even the punctual are carried

....

136

away on a stream of warped time perceptions. One rock-and-roll song takes about an hour to play, whereas a movement of a symphony is over in fifteen seconds. I felt that time had a form – the form of a chiffon scarf floating aimlessly down a large water slide; or that it was oblong but slippery, like an oiled football. I got home late, having forgotten to do the shopping. Since I had freely opted to be Thorne's housewife, he was perfectly justified in getting angry with me. My problem was, he thought I was having an affair.

It is one thing to tell your husband that you are sleeping with another man, and it is quite another to tell him that from the very instant of your meeting you have been under the influence of a mind-altering substance, no matter how mild. An astonishing confession next to which the admission of an afternoon or two in the arms of another man is nothing. Nothing!

What was I to do? My only real talent in life appeared to be getting high, and I was wonderful at it. Ostensibly I was supposed to be nurturing a talent for drawing – everyone had a skill, it was assumed. Every day I went upstairs to our attic room, lit a joint, and drew tiny, incoherent and highly detailed black and white pictures. This was not my idea of an occupation. It was hardly my idea of a hobby. Of course it is a well-known fact that drawing while high is always fun, which only made it more clear to me that my true vocation lay in getting stoned.

And so when dinner was late, when I was late, when I had forgotten to do something I had said I would do, Thorne liked to get into a snit, but he was terrified of getting furious with me. After all, my role was to look sort of dangerous. In some ways, Thorne treated me with the respectful and careful handling you might give to something you suspect is a pipe bomb: he didn't want to tempt fate because the poor thing was in some ways enraptured with me and he was afraid that if he got mad enough, I might disappear. That was the way the scales of our marriage were balanced.

....

When he looked as if he were about to shout, I would either get a very dangerous look in my eyes, or I would make him laugh, which was one of my prime functions in his life. The other was to behave in public.

Since I was stoned all the time, I tried in all ways to behave like Queen Victoria. Thus I probably appeared to be a little cracked. At public functions I smiled and was mute – no one knew that at home I was quite a little chatterbox. The main form of socializing on campus was the dinner party. I found these pretty funny – of course I was high and didn't know the difference. Thorne found them pretty dull, so I tried to liven them up for him. If we were seated together at dinner, I would smile at the person opposite and then do something to Thorne under the table. I tended, at these parties, to smile a great deal. This unnerved Thorne. He wore, under his party expression, a grimace that might have been caused by constant prayer, the prayer that I would not say something I had said at home. That I would not talk about how a black transvestite hooker should be sent as a present to the president of the college for his birthday. He prayed that I would not say about this gift: 'With my little inheritance and Thorne's salary I think we could certainly afford it.' Or I would not discuss the ways in which I felt the chairman of the history department looked like an anteater, or, on the subject of ants, how I felt his wife would react to being rolled in honey and set upon by South American fire ants. I did think that Professor X stole women's clothing out of the townie laundromat and went through the streets late at night in a flowered house-coat. I knew why Professor Y should not be left alone with his own infant son, and so on. But I behaved like a perfect angel and from time to time sent Thorne a look that made him shake, just to keep him on his toes.

I actually spoke once. This was at a formal dinner at the chairman of the department's house. This dinner party was so unusually dull that even through a glaze of marijuana I was bored. Thorne looked as if he were drowning. I myself

....

began to itch. When I could stand it no longer I excused myself and went to the bathroom where I lit the monster joint I carried in my evening bag and took a few hits. This was Lionel's superfine Colombian loco-weed and extremely effective. When I came downstairs I felt all silvery. The chairman of the department's wife was talking about her niece, Allison, who was an accomplished young equestrienne. At the mention of horses, I spoke up. I remembered something about horses I had figured out high. Lionel Browning called these insights 'marijuana moments' – things you like to remember when you are not stoned. Since no one had ever heard me say very much, everyone stopped to listen.

'Man's spatial relationship to the horse is one of the most confusing and deceptive in the world,' I heard myself say. 'You are either sitting on top of one, or standing underneath one, and therefore it is impossible to gauge in any meaningful way exactly how big a horse is in relationship to you. This is not,' I added with fierce emphasis, 'like a man inside a cathedral.'

I then shut up. There was a long silence. I meditated on what I had said, which was certainly the most interesting thing anyone had said. Thorne's eyes seemed about to pop. There was not a sound. People had stopped eating. I looked around the table, gave a beautiful, unfocused smile, and went back to my dinner.

Finally, the chairman of the department's wife said: 'That's very interesting, Ann.' And the conversation closed above my head, leaving me happy to rattle around in my own altered state.

Later, at home, Thorne said: 'Whatever made you say what you said at dinner tonight?'

I said, in a grave voice: 'It is something I have always believed.'

The nice thing about being high all the time is that life suspends itself in front of you endlessly, like telephone poles

....

on a highway. Without plans you have the feeling that things either will never change, or will arrange themselves somehow someday.

A look around the campus did not fill the heart of this tender bride with visions of a rosy adult future. It was clear who was having all the fun and it was not the grown-ups. Thorne and I were the youngest faculty couple, and this gave us – I mean me – a good vantage point. A little older than us were couples with worn-out cars, sick children and debts. If they were not saddled with these things, they had independent incomes and were saddled with attitudes. Then they got older and were seen kissing the spouses of others at parties, or were found, a pair of unassorted spouses, under a pile of coats on a bed at New Year's Eve parties. Then they got even older, and the strife of their marriages gave them the stony affection battle comrades have for one another.

There were marriages that seemed propped up with tooth-picks, and ones in which the wife was present but functionless, like a vestigial organ. Then the husband, under the strain of being both father and more to little Emily, Matthew and Tabitha plus teaching a full course load, was forced to have an affair with a graduate student in Boston whom he could see only every other weekend.

The thought of Thorne and my becoming any of these people was so frightful that I had no choice but to get immediately high. Something would either occur to me, or nothing would happen. Meanwhile, time drifted by in the company of Lionel Browning – a fine fellow and a truly great pothead for whom I had not one particle of sexual feeling. He was my perfect pal. Was this cheating? I asked myself. Well, I had to admit, it sort of was. Thorne did not know how much time I spent with him, but then Linnie was soon to graduate, so I had to get him while I could, so to speak.

In the spring, Thorne went off to a convention of the Historical Society and I went on a dope run to Boston with

....

Linnie. I looked forward to this adventure. It did not seem likely that life would bring me many more offers of this sort. The purity of my friendship with Linnie was never tainted by the well-known number of motels that littered the road from school to Boston. Sex was never our mission.

We paid a visit to a dealer named Marv (he called himself Uncle Marv) Fenrich, who was somewhat of a legend. The legend had it that he had once been very brilliant, but that speed – his drug of choice – had turned his brain into shaving cream and now he was fit only to deal grass to college boys. He also dealt speed to more sinister campus types, and he had tried to con Linnie into this lucrative sideline. But Linnie wanted only quality marijuana and Uncle Marv respected him, although it irked him that Linnie was not interested. He sold what he called 'The Uncle Marv Exam Special – Tailored to the Needs of the College Person'. This was a box containing two 5 milligram Dexamyls, a Dexamyl Spansule (15 mg), two Benzedrines (5 mg), and something he called an 'amphetamine football' – a large, olive-green pill which he claimed was pure speed coated with Vitamin B. On the shelves of his linen closet were jar upon hospital-size jar of pills. But his heart, if not the rest of his metabolism, was in grass, and he never shut up.

'Man,' he said, 'now this particular reefer is very sublime, really very sublime. It is the country club of grass, mellow and rich. A very handsome high can be gotten off this stuff. Now my own personal favorite cocktail is to take two or three nice Dexies, wash them down with some fine whiskey or it could be Sterno or your mother's French perfume, it makes no difference whatsoever, and then light up a huge monster reefer of the very best quality and fall on the floor thanking God in many languages. This is my own recipe for a very good time. I like to share these warm happy times with others. Often Uncle Marv suggests you do a popper or two if you feel unmotivated by any of the above. Or snap one under the nose of a loved friend. Believe me, the drug-

store has a lot to offer these days. Now a hundred or so of
those little Romilar pills make you writhe and think insects
are crawling all over your body – some people like this sort
of thing very deeply. I myself find it a cheap thrill. Say,
Linnie, have you authentic college kids gotten into mesca-
line yet? Very attractive stuff. Yes, you may say that it is
for people with no imagination, but think of it this way: if
you have no imagination, a Swiss pharmaceutical company
will supply one for you. Isn't that wonderful what modern
science does? Let me tell you, this stuff is going to be very
big. Uncle Marv is going to make many sublime shekels off
this stuff as soon as he can set it up right. You just wait
and see. Uncle Marv says: the streets of Boston and
Cambridge are going to be stacked with little college boys
and girls hyperventilating and having visions. Now this
lysergic acid is also going to be very big, very big. God bless
the Swiss! Now, Linnie,' he began rooting in various desk
drawers. 'Now, Linnie, how about some reds for all those
wired-up college boys and girls to calm down after exams?
I personally feel that reds go very well after a little speed
abuse and I should know. Calm you down, take the reptile
right out of you. Uncle Marv is so fond of these sublime
red tens.' He paused. 'Seconal,' he said rather coldly to me,
since it was clear even to a person who was out of his mind
that I did not know what he was talking about. 'I like to
see a person taking reds. This is a human person, a person
unafraid to admit that he or she is *very nervous*. You don't
want any? Well, all right. But you and this authentic college
girl have not come to pass the evening in idle drug chatter.
This is business. Reefer for Linnie, many shekels for Uncle
Marv. Now, Linnie, this reefer in particular I want you to
taste is very sublime. You and this authentic college girl
must try some this very instant. Now this is Colombian loco-
weed of the highest order. Of Colombian distinction and
extremely handsome. I also have some horse tranquilizers,
by the way. Interested? Extremely sublime. They make you

....

lie down on the floor and whimper for help and companionship. Uncle Marv is very fond of these interesting new pills.'

He cleared a space on his messy kitchen table and proceeded to roll several absolutely perfect joints. It was extremely sublime grass, and Linnie bought a kilo of it.

'Linnie, it will not fail you,' Uncle Marv said. 'Only the best, from me to you.' Linnie paid up, and Uncle Marv gave us each a Bennie for a present, which we were very glad to have on the long ride home.

When Thorne came back from his conference, the axe, which had been poised so delicately over the back of my neck, fell. This marked the end of my old life, and the beginning of the new. Thorne had called me from Chicago – he had called all night – and I had not been home.

'You are sleeping with Lionel Browning,' he said.

'I never laid a hand on him,' I said.

'That's an interesting locution, Ann,' said Thorne. 'Do you just lie there and let him run his grubby undergraduate hands all over you?'

This was of course my cue. 'Yes,' I said. 'I often lie there and let almost any undergraduate run his hands all over me. Often faculty is invited, like your colleague Jack Saks. Often the chairman of the department's wife pops over and she runs her hands all over me too.'

The effects of the beautiful joint I had smoked only an hour and a half ago were beginning to wane. I was getting a headache. I thought about the sweet little stash I kept in my lingerie drawer – all the grass I smoked at home tasted vaguely of sachet. I was longing to go upstairs where, underneath my socks, I had a little lump of African hash. I saw my future before me – a very depressing vision. I was fifty. Grown children. Going to the hairdresser to have my hair frosted. Doing some genteel work or other – I couldn't think what. Wearing a knit dress – the sort worn by the wife of the president of the college. Calling grimy boys from

....

pay phones: 'Hello, hello? Kenny? Steve? This is Mrs Speizer calling. Do you have anything for me?'

There I would be in my proper hairdo. Facing change of life and still a total pothead. Locking the bathroom door behind me to toke up. By then Thorne would be the chairman of his department somewhere.

'That wife of mine,' he would say – of course he only spoke this way in my fantasies – 'does say the oddest things. Can't keep track of where that mind of hers is meandering to. Goes out at odd hours and what funny boys she gets to do the lawn work. I can't imagine where she gets them from.'

In fact, this was the most depressing thought I had ever had. If you stay high enough you never wonder what will become of you. A large joint was waiting in my jacket pocket. How I longed to smoke it. Somewhere near me was adult life: I knew it. I could feel it breathing down my neck. Professor's wife smokes dope constantly. Must see shrink. Must grow up. Must find out why she cannot be straight. Why she refuses to enter the adult world. And so on. And Thorne – much sympathy for Thorne – for example, the chairman of the department's wife: 'Dear Thorne, you poor thing! All alone in that house with a drug addict! When Ann has been sedated why don't you come over and have dinner with us and our lovely niece Allison and after Ann has been committed to a mental institution, you and Allison can establish a meaningful and truly adult relationship.'

The thing that divides the children from the adults is that children know it's us against them – how right they are – and adults are children who grew up and are comfortable being *them*. Two terrible images flashed before me. One was that life was like an unruly horse that rears up and kicks you in the head. And the other was that my life was like a pane of glass being carried around by a nervous and incompetent person who was bound to let it slip and shatter into zillions of pieces on the pavement. My futureless life, besides being shattered and rearing up, unwound endlessly

....

before me. What was around for me to be? There did not seem to be very much of anything. Suddenly I felt a rush of jaunty courage, the kind you feel when everything has bottomed out and just about every old thing is lost.

'Thorne,' I said. 'I smoke marijuana unceasingly and always have. What do you think of that?'

'Incessantly,' said Thorne.

'Thorne,' I said. 'I have been stoned from the first minute you laid eyes on me and I am stoned now.'

He regarded me for a moment. 'You mean, you came to my class high?' Thorne said. 'And you're high now?'

'Yes,' I said. 'I was stoned in your class and I am stoned right now but not as stoned as I want to be. So I am going to take this great big gigantic reefer out of my pocket and light it up and I am going to share it with you.'

He looked shocked.

'You can get in jail for smoking that stuff, Ann,' he said in an awed voice.

'An interesting locution, Thorne,' I said. He stopped looking awed and began to look rather keen and hungry. I realized with a sudden jolt of happiness that I could very well change my husband's life in one easy step.

'Take this thing and inhale it,' I said.

'How can I when I don't smoke?' Thorne said.

'Make an effort. Try hard and be careful,' I said. 'Go slow and don't exhale for a long time.'

'How long?' Thorne asked.

'Oh, a half an hour or so.' He inhaled successfully several times. In a little while he was high as a kite.

'My,' he said, 'this certainly is an interesting substance. I feel I've been standing here for a few centuries. My hands are cold and my mouth is dry. Are these symptoms?'

For an hour Thorne went from room to room having impressions. He was having a wonderful time. Finally, he sat down.

'Were you stoned on our wedding day?' he asked.

'I'm afraid so,' I said.

....

'On our honeymoon?'

'I'm afraid so.'

'I see,' said Thorne. 'In other words, you're like this all the time.'

I said more or less, mostly more.

'In other words,' said Thorne, 'since you are like this all the time, you have no idea what it's like to be with me when you're not like this.'

That seemed logical to me.

'In other words,' Thorne said, 'you have no idea what it's like to be with me when you aren't like this.'

I said that sounded very like his previous other words, and that such a thought had never occurred to me.

'This is terrible, Ann,' said Thorne. 'It isn't normal. Of course, this stuff is pretty interesting and all, but you can't be stoned all the time.'

'I can,' I said.

'Yes, but it must be wrong. There must be something terribly wrong, don't you think?'

'Actually, no,' I said.

'But, Ann, in other words, this is not normal reality. You have not been perceiving normal reality. How long has it been, Ann, since you actually perceived normal reality?'

'This is normal reality, silly,' I said.

'Yes, well, but I mean I'm sure there is some reason why it's not right to be this way all the time.'

'There may be, but I can't think of it. Besides,' I added, 'you seem to be having a swell old time.'

'That cannot be gainsaid,' said Thorne.

'Or cannot not be gainsaid.'

'What does that mean, anyway?' said Thorne. 'But never mind. The fact is that if you've been high all this time, we don't know each other at all, really.'

'What,' I said, thinking with sudden longing of the hashish upstairs, 'is knowable?'

'An interesting point,' said Thorne. 'Maybe in the open knowableness of things their sheer knowableness is

....

146

obscured. In other words, light darkening light, if you see what I mean.'

I did see. I looked at my husband with great affection, realizing that he had possibilities I had not counted on.

'What about your affair with Lionel Browning?' Thorne said. 'Is that knowable?'

'Yes,' I said. 'Lionel Browning is responsible only for the very substance that has put you in this state of mind, see?'

'I do see,' Thorne said. 'I see. In other words, you sit around and get high together.'

'Often we stand up and get high together.'

'And I as a professor can never join you since that would be undignified, right?'

'Right.'

'Well, then, in honor of Lionel and in the interests of further study, let's have a little more of this stuff, OK?'

'A very good idea,' I said.

'Yes,' said Thorne, stretching out on the couch. 'Let's carry this one step further.'

'An interesting locution,' I said. 'I wonder how it works. In what way can a step be carried?'

Thorne sat up. He looked puzzled. 'It must go like this: the step is the province of the foot, without which there can be no step. The foot is carried by the body, but the action of the step is carried by the foot. Therefore the step is to the foot as a baby is to its mother. And so it can be said that the foot is the mother of the step, or rather, the step is the potential baby of the foot.'

I thought about that for a very long time.

'Say, Ann,' Thorne said. 'Where's the more we're supposed to have?'

'It's illegal, Thorne,' I said. 'We could get in jail for simply being in the same room with it.'

'Get it if you have it,' Thorne said.

I brought down a bag of Linnie's top-quality and my lump of hash. This I scraped with our sharpest kitchen knife and sprinkled deftly on the unrolled reefer. I rolled wonderfully.

....

Thorne was impressed, and he was intrigued by watching me do something I had obviously done millions of times but not in front of him.

'You're awfully good at that,' he said.

'Years of practice,' I said. 'Now, Thorne, why have you never told me how much Lionel Browning looks like me?'

'Because he does *not* look like you,' said Thorne. 'You have the same loafers, that's all.'

'We are virtually identical,' I said.

'Ann, this mind-impairing substance has impaired your mind. Lionel Browning and you look nothing alike. Now are you going to roll those things all night or are you going to smoke them?'

The thing about history is, most people just live through it. You never know what moment may turn out to be of profound historical significance. When you are meandering near the stream of current events, you do not know when you have dipped your toe into the waters of significance. I like to think that as I passed that joint to my husband, a new era opened. The decade was fairly new, and just about everything was about to happen. In what other era could a nice young thing pass a marijuana cigarette to her strait-laced husband?

In those days potheads liked to try to track down their fellow heads. Everyone had a list of suspects. William Blake was on everyone's list. On Linnie's list was Gerard Manley Hopkins. It amused him inexhaustibly to imagine the Jesuit father smoking dope and writing in sprung rhythm. I myself could not imagine any straight person writing those poems and as I watched a happy, glazed expression take possession of my husband's features, I had cause to think of my favorite Hopkins poem – 'The Windhover' – which contains the line, 'my heart in hiding/Stirred for a bird, – the achieve of, the mastery of the thing!'

I felt full of achievement and mastery – Thorne being the

victim and beneficiary of both. Getting him stoned was a definite achievement of some sort or other.

I said to Thorne: 'What do you think of it?'

'It produces a strange and extremely endearing form of cerebral energy,' he said.

'Yes,' I sighed in agreement. 'Wonderful, isn't it?'

'It produces unhealthy mental excitement,' Thorne said.

Suddenly I was full of optimism and hope for the future.

'Oh, Thorne,' I said in a happy voice. 'Isn't this fun?'

And as Thorne has frequently pointed out, that very well could have been the slogan for the years to come.

Gone

. . . .

CHRISTOPHER HOPE

Arnaldus and his wife, Ina, had been driving home from a big wedding over Scorpion Point way when their blue Oldsmobile 88 left the road at Bushman's Bend. So empty is the hot, high, dry country between Lutherburg and Beaufort that it was three days before they were found bolt upright, the radio still playing selections from the Don Elliot Sextette.

People shivered. Happen to a government senator, happen to anybody. Still, they tried to look on the bright side. A bloody miracle they weren't robbed by passing natives. Left a boy, young Nico, away at boarding-school some place.

The unfairness of it upset everyone. Arnaldus had been modern. But modernity had not saved him. 'This is 1954 and I love it,' he liked to say. His wife had one of the first fully integrated kitchens in Beaufort.

Yet there was his queer old sister, Aunt Betsy, in a mud-walled cottage without running water: kept a skivvy-girl, and treated folks with roots and herbs, like a Hottentot bush doctor. Even though Lutherburg had a perfectly good medical man in young Dr du Plessis, who ran a proper surgery with modern, separate entrances for all the races. Man, that guy was so modern, when the Moosah family moved to Lutherburg, he said, 'I'm gonna have to make me a third entrance now: one for Whites, one for Browns and one for Coolies!'

After Arnaldus died, considering how she got the news on a neighbour's phone, otherwise she mightn't have heard

. . . .

GONE

for *weeks*, Bill Harding very kindly asked again didn't she want to go on the party line now?

Aunt Betsy asked straight back: 'For why?'

''Cause that way news of any further tragedies reaches you directly.'

Bill Harding had been the pole planter for the PO, stomping the empty country between Eros and Compromise, Lutherburg and Zwingli, Scorpion Point, Mutton Fountain and Abraham's Grave. Behind him came two chainmen dragging a line of heavy steel wire, forty-four yards long, for measuring the distance. One chain's length between main-road poles; two for farm lines.

The poles Bill planted strode across koppie and gorge, from the Karoo to the Kalahari desert, on and on into the powder blue horizon where no one had ever been. And remote villages, hamlets, farms and baking railway sidings where a goods train once a week was a big deal, were suddenly jabbering away day and night on the party line, run by an operator in a room behind the Lutherburg post office who cranked a handle and buzzed your own special ring-code. It was a triumph of science and shoe-leather.

But Aunt Betsy didn't see the point – then or later. She told Bill Harding, 'Bad news always got fresh horses.'

Soon after she lost her brother, she began emptying out her consulting room, storing her herbs and potions in the stable with Balthazar, her chestnut. The roots she dug up in the veld, the twigs and grasses and *muti*s she'd collected for years; and bottles of Horniball's Patent Wonderful Extract; boxes of Fisher's Balsam of Life; packets of permanganate of potash crystals against snake bite.

On her garden gate, she hung a notice painted in indigo capitals:

NO PATIENTS
UNTIL LATER

....

Dr du Plessis in the big house at the top of the street, young smart-arse, said he hoped this was an end to her quackery.

Aunt Betsy sniffed: 'In three months you been here, you've lost more patients than I've ever treated.'

The floor of her consulting room, roughened by the feet of generations of patients, needed fixing, so she sent her girl to gather fresh droppings in the goat pen behind the abattoir, showed her how to tamp them flat, seal the surface with white river clay and polish the new floor to a gleam.

The room was furnished with an old six-drawer mahogany tallboy on which stood a blue pitcher and basin painted with cosmos flowers, deep red faces on feathery stems.

A bed of maple wood with leather thongs was made by Ezekiel, the carpenter. A mattress, striped blue and white, stuffed with coir, purchased from Levine's General Traders (Now under New Management) was carried to the cottage by Levine's boy, Harry, draped over his head so he looked like a fat blue sandwich walking. When he knocked at the door of the cottage, he was singing an old song about a lass who nearly drowned in a waterhole but was saved by a farmer's son who loved her upturned nose.

'A little less foolery, if you don't mind,' Aunt Betsy said.

The bed was covered with a mohair blanket and a kudu skin, from last year's hunting. The girl lined the drawers of the mahogany tallboy with pages from *Reader's Digest*; one showed a semi-dressed woman in long gloves, leaning over a balcony under a starry sky, pointing her bra at the heavens.

'Not to worry,' said Aunt Betsy. 'People from the city, they see that sort of thing constantly.'

Then one morning she met the bus from Beaufort, down by Bokkie Bok's Butchery, and walked home with a blond boy. And it was around town in minutes: Aunt Betsy was taking her dead brother's son, the orphan Nico, for the school holidays.

She wanted Nico to feel at home, as quick as lightning. So she started setting him right then and there. Passing under the willow tree in Voortrekker Street, Aunt Betsy mentioned that a man with a big beard sometimes jumped out of the tree.

'If he asks you your business, don't fret. It's only Nephew.'

Nico said it was amazing in the mid-twentieth century, to hear of a man who lived up a tree.

'Ag, he's done it for years. Keeping an eye on things,' Aunt Betsy said. 'Now the police went and made him a special constable so's he may at least be of some use with his questions.'

She walked him around the cottage. At first he pretended he didn't see the girl. He asked questions about her as if she wasn't there, without bothering to keep the amazement out of his voice.

'But why does Auntie call her Me?'

'Because she's mine.'

'Did you really and truly buy her for seven cakes of soap?'

'Six,' said Aunt Betsy. 'Made 'em myself. Blue cold-water soap. Of course, that was before the war.'

When she showed him round the cottage Nico stopped asking questions aloud but Me could hear them anyway:

'You've never had running water?'

'Don't you miss electricity?'

'You never heard of the twentieth century?'

He was silent before Aunt Betsy's treasures; her glass case containing old South African republican flags, assembled from coloured matchsticks by Italian prisoners of war, captured in North Africa; her sketches of bearded Boer prisoners in British concentration camps. He was scared of Balthazar, the chestnut, but tried to pat his nose.

Aunt Betsy walked him into the corner of the garden and showed him the dark-green wooden outhouse, with pages of *Farmer's Weekly* spiked to the back of the door. His pale cheeks turned pink as if looking too hard made him hot.

Shown the alcove beside the fire where the girl spread

....

her blankets at night, he asked: 'Doesn't she – I mean Me – have a real bed, even?'

'That's it,' said Aunt Betsy, 'except when she sleeps with me.'

The next morning Nico came to breakfast wearing red jeans with pockets which were closed with silver zips on each hip. His black shirt had a broad collar picked out in white saddle-stitching. When Nico asked for golden syrup on his porridge Aunt Betsy sent Me running to the Co-op for a tin of the green and gold, even though she was always saying it rotted the teeth sure as shooting.

Nico asked why his room smelled of liquorice.

'That'll be the dog's-blood bush we stored in your cupboard for all those years,' said Aunt Betsy.

Me said: 'You chew the twig of the dog's-blood bush if you've a cold or a bad chest.'

'That's not very twentieth-century, is it?'

He kept a steel comb in his back pocket and swept his hair in two waves round the sides of his head, closing like curtains above his nape.

Me was reminded of the tailfeathers of an Egyptian goose.

'It's called a ducktail,' said Nico.

Aunt Betsy nodded hard: 'I never in my life saw better on a duck.'

And she listened proudly to all his plans. How he'd get a radiogram one day, with the cash his dad left him. He'd also buy a Pontiac Starchief. Back at school he'd got this Trans-Oceanic Standard and Short-Wave Portable Radio so incredibly powerful it could pick up America, where you paid seven and six for a Coke. After lights out in the dorm in his boarding-school he listened secretly on his special built-in earphone, which was no bigger than a dried pea.

Breakfast over, Nico nodded to Me to follow him to his room. He sat on the bed, opened the fat black case with its silver handle sticking out of the side of the box. From a drawer inside the lid, Nico slid a shining black record and laid it gently on the turntable.

....

'Regiontone, real English record player,' he whispered.

He cranked the handle like you did a meat mincer and the record began to spin.

'78 r.p.m.,' Nico said, and he lowered the silver arm.

A man started singing. High and blurred. He told how he woke up one morning and looked out the door, his cow was missing. Suddenly the singer stopped and said he wanted to start again, but this time he was going to get real gone!

Nico sang with the man, holding his fist to his frozen lips, rolling his eyes so far back they vanished under his lids. Clicking his fingers and shaking his head and jerking his hips, his face full of pain as if he was crying and dying. Me thought maybe it made him remember his dead mother and father. The song said there'd been trouble on the farm: that old Milk Cow was mean to her lovin' Daddy. Left him without milk or butter. Well, now it her turn to cry because her lovin' Daddy's leaving. And if she don't believe it, she can count the days he's gone.

The music stopped. Nico was kneeling on the floor, his eyes screwed closed. He opened his eyes slowly. 'You ever been gone?'

'You mean like your loving Daddy's gone?'

Nico said she was crazy, and showed her how to wind the machine and they ran the song again.

Aunt Betsy told Me to be really kind to Nico: 'Death knocks the shoes off a fellow and he needs reshodding.'

Me could never remember her mistress in this bright and laughing mood. She was forever encouraging Nico; she waved to him from the other side of the glass when he combed his hair in the sitting-room windows. If Nico broke off hot dripping wax from the mantelpiece candle and chewed it she never told him: 'Wax, wisdom and water's precious, child!' And made him spit it in the box above the fireplace. And when he checked over his spots in the glass of her *Jesus Feeding the Five Thousand* oleograph, all she

....

said was 'Verbena tea's good for acne if ever you want a treatment.'

And when Nico saw the Bassons arriving at their place across the street and out tumbles this little servant girl, he watched her for a few minutes. Their blue Hudson Hornet pulled into the carport and out she climbed, about thirteen with very wavy lashes and a sturdy body under a thin pink dress. In two minutes he knew her name was Childie and she was the Bassons' townhouse maid, in special training. Then he trotted right indoors and got Aunt Betsy to invite her over.

And she did! Even though it was years since she'd spoken to Basson. Not since she'd thrown coffee in his face for placing his hand on her knee as they sat round the campfire after shooting springbok; six, seven years ago; not since he'd thrown Me off his farm as a dead loss; and Aunt Betsy had snapped her up for six stones of cold-water soap.

But if Nico wants Childie to come over, that's fine by Aunt Betsy, even if it means smiling and going on smiling at Bananas Basson while Bananas tells her how clean Childie is, and she's no skivvy, she's on a regular wage and so clean like no one would believe. 'I'd say,' says Basson. 'She's cleaner than any maid in forty miles, true as God.' Because before they leave the farm she's stood up on a milking-stool by Mrs Basson, and she takes off every stitch and Arletta Basson makes her scrub herself all over. 'How about that?' Bananas Basson gives Me this sideways look. 'Do's you like with yours. But mine's clean!'

If Basson remembered the day he lifted his rifle and fired at the feet of Me and old Daisy, sending them running out of the farmyard with the shale stinging their ankles as the bullets popped, he gave no sign of it. Close-up, the black and yellow mottling of his round, fleshy face was even more visible and scary than she remembered as he started firing off orders to Childie.

Aunt Betsy is in sole command. Anything she says, and

....

Childie better jump. She better not even look the wrong way, unless Aunt Betsy gives express permission.

'I'll be watching, and Mrs Basson will be watching . . . and if you step out of line, God help you – because I won't,' said Bananas Basson.

Though she was about the same age as Me, Childie's breasts were very big and shifted beneath her light cotton dress. The closest thing to Childie's breasts were to be seen in the advertisement Me used to line the chest of drawers in Nico's room. The lady wore white gloves to her elbows, like Aunt Betsy's; she stood on a balcony pointing her bra-clad breasts at the moon, while saying to herself: 'I dreamt I was a Social Butterfly in my Maidenform Bra.'

Childie visited every Saturday afternoon, and Nico dressed in his pink shirt, and he polished his black leather shoes on the backs of his black jeans. The pattern was more or less always the same. They sat in Nico's room and listened to the Cow song; Childie and Nico got gone. Childie knew how, tapping her feet, she snapped her fingers, her face creased, she was in pain. She wasn't in pain; she was gone. Sometimes Nico turned the record over and sang that Childie was a heart-breaker and Childie smiled. Sometimes Nico and Childie danced and when the singer got slower and slower and sounded sleepy or drunk, Nico would call out: 'Hit me again, Sister,' and Me's job was to wind the silver handle real fast so the music speeded up, and Nico twirled Childie and when her skirt lifted Me always looked away because Childie never wore pants.

But Aunt Betsy said not to worry: 'If Mrs Basson stands Childie on the milking-stool before they set out from the farm for town, and makes her soap herself all over, maybe she's OK without.'

And she would send Me back to the others, who would be laughing to themselves in the garden under the pear tree.

When Nico got smart, he'd ask: 'Is it true, hey, you haven't got a mother and Aunt Betsy bought you for six bars of soap and you're a sl-a-ve?'

. . . .

It sounded horrible, the way he dragged it out.

Childie would cock her round head to the side and her long lashes would go blink, blink, blink as she drank Nico in.

Me shot back, 'I'm not.'

'So what are you?'

'I'm the girl of the house.'

'Some house!'

'And I have got a mother.'

'Then where's she?

Me had her answer ready: 'She's in Beaufort.'

'If she's in Beaufort I'm a banana,' said Nico, and he and Childie climbed the pear tree. They sat in the higher branches where they thought the leaves hid them and Me's job was to keep an eye out for anyone approaching.

The leaves didn't really hide them. Childie was munching a pear, and she let go the core, and it fell bouncing on the branches, and she looked at the sky, seeming not to notice that Nico had his hand down her dress.

People came by sometimes when Nico was in the garden, wearing zipped jeans and pink shirt; leaning over the fence they stared at him combing his hair with a steel comb, the way they stared at a snow-white springbok; or a calf with two heads or the albino from Carnarvon who juggled soup cans.

One day Nico asked, could he take the girls to town? Aunt Betsy, who never let Me out of the yard alone, said: 'Only with pleasure.'

Me didn't want to go: when the Brown children from Silver Street ran by, she never went, yet here was Nico proposing to walk down the road with two Brown girls. It didn't seem right and anyway she could see the Venetian blinds twitch over the road at Basson's place the moment they got outside the gate and she had a terrible fear of the open street. Nico's zips flashed, and he had his guitar slung over his shoulder. He made it worse by putting his arms round their shoulders and Me wanted to die.

They were passing under the willow tree when, with a

....

crash of green leaves that made Childie scream, Nephew with his huge blond beard and leather trousers tumbled out of the branches.

Holding on to his cap and gun, he said to Nico: 'I know you! The senator's son. What you doing, out with these?' He jabbed his finger at Childie and Me. 'Us is Herringfolk, not them.'

Nico was puzzled. 'What's this Herring, hey?'

Nephew was amazed. A senator's son and he didn't know! 'White folk's Herringfolk; others isn't. End of story'.

Nico thought it over a while: then he grinned. 'Not Herrings, man! *Herrenvolk*. It means: Higher People.'

'Same difference,' says Nephew. 'We don't fool about with folks who aren't.' Nephew taps his police reservist's badge. 'I'll have to report this.'

Nico sat down right there on the kerb, unloaded his steel comb and fixed his hair.

On the corner of Leibrandt Street, a crowd was gathering on the stoep of the Hunter's Arms: Pop Haaroff, the pastor and Bill Harding, the pole-planter from the PO, gathered at the end of the broad, sandy street like statues or sentinels. Ma DuToit from the Co-op was wearing a yellow and white frock, frozen like lemon meringue tart; Bill Harding in Western Desert army-issue khaki shorts flapping above his bald knobbly knees; Pastor Greet, as always, well wrapped in heavy brown serge whatever the weather and black tie, in case a sudden burial was needed.

Across the road a crowd of Brown guys, who always sat there hoping some farmer driving by would load them on his truck for a day's shearing or lifting potatoes, watched the white boy with his feet in the street unsling his guitar and let rip. And they liked what they saw. They whistled.

Nico had two audiences, on opposite sides of the street, which should have been nice. The Brown guys were clicking their fingers: the White crowd quiet, but listening hard as Nico lit into the Cow song. When he promised they'd miss him when he was gone, the Brown guys cheered, but

....

159

someone on the other side of the street, probably Pop Haaroff, yelled, 'No, we bloody well won't!'

Then Bananas Basson turned up, sun gleaming on the ridges of bone where his hair was shaved above his ears. Childie's golden face turned grey when she saw him and she hid her face in her hands. She tried to get Nico to stop but his eyes were closed and he was real gone. When he finished and stood up, all the Brown people clapped but someone from the other side – perhaps Bill Harding – yelled: 'And get your bloody hair cut!'

Childie cried all the way home and when they got there she screamed because Special Constable Nephew was standing outside the gate fingering his revolver.

'I'm a sentry,' he told Nico. 'This house is under guard.'

The house was full of people. Sergeant Roux said he had searched Nico's room. He had found this newspaper under his mattress.

'It's from Memphis!' cried Nico.

'D'you hear?' cried Aunt Betsy. 'That's in Egypt!' She grinned proudly at Nico.

'What you been doing in Egypt?' demanded Sergeant Roux. He read out carefully: 'Suddenly Singing Elvis Presley Zooms into Recording Stardom'.

Nico groaned loud and low, full of contempt. 'Memphis, Tennessee, not Memphis, Egypt.' He sat down at the kitchen table with his arms folded. This was not the bloody twentieth century.

Bananas Basson arrived then and stood staring at Childie and breathing loudly. Childie got under the kitchen table. Me moved behind Aunt Betsy's chair because, usually, it felt safer there. But she knew nowhere was safe tonight.

'What's a Suddenly Singing Elvis?' Sergeant Roux demanded.

'It's not a what, he's a who,' said Nico.

Bananas Basson came over and read from the paper: 'Listen here. What's this paper write, OK? It writes this guy's – Elwhatever – "got a white voice that sings negro

....

rhythms". Know what's that – *a negro*? That's to us a native. Isn't it?'

'In that case,' said the sergeant, 'I'm confiscating this paper.'

Nico tried to snatch it away and it tore in two ragged pieces. Holding his half he ran to his room, sobbing, and locked the door. Me was horrified at the way he disappeared. Now she and Childie were alone with the police and Bananas Basson was breathing loudly still and staring at the table under which Childie was hiding herself.

Aunt Betsy usually so good at knowing what to do, seemed at a loss. Normally she would have thrown them out, but she just stood there, rubbing the hairs on her chin and looking from the sergeant to Basson to the table where they could hear Childie sobbing.

'What's your case? What's wrong with Memphis? Why can't he sing native rhythms?'

Sergeant Roux never answered; he was placing the fragments of newspaper in a large sack. Bananas Basson suddenly reached under the table. When he withdrew his hand he had Childie fast by the hair, wrapped round his fist like black rope. He lifted her off her feet. She was making a yipping sound like a frightened puppy as Basson backed out of the kitchen door, eyes on Aunt Betsy as if daring her to try and stop him.

His voice was thick with joy. 'Do what you like with yours' – Basson jerked his chin towards Me – 'but mine's not sitting in no damn gutter singing native rhythms. No way!'

Afterwards Aunt Betsy paced round the kitchen punching her fist into her palm and sucking her teeth. They could hear across the road Basson's belt coming down with a dead-meat slap on bare flesh. Childie's cries floated across the road. For the first time Nico looked scared. He wound his Regiontone and played the Cow song so loud the needle jumped and you could hear it halfway across town. The louder he played it the harder Basson's belt came down.

....

Aunt Betsy growled in her throat. She knew she'd let Childie in for this but there was nothing she could do. She hadn't cared if she wore no pants, or walked down the street with Nico or got gone in the bedroom. Finally, she went into the yard, rolled up her sleeves, grabbed the axe, swinging it under a fat creamy moon that made her muscles glisten as she chopped logs from an old branch off the pear tree.

Me climbed into her cubbyhole beside the firewood, and rolled her blankets round her head to block out the music and the screams and the axe slamming into the pearwood.

Next morning Aunt Betsy took Nico to the bus and he never came back. Me never actually saw him go but she had this picture; his guitar was slung, his zips were shining, and he was hefting his record player on his shoulder. When the cops gave him back his newspaper he Sellotaped each page and ironed it flat. In her picture of his leaving, Nico climbed on to the bus and opened the *Memphis Scimitar*; he didn't look back.

She tried counting the days he'd been gone. But somewhere on the other side of ten she lost track.

Just Breathing

DIANA HENDRY

It was only while she was ill and vulnerable that Nina thought about possession. About being possessed. If it really happened. And if it had happened to her.

Back home and convalescing from the asthma attack that had whisked her off to Lark Green hospital in the middle of the Easter holidays (why did illness never strike in term time?), Nina was able to rationalize it all. Talking to friends she described Madge as 'this old woman who took a real shine to me'.

But it had been more than a 'shine'. And what Nina never repeated to anyone was Madge's last words. 'I'm going. You've come to take over.' That's what Madge had said before her eyes went wide – with astonishment or terror, it was hard to tell – and a noise like someone gargling on phlegm came from her throat. Nina had pressed the buzzer for the nurse. Then there'd been curtains round Madge's bed, more awful gargling and the nurse apparently slapping Madge's hand and trying to call her back from the brink. 'Mrs Dawson! Mrs Dawson!' How odd, Nina had thought, to be called Mrs Anybody on one's death bed. Then there'd been a final terrible retching, as if Madge were coughing up her lungs and it was all over.

Or rather it was just beginning. Nina had gone back to her own bed and listened to the awful sounds coming from behind the curtains while Madge's last words bound her like a petrifying kind of spell. A spell, Nina had thought, was not an instant thing, as it was often made out to be in fairy tales. Rather it was something that worked on you slowly

....

and you didn't know it was happening until the final magic words were spoken and then it was too late.

Thinking about this now, in the study which was really Tom's but he allowed her a corner, and trying to prepare next term's school work – though her usual enthusiasm seemed entirely lacking – Nina told herself it was ridiculous to think of Madge casting a spell. She herself had been in a state of nervous shock. What with Tom not wanting to call the GP, then the ambulance in the middle of the night and the oxygen mask – just like the one her father had died under. Then the hospital itself and the nurses, sailing up and down the ward, their little white hats like paper boats on a river, casting rhetorical 'all rights?' to the left and right of them and not wanting to disturb the houseman. Nina spent the whole night heaving for breath and thinking she was going to die – not of asthma but of mortal carelessness; of the English dislike of making a fuss, shared, apparently, by nurses, GPs and Tom. At a certain point in the night she had felt as if the world had shifted on its axis.

And then there had been Madge, lying there like a Government Health Warning personified. Nina was not a heavy smoker. Never more than ten a day. Not what you could call an addiction. And Nina didn't. To herself, to that part of herself that somehow remained rootedly Catholic, she called it a sin. To smoke was to commit slow suicide, therefore, *ipso facto*, it was to be guilty of the sin of despair. Had she still been in the habit of going to confession, this is what she would have confessed to. Despair. (Possibly not mentioning the fags.) Nina liked the romantic flourish of 'sin of despair' compared to the flat metallic sound of 'addiction'. Psychology had done nothing for the language. Consider melancholia/depression. Listlessly, Nina turned the pages of the National Curriculum advice on English Literature.

No doubt it had been a combination of terror and residual Catholicism which, that night, had magnified Madge into a personification of the twentieth century's eighth deadly sin.

....

Smoking. Propped up by a stack of pillows, all skin and bone, hair sweated to her head, two black pools for eyes, a green Ventolin inhaler fixed (with a permanent look) over her mouth, Madge had gazed out at Nina like a latter-day Cassandra. Indeed it had been Madge who had kept vigil over Nina all night. Madge who had pressed the buzzer for a nurse when Nina, too breathless to call out, had realized – and really it was the last despairing piece of carelessness – that her own bed was not fitted with this essential piece of patient equipment.

Nina abandoned the National Curriculum and went downstairs to make herself a cup of coffee. Not that coffee was worth having without a cigarette and she and Tom had quit. To quit. What a quick, cutting verb – onomatopoeic, in a way but wholly inappropriate for the long, shaky, gut-gnawing, hand-trembling process of giving up fags. The kitchen – indeed the whole house – felt curiously claustrophobic this morning. Nina was tempted to wonder if it was claustrophobia rather than fags that had prompted the asthma. Or was this yet another wriggling evasion of the addict's mind?

She nibbled an unpleasantly hard ginger biscuit and thought about Madge. It had been that first night, that vigil, that had bound them together, one breathless soul to another – Nina with her feeling of 'there but for the grace of God . . .' and Madge? Nina tried to put herself in Madge's shoes. Or rather Madge's bed. In which (so she had learnt from the young gossipy nurse) Madge had been lying – and dying – for four months. January, February, March, April, literally and slowly passing away with the effort of just breathing. It was a stint of suffering long enough to test anyone's belief in a loving God. In four months He would become punishing. Or indifferent. An inexplicably slow sort of death, like Madge's, would drain away not only your health and strength, but any possible meaning life once might have had.

Nina took her coat from the back-door peg. A walk, some

....

fresh air, was what she needed. There was nowhere really to walk except towards the park, up past a long row of shops that seemed to change every other week; charity shops and second-hand clothes being the most long-lasting.

The thing was that her arrival in the ward had given Madge an explanation, given meaning to those long months of terrible endurance. You see what you feel, thought Nina, finding herself, automatically and seemingly without intent, in the tobacconist buying twenty Benson & Hedges. (Twenty!) She had felt guilt and therefore had seen Madge as a Government Health Warning. Madge, feeling God-forsaken, had seen Nina as – as what? Daughter? *Doppelgänger*? Beloved? Heir? 'I'm going. You've come to take over.' The one she had been waiting for – like in a relay race when you have to hand on the torch. The Lord had it all planned really. There was a reason for suffering. Or rather, the human heart had to find one.

'I'm so glad you've come,' Madge had said, the next morning when, after a powerful injection of steroids (the doctor having put in an appearance at last), Nina was up and breathing and sitting by Madge's bed, holding her hand. And Nina had heard no more in this statement than ordinary politeness, something a hostess might say to a guest at a party – 'I'm so glad you've come' – not the unspoken 'at last'.

Nina paused at the corner by the park and lit up. A sweet giddiness overtook her. A month without nicotine and this was like her first ever Woodbine, bought illicitly in her teens, smoked with the gang, walking along the sea-front on a Sunday evening after church. Ciggies, they were called then. Not fags. Nice friendly ciggies. How she and Madge had laughed about Woodbines. (Not that Madge *could* laugh, though you could tell from her eyes she was trying.)

'Wild honeysuckle,' Nina had said. 'Imagine calling a cigarette that today!'

'More like cancer-suckle,' said Madge, which was brave, considering.

....

After Madge's death, Nina had wondered, briefly, if she should try to find out more about Madge's past. What she had inherited, as it were. Just who and what she was 'taking over' from. 'A woman of enormous emotional energy,' Nina said out loud, sitting down on a park bench under a dead elm and lighting a second Benson & Hedges. Because of course that was what had been so astonishing about Madge – the quality you could, well, love her for. Almost nothing of her left, physically, yet what you felt was this energy, this still passionate desire to love and be loved. Madge was not a woman who would stay stuck in a school for fifteen years trying to cram Eng. Lit. into reluctant ears. No. And nor would she stay claustrophobically married. . . .

Nina stamped out the cigarette. If she had learnt some *facts* about Madge's life, she wouldn't now be in danger of making her up. She could have asked the young couple who had visited Madge one evening. They'd stood silently at the end of Madge's bed as if they feared death might be infectious. Which of course you could say it was. The whole human race caught it. Madge herself seemed indifferent to their presence, feigning sleep, not attempting to remove her oxygen mask and talk. Nina saw the young couple looking at each other as if trying to decide how long a stay constituted a duty done.

Leaving the ward, the girl had looked at Nina as if, after a silent half-hour with Madge, she had to speak to someone. 'You wouldn't think she was a fine musician once, would you?' she said. She had spoken bitterly as if it was all Madge's fault that she could no longer play whatever instrument it was she'd once played so finely. And maybe it was. All those friendly ciggies taking over from flute, clarinet, oboe, whatever. Perhaps the girl was a distant niece. It would have been possible to get her name and address from the nurse. But Nina hadn't. She hadn't wanted to know. Had been too frightened by then. Instead she'd gone off into her own memory of applying for a place at a music college and failing and having to abandon the dream . . .

. . . .

By the fourth day in the ward, the 'thing' with Madge – Nina still preferred to call it this, the only alternative suggesting itself being 'a whirlwind love affair', which was somewhat ironic considering its short and static nature – had somehow got out of control. It had been like finding yourself the unwitting object of someone's passion, thought Nina, walking moodily out of the park and back up the main road of shops.

But had she been unwitting? And why, try as she might to explain away the whole brief encounter as just the product of Madge's desperate, dying delusion, could she not do it? Instead she found herself facing that old and foolish question continually asked by the abandoned lover: 'Did she really love me?' And there was no clear answer to this except that something had got so close to Nina's heart that it hurt. She'd been moved and repelled.

It had happened in the afternoon. Nina had been reading to Madge and Madge had fallen asleep. Nina was just about to go back to her own bed when Madge woke, pulled the mask away from her face and nodded towards the third patient in the ward. 'She's jealous of us,' she said. That was all. But it was grotesque. And grand.

The third patient was Mrs Doreen Biddle. Speechless and semi-paralysed after a stroke, the large grey lump of Mrs Biddle lay in bed with a plastic sack of urine hanging from her side. Every now and then, when Mrs Biddle scratched herself with her one working hand, the sack fell on the floor and then the nurse came and tutted and attached it to Mrs Biddle again and tucked it back in the bed, tidy as a miniature hot-water bottle.

Most days Mr Biddle came and sat by Mrs Biddle's side and then her eyes spat with silent hate. 'It was all his fault,' the gossipy nurse explained to Nina. 'He left her on the floor all night.'

The idea that Mrs Biddle, preoccupied with hating her husband and no doubt desperate to know if she would ever recover the use of her limbs and larynx, had the emotional energy left to be jealous was preposterous. And the small gloating smile of power that accompanied Madge's words was shocking. And what, oh what, could Mrs Biddle have to be jealous *of*? In one of those awful moments of recognition, Nina knew the answer. That even in extremis, paralysed, speechless or dying, the human heart hungers for love. For intimacy. Madge had claimed Nina as her own. And Nina had allowed it. How else explain the fact that she had never once crossed the ward and sat by Mrs Biddle's bed; held Mrs Biddle's hand? Mrs Biddle had seemed to belong to another world.

Nina stopped outside the Violin Shop. She often stopped here. The window was appealing. A cello was set up on a plinth with a music stand in front of it and behind the cello hung a line of violins, shapely as nudes, their wooden torsos polished, the dark holes of their mouths saying, 'O, O, O. Play us! Play us!' Nina went in. She half expected to find the distant niece there, but she wasn't, of course. It was a man in a brown apron, polishing a bow.

It was unreasonable to be frightened of Madge's last words, to fear possession. So thought Nina now, walking down the line of violins and selecting three to try. Years since she'd played, but she hadn't lost her touch. The man in the brown apron looked quite impressed. In the hospital, still in a nervous state, she hadn't been able to see beyond Madge's death. The only thing she could see herself 'taking over' was the manner of Madge's death. As though she too was destined to spend four months gasping for breath, dying as slowly as a human being knew how to die. That was all nonsense, of course.

Nina paid for the violin with her Access card. Tom would probably create, but it would be too late by then. She'd be gone. Off to seek whatever it was Madge was still seeking when she died. If she was taking over anything, it was surely Madge's energy.

Nina smoked half the Benson & Hedges with several glasses of pre-supper wine. Tom had shaken his head over

....

169

it and then joined in. He'd been nice about the violin. Said he'd been thinking of buying her one for her birthday. This could be it.

'You seem like a new woman since you came out of hospital,' he said.

'Do I?' asked Nina. 'I feel quite like my old self.'

A Woman is Born to Bleed

JOYCE CAROL OATES

Laughed at me the way I was dancing, throwing my body to the beat. Slick with sweat and my long hair slapping. Like an eel being boiled, one of the guys said. Maybe they weren't laughing at me, maybe it was just general laughing. These were hilarious times. These were happy times. They're vanished now, just litter and ripped-out wiring in houses marked NO TRESPASSING THIS PROPERTY CONDEMNED, but they were alive then, we all were.

I was high on two tabs of LSD, smashed so I didn't know my name. When I felt for my face, it was just nothing – smooth as a plate, and a sucking hole where the mouth had been. There were lights, lightbulbs turned to actual flames making the air quaver. The faces of my friends turned liquid like fluorescent rot running down their bones. I didn't judge! I saw it was the natural law of the universe. My own bones, my long slender forearm bones, showed glimmering through my flesh like an X-ray. My soul was the size of a pea rattling inside my hollow head. *Better bring her down*, somebody said. *She's gonna burst a blood vessel.* Another guy said, *Who the fuck is she? Who brought her here? She's just a kid.* Somebody called somebody else *asshole, fuckhead.* There was a sound of breaking glass like you'd imagine a xylophone. Voices screaming but mine wasn't one of them. Where my tank-top was off my shoulder showing one of my breasts, my skin oily like you'd imagine an actual eel, somebody took hold and the fingers sunk in, right into the flesh like it was putty. I laughed and pulled away and what's he left with but the shoulder bone? – laughed and laughed.

Later, it might've been another time, they sat me on the knee, then it was the hard shin bone, of this guy Jax who was Opal's boyfriend. *Giddyup*! *Giddyup, horsey*! Jax was laughing. He was a shaved-head boy, with the most beautiful eyes, and a moustache. His face shiny like it'd been scrubbed and his big strong fingers had bleached-looking nails, big blunt square-cut clean nails like you never see on a man. Worked at Yewville General and smuggled out pills and syringes in his pockets. Baggy khakis. Wrapped in used Kleenex is the trick, Jax said, if anybody stops you they'd be disgusted to examine a snot-dried Kleenex, right? Some of it he sold but most he gave away to his friends, there was such a strong love of friends for friends, these were the people you'd die for. Opal laughed and squealed making a face, she was fastidious about certain things said aloud, given voice to, crude vulgar things, it was OK to perform certain actions but not to speak of them. Like going to the toilet, and she'd had an abortion (I knew of this but Opal wasn't the one to tell me, she'd have been furious to know people spoke of her behind her back) but you'd never guess from how she talked. Jax was a big boy, younger than Opal with upper arms big as another man's thighs. And that sand-colored moustache he was always chewing, like it helped him to think. I wanted him to like me, though. All of them, Opal's friends. There was Opal's ex-husband, too, people were scared of, not to his face exactly but he'd been eight months at Red Bank, a drug deal gone sour so he had certain grudges to repay. Somehow, that was understood and accepted. Jax was my special friend, I'd thought, the way he smiled calling me *sweetheart*. And Opal would laugh and kiss me like I was some discovery of her own. *Isn't she! She is!*

Opal liked to kiss me in the beginning, the way Momma did years ago. Now she was Mother, not Momma. We fought all the time.

Begging Jax to let me go, it hurt me between the legs, my tender parts between my legs, I was wearing white shorts, and thin panties underneath. It'd been a hot summer day but now cold in the night and my legs pimpled with goosebumps and insect bites and scabs and bruises but nobody could see, it was too dark. I was sort of in love with Jax and this was my punishment maybe. *Giddyup, baby!* Jax was saying. And everybody laughing, the look on my face maybe – I'd be trying to smile, trying not to show hurt, or that I was scared, sometimes that's funny in others' eyes. And Jax so big, my hands hidden inside his gripped tight so you could see just my wrists and no hands at all. I begged him let me go but it was loud in the room, in all the rooms they were partying, a speaker blaring rock music so loud you couldn't hear except for the heavy downbeat, the pulse, vibrations in everybody's bones like an earthquake. Tried to slide off Jax's shin bone and he'd grab me and position me, pumping his crossed leg like a seesaw. Sometimes when you let them do what they want to do and don't try to stop them the evil energy runs through them like an electric shock. And it's over. The shine on Jax's face like something hot inside his skin pushing out. And his eyes. *Giddyup horsey! Baby-horsey!* Pumping his leg faster and faster and finally I started to cry and Opal came over and grabbed Jax's bald head in both her hands laughing telling him to stop.

I wanted them to like me, so badly. And this was one of my secrets from Mother who didn't have a clue what I was doing, all that summer staying with a cousin in Yewville, working at a fruit stand on the Shaheen Road.

Selling fruit, pint baskets, quart baskets, bushel baskets. Tomatoes, pears, peaches, apples, cantaloupes, the smell of the cantaloupes so strong, the rear of the stand where the overripe melons were tossed, buzzing yellow jackets, flies, the smell of the rotting fruit, so the smell of cantaloupe would sicken me, and make me angry God knows why, all

....

my life. Try to eat it, are you kidding? – right now, remembering, I'm nauseated.

Jax let go, and forgot me, in one minute they can forget you so you know no harm's meant. It was hard for me to walk without doubling over. Like my insides were hurt. But I'd be smiling, I had this smile people said was so sweet, Opal touched my face sometimes staring at me like you'd stare into a mirror. I was crazy for Opal and later on, hearing what happened to her, I just wouldn't think of it at all, I had the power to make my mind go blank, that's always in your power. That night is confused in my memory like so many. I didn't have sex with anybody, any of the guys, I went away crying, the pain scary like I'd been pounded there, between my legs, I wasn't even sure what it was called except *vagina*, wasn't sure what that meant exactly, was it the whole thing, *reproductive organ* the biology textbook called it, or just the outside of it, there was *uterus* too, *womb*, the woman Mother worked for owned a fancy women's clothing store in Mt Ephraim, Flora Wells – she had *uterine cancer*, an operation and some treatments but in a few years she'd be dead. I went into the bathroom trying to pee and there was a numbness like needles, and burning. And next day when I woke up wrapped in a blanket on the front porch, it was an upstairs porch overlooking the cracked sidewalk, already it was afternoon of whatever day and I'd missed hours of work and had a hard time getting to my feet my head was so heavy, my eyes out of focus like trying to see underwater. When I went to the toilet this time the pain was like fire, and a knot deep in my belly, and I saw it, the blood, in the toilet bowl, and freaked, calling Opal's name, just freaked seeing the swirls of blood in the water, thin and curling, streaks of red like long thin worms swimming languidly and Opal came in and grabbed me to quiet me, calling me *baby*, *sweetheart*, saying I was just having my period, that's all. I was trembling, couldn't seem to stop, and my teeth chattering, I told Opal it was my first time, it hadn't ever happened to me before,

....

I was talking fast and nervous and Opal asked if I was serious, this was my first? – looking at me like I had to be lying. Standing there half naked my legs bruised and scabby and my knees bent, like my body was made of something brittle like ice that would shatter if I moved the wrong way, and Opal asked hadn't my mother prepared me, and I lied and said no, and Opal said she had some Tampax she'd give me, and one of Jax's codeine tablets would take care of the cramps. Saying getting your period is no big deal, it's great news usually you're not pregnant. Saying *It's just a fact of life, baby, like any other. A woman is born to bleed.*

....

Postcards of the Hanging

MICHAEL CARSON

'They're selling postcards of the hanging,' I said to Lady.

Lady looked at me. She'd seen my lips move but I knew she hadn't heard what I'd said. 'Lady,' I wrote on the pad, 'turn down the vol on the implant and listen to me for a minute.'

I knew Lady didn't want to from the way she took her own sweet time to press the vol minus button under her left thumb-nail. 'Nothing's happening, Boss,' Lady said – or rather, shouted. 'The vol minus is on the blink now; gone the same way as the graphic equalizer. I could murder those Radio Rental people, I really could.'

I didn't want to get into all that. I try to leave litigation to Lady. I put the faxprint down on the auto CD selector which is also a coffee table, though there's no coffee in any of the MacMony outlets these days, and every single one of our CDs jumps and skips – only good for mirrors and coasters and good time sparkers. Still, you know all that. *What To Do With Your Useless CDs Monthly* didn't get to be the hottest title on the faxprint circuit without people like you buying it. Anyway, I swivelled the paper round so's Lady could read.

'They're selling postcards of the hanging!' Lady said or – like I said – shouted. 'It's disgusting! He was just a bloke who wouldn't be parted from his personal stereo and fought back when the Angry Commuter Brigade tried to give him a bollocking for leaking on the Northern Line. Wasn't his fault if one of them had a stroke.'

Well, it was pointless for me to try and go on while Lady

was having trouble with the volume of her implant. The digital display on Lady's wrist said that the selection now playing was 'Hit Me With Your Best Shot' – a ditty I've never liked due to it being the anthem of the orphan-hunting lobby. And this is a safe house for orphans. My dad didn't bounce us on his knee to the *Joan Baez Songbook* for nothing.

Still, the hanging reminds you that it's a whole different world out there. Me and Lady are well out of it.

Until the hanging we thought it was the Plods who were out of it. Funny that. They always seemed to the Rockers to be so far out of it they had ceased to exist. The Plods, despite all evidence to the contrary, didn't even know something was happening, let alone what it was. What it was, was Rockers in their own world.

No messing about, I think it was a grave mistake for Lady to rent her implant from Radio Rentals. They offered all these extras – controls on finger-nails and the rest – but they didn't mention that these things wear out and would be a pain to replace, nor that they'd go and go bust in the last recession but two. Baby, Baby, it's a hard world. Wild, too, once you're past the garden mural to The Dead – now just that . . . and not that grateful from what I heard of their last words.

Mind you, I've made lifestyle mistakes same as you I expect. For instance, it's going to be tough for me to get this down 'cause my own implants are playing up and the static's giving me a shocking time. Still, even the glitch in the implant can't disguise the raw yet warm acoustic of Janis doing 'Moan Over Me', the ultimate greatest track on *Joplin from the Other Side (The Concert) LIVE!* I still can't get my head round the way they did it. This medium in Carmel like got in touch with Janis – who'd got into heaven's fifth mansion, in case you'd been worrying yourself sick – and Janis communicated the album to this medium. In One Take!

. . . .

It's making my fingers mourn over every letter I beat out. I miss Janis like crazy. I'm ululating like Sahila who is, in this Rocker's book, the greatest of the New Wave Saudi Women rockers. Hard to credit that we've never seen her! Wow! Janis Lives!

Better now. 'Summertime [The Remix]' and it's not the cruddy NYC Version done at the Murdoch studios, neither. This is from the Funky Young Tory lab in Rotherham and it makes me into a stylist for this my first – and probably last – venture on Rocknet International.

But it ain't summertime and the living ain't easy. They're selling postcards of the hanging for a start. What's that all about?

I don't regret having the audio implant put in. I was one of the first to check out then check into the MacMony Clinic when headset implants were right on the cutting edge of surgical procedures. When I heard that MacMony had come up with a way of doing away with earphones by putting this tiny – well it seemed tiny then – chip into the inner ear, I said to my lady, 'Lady,' I said, 'do they know it's Christmas? With one of them neat brillo-dillos, Christmas will be every day for your old Rocker of a lover-man!'

My lady was going through a phase of playing her Helen Reddy records like on random access twenty-five hours a day eight days a week and that always meant something bad going down.

'No way to treat a lady,' sang my lady.

Anyway, I calculated that having the implant would save me and Lady in the long run. It would open the door to all the rest of the state-of-the-art technology available. Out would go the earphones, the people-walkers, the tapes, the CDs, the batteries and the bum-bags. And in would jive this great Library of Rock, owned by MacMony, accessed through your trusty pendant computer and able to deliver in split seconds every track of your choice from Jimmy Crumit to The Sicking Portillos.

'Course, there's always people around ready to spoil the

fun. Lord Richard of Walsingham backed by Sir Sting and Lady Faithfull came on the Telescan to warn of the dangers of a constant diet of the sort of music then in vogue. Sir Sting – always a closet Plod I reckon – said that it was absolutely disgusting that MacMony were even contemplating fitting audio implants because they could then get at you subliminally and murmur: 'Mahogany furniture is the best thing since sliced Meatloaf!' and other subversive sentiments. He was right, but for every advance there's a retreat. Times don't really change, you know. Old man, look at my life. I'm a lot like you were. Mind you, having said that you haven't said very much.

I suppose a few took some notice of these old geezers but, as I said to Lady – not that she listens – not that she hears, 'Rock on, Lady!' I said.

I had to stop just then. 'The Wall' was on. I'd forgotten that I'd ordered it up. Christ, it holds up well! The new recording for the Let's Keep Teachers Live! charity improves on perfection. 'All in all you're just another brick.' It really knocks me out. Ha ha. Hum. Anyway I had to get up and just walk about. Lady mimed me to hoe the kale, so that's what I did. Hardly any sign of the damned buzzing in the implant.

But I'm back now. No worries. *U2 Play Percy French Favourites*. 'Have you heard of "Phil the Fluter from the Town of Ballymuck?" ' Too much I have. Have they gone off or have they gone off? Since Bono straight-bananaed over that bent Brahmin Rampal it's been hopeless. Still, there's art in the badness. It's like a Damien Hirst. Rot and decay and how are the mighty fallen. They've put his body in a vat of Silver Shred. Surrounded by smiling animals done by that Yank chap who married the Itai porn star and came to a bad end. It's in the Tesco Gallery in Scunthorpe. Yo, Rinny! Ah, yes, but is it art? Art-fart-mart-tart. That toast ready yet?

'Course, implants have made these great strides since I

....

had mine. And wouldn't you know it, they've been down-priced by a factor of fucking five. *You're just another brick in the wall ... all in all ...*

Sorry about that. I slipped back. That happens a lot. The heavy metal lament on U2's 'Mountains of Mourne' just couldn't hold me. Back I went to the last track. Mentally, you dig.

I like bands that put their life on the line. Ever since Peaches and Spunk, seeing as how they were fading off the world, put it about that they were going to end it all – and I mean END IT ALL – for charity on Worldwide Rupert and the whole fucking world tuned in and the Donkey Sanctuary suddenly had twice the assets of the NatWest and every donkey in the whole goddamned world was given sanctuary on a private island in the Indonesian archipelago ... ever since then I've had a soft spot for them. Peaches and Spunk did do themselves in. No one actually thought they would. The whole world was kind of of the opinion that when the cloud following this mega-explosion on stage had cleared there they'd be looking like Abba with Aids. They'd never had street cred – never recovered from that New Labour gig back in '97 – but in death they saved themselves as well as donkeys worldwide. And ever since on the anniversary fans gather in reality or virtual at the Peaches and Spunk chapel where they pray to them – Jimmy, Coalface, Peaches and Grid – for their own special intentions. In my case, it's *More Rock! More Roll! More music for my soul! Amen.*

Wait. I want this right. Plainchant for twenty-first-century needs. It takes a bit of time to bring it up on my old set-up. There.

Ad DEUM qui LAETIFICAT juvenTUTEM MEAM!

Ginger Baker joining the Cistercians was the best thing that could have happened to the Christo-Rock fusion. There was a time when I thought that something great would come

....

out of the link-up between Motown and the Benedictines
but it ended up being mulched into lift-silt and home-
shopping lull. Buckfast monks who had once been idols –
The Fast Bucks were huge on the Pacific Rim – are now
back making – and probably getting stoned on – their tonic
wine. And meditating on how all things pass.

I've not been a great one for the Rock and Roll Saints.
I know that puts me out on a limb at a time when Rock
sanctity is big business . . . and when they're painting the
passports brown. But, hey, I'm a groaner from the old school
– it's only Rock and Roll. I can't keep it in; I gotta let it
out and I say – and I can hear the yucks in quad but what
can you do? – Just a (shrugs helplessly) FAN. That's me.
I'll fan the Rockers til their egos are cooked right through,
but worship? No way. No fucking way. I mean, I was an
altar boy; I know where it leads.

That's what really pisses me off about the generations of
Rockers behind me. They've swallowed the whole Rock
religion whole. Of course me and Lady could see it coming;
we lost our kids pre-teen to the Church of the Bay City
Rollists. It's like I said to Lady at the time. 'It must come
from your genes, Lady. Your folks were always great
believers in lost causes. They took *Marxism Today* long
after it was "Marxism Long-Gone" for the rest of us. They
followed Freddy and the Dreamers into the terminal care
home where they did everything for them. Is it any wonder
that our kids've gone in for a really naff Rock religion?'

Well, Lady had no answer to that. Like I was saying, I
don't think she was listening; I don't think she heard. You
see, we did know that it was kind of inevitable that the kids
would fall for one or other of the rock religions. It was like
I said to Jason (I know! I'm SORRY! OK?) 'Look, Jason,' I
said, 'I know you think your daddy's a washed-up old
Rocker, listening to his orchestral Blur records, but couldn't
you – if you have to become a Rockist – join one of the
more middle-of-the road sects? How about the AC/DCists?
Their CDs are sensibly priced and Teflon-covered, their

. . . .

liturgy is middle-of-the road, and they don't grab a hundred and ten per cent of your attention?'

'No, Dad,' Jason said, 'it's the Bay City Rollists for me. I accept it all, Dad. It's not just the tartan and the scent of Old Spice, believe me. OK?'

Kids, what can you do with them? Jason already had an audio implant that made mine sound like rubbish. Permanently tuned to his band of preference. And the others went the same way. Elton and Cocker had their implants put in the day they were circumcised. By some NHS cowboy. So they were in a world of their own from very early on and grew up buying everyone Coke, teaching the world to sing, and talking all Oz. Still, they've turned out well enough. They close the door, light the lights, stay home every night and read their Seekers tracts. Paid for by standing order. Fit right in. Do no harm to anyone. Drive me and Lady nuts.

It's the youngest – Nebraska – that really worries me. You see, she came along when me and Lady thought Bruce Springsteen was God – and let everyone know it. The Bruce cult was the last gasp of monotheism before the world went back to its galaxy of stars, its dawn-of-history divergence. We hadn't been so electrified since Dylan went electric, though according to the latest biographer – and he had access to the Dylan Papers – Bobby never wanted to go electric at all. He was forced into it. By the Mob.

Christ, the static is bad today.

Lady's back from the Billy J. Kramer precinct. The MacMony technicians laughed at her volume problem and pointed to their logo – they never speak due to their state-of-the-art implants:

> *When you've been screwed by the rest,*
> *You will know*
> *MacMony's*
> *simply the best.*

....

Well, seeing as Lady is stuck with her Radio Rental number stuck on max and locked into random continuous play mode, she couldn't really argue with that. But, as she wrote on the pad just now, she gave them one of her gestures. People have really come on in the gesture department. Rockers in their private world meant that an alternative form of communication had to be found. Not that people have much to say to one another, but there are times when it's still necessary. Sometimes, it's even necessary to communicate with the Plods.

She also mentioned that the beauty parlour in the precinct was full of sailors. That pissed her off rather because it meant that she wouldn't be able to have her hair done for the Ringo concert. He's the only one left – contrary to all expectations. Shame how Paul went. A chick-pea went down the wrong way. I've not heard 'Pin Ball Wizard' in a while. The Who have lasted well. Old as the hills and, despite hope against hope, still in the land of the living. Advertising All-Bran.

But I was telling you about Nebraska. She fell hook, line and whatsit for Bruce and his cult. She started looking for enlightenment in fading seaside resorts and along lonesome roads. Being strapped for cash at the time, the best she could manage was the A44. Still she yearned for the space of America where a man's a man and free to worship Bruce as his chip company intended.

OK so far. Sort of standard issue. But then the silly cow bought herself the latest virtual reality compu-scan on the never-never in Dixon's sale. And before me and Lady knew where we were, Nebraska had gone through a virtual reality wedding with all the trimmings to a hillbilly from the badlands of Montana and all hell was let loose in the compu-scan on Nebraska's bed and the phone bill went so far through the roof that this bint from Telecom got on the blower to ask if everything was all right. That's how bad it was.

....

MICHAEL CARSON

Well, as far as Nebraska was concerned everything was fine and dandy. We'd hear her moaning like a coyote up there, enough to strip the Laura Ashley off the walls.

In those days, of course, me and Lady still talked. Not often, but we did sometimes.

Lady said as how – call her old-fashioned if I liked – she didn't think virtual reality marriage was what you'd call moral. She can sound like the spitting image of Lady Faithfull when she gets up on her soap-box.

'The times they are a-changing,' I said, like I always did. 'I mean, Lady, as long as it's a virtual marriage Nebraska won't get herself banged up. It's just Red Hot Belgian with commitment,' I said. 'Don't worry; Be Happy!' I said.

Looking back I think it was about then we gave up on conversation. Lady frowned, pressed her left thumb-nail to max, grazed forward with the index nail of her right hand – I knew she had chosen something really mind-blowing – and went all silent.

And Lady was proved right when the circus came to town and TNT delivered this frozen sperm and before we knew what hit us the Vege-roast baster had disappeared from the kitchen cupboard and Nebraska had embarked on the first of her pregnancies.

And Bruce and Brucilla are fine kids, don't get me wrong. Still, you've guessed it, the hillbilly is no more. They just ran out of programmes to run. They had an amicable virtual divorce. Even me and Lady banging on the bedroom door and shouting, 'What about money for the kids?' – not that Nebraska could hear us – didn't do anything to sour things. Nebraska hasn't got a litigious bone in her body. About the only person on the planet who hasn't.

I've got to do something about the implants. They're driving me nuts.

It's always interesting to think about how we got where we are. If you ask me, the first personal stereos led seamlessly to the silent outside world and everyone rocking to

....

184

their own tune. I can remember – just – back in '79 seeing the first set in the shop and thinking, 'My life has been leading up to this moment.' I bought it – over a hundred quid it cost – and from the first moment I was hooked. I mean, it was an answer to prayer. We were able to go through life like film-stars; able to accompany the screen-play of our lives with the soundtrack of choice. A world of our own that no one else can share – like The Seekers say.

This is not to say that I didn't have reservations. I mean, when stereo became personal I won something but I lost a bit too. There was no way to share my enthusiasm for a start. And that was a loss. I used to love to bring joy to the Plods by pumping up the volume on the car stereo, by opening all the windows of the house. The personal stereo stopped all that.

Trouble was, of course, the Plods heard a buzz and didn't like it. They just didn't fit in with the screenplay and the soundtrack and they started appearing on the Telescan going on about how marginalized they felt. We told them to get themselves a life, which didn't go down well. The Stereo Murders of '98 – a succession of wicked acts on the Northern Line – was the lead-up to the war of the headsets. AA batteries were made illegal as a result of the Battle of Tottenham Court Road. They were bad times. We were in a pretty uncool situation until the new technology came to our rescue. But God only knows what's going to happen. Did I mention that they're selling postcards of the hanging? What's all that about?

There are still Plods about who could tell me. Not that we see much of them. We've got nothing to talk about – even if we could hear them. There's no common ground. I mean, once the Rockers had the implants the rest were stuck. The old ways go on. Sometimes I can see the geezer next door tuning his Roberts, so there must be something happening. Only the other month – and you're probably

....

not going to believe me – I caught sight of a woman reading a *book* for Christ's sake.

I had to stop there. Things are going really weird. The implant went back to normal for a minute and I had this Prince album (he's called pi r squared these days) from start to finish with gorgeous clarity. Then there was silence, which really set me on edge and then this bloke talking – TALKING. For a while I thought it was just a new wave of Rock – an intro before it broke into something really mind-drilling. But no. On and on this chap went and, once I'd settled myself into it, I realized that he was comparing different recordings of – scuse me while I honk into my Charles and Di Divorce mug – 'The Nuns' Chorus'. After half an hour of it I decided that it was really so bad that it was quite perfectly excellent. The bloke thought that, on balance, the Mormon Tabernacle Choir had it over this choir called, I think, the Oily Cart.

He signed off and then we got a programme called *The Most Beautiful Music in the World* – though which world wasn't clear. Not this world. Not me and Lady's world.

Then this really posh bloke came on and said there had been a hostile buy-out of the MacMony music archives by a consortium of concerned international leaders of the business world who were dismayed at the damage done to society by the Rock Revolution. Well, that came as a shock to me and Lady – who was picking it up too – I mean, the way we'd been taught there was no such thing as society anyway. Still, we were not to be alarmed, they said; a normal world would be resumed as quickly as advanced audio-indoctrination procedures allowed.

A minute or two of Nigel Kennedy. I ran to the bathroom for a Hendrix, but Lady was already there. Then this bloke announced that Lesson 1 of the Reorientation to Life series was about to commence. 'Module 1 of "Your Rock-Free Life", Lesson 1: Coming back to People. Part 1: Introductions.'

....

*

I've just come back from the public library – THE PUBLIC LIBRARY FOR CRYING OUT LOUD! – where Lady and me took our Intermediate examination in Sensitivity to People in Public Places. I got a C– for the beginners' course. Lady surprised herself by getting an A. On the way out we saw an ad for implant removal. It's free, once you've worked your way up the waiting-list. We signed on – well, we might as well. I can't stand the prospect of the Three Tenors coming in uninvited all the time – and I mean all the time.

The kids seem to have taken to the change in circumstance. Never having known anything else except Implant Culture and wall-to-wall Rock, they see books and discipline and Classic FM as something novel, even a bit on the rebellious side. Not me, though, not me, not Lady. Me and Lady, we're too old to change. When we get home from Charm School we go upstairs, close the curtains and hum 'Never Mind the Bollocks'. Then we hand-jive the night away.

Still, it's not the same. The soundtrack's gone; the heartbeat of life is fading. Wouldn't it be nice if we were older, then we wouldn't have to wait so long? Speaking for myself, I'm quite prepared to drop off my perch any time I'm told. I got a D– in Module 2 of Mantovani Studies last week. My time for dropping off can't be that far off.

I got a postcard of the hanging the other day. No message.

....

Friends in Berlin

CHERRY WILDER

Frank had flown on ahead to liaise with the Berlin management and work up something dark and feathery at the airport. The rest of the poor sods had to front up – Heathrow at sparrowfart, per usual. At least, said Long, the minibus was still in good nick. Only Long, David, Cam and Tony were on the bus. James and Fiona were coming on from the Dorchester separately. This was another of Frank's ideas.

David, who was doing all the PR while Frank was in Germany, had scored a big bundle of *Music Notes* with good pictures. There was one of James playing guitar in Highgate Cemetery, 1994, and one of the band, 1992, fooling around with Ray Cokes on a merry-go-round. The headline read: 'AS THE RAVEN FLIES!! Nightwings over Berlin'. They all sat there signing the copies like good lads to make a nice souvenir handout.

Then as they were going under an underpass about fifteen minutes from the airport David spotted Jenny and half a dozen old faithfuls struggling along through the drizzle. Long clapped old Dan, the driver, on the shoulder and he stopped dangerously in a shot-at-dawn zone while the little bunch of fans scrambled in. Besides Jenny there was her friend Maureen, couple of new girls and couple of younger boys. One of them asked straight off about James. Where was James? – stood to reason. Leader of the band. It was his band. James Raven and the Nightwings. David spoke up and said sure, James would be at the airport.

Long stayed in his seat and Jenny came to sit beside him.

They went a long way back – thousands of miles south of Earl's Court.

'How's it going, Gary?' she said.

'Tip-top!' he said. 'Nice to see big Berlin, no wall at all. We're doing fine.'

'I believe you, thousands wouldn't,' she grinned. The Australianism almost made him cry. He sat there choked up, felt his face working.

'Jesus, Jen,' he breathed.

'Come on,' she said, squeezing his hand tightly. 'We know how bad it was.'

The bus was already turning into the dark tunnels that led into the airport. The fans were having a great time – Cameron Taylor's mum had sent along enough sticky buns and doughnuts to feed an army; there was a whole tray of Coke cans.

'Gary,' said Jenny, 'you should just stop. I love the group, you know that, I think James is absolutely the greatest. But if he's that far gone . . .'

Long knew she was sincere, a nice sensible girl, good sort, but if he went along with her it would be wrong. A betrayal.

'I know him pretty well, Jen,' he said. 'The rat of a reporter blew up that bad scene out of all proportion. You've been a tower of strength for us all from the old days – from when we were The Magic Runes. Don't believe all this deathwish, depression, designer drugs story – OK?'

She leant over and kissed his cheek.

'OK, love,' she whispered.

Then they were crawling out of the van – couple of local roadies had made it on time, and were heaving the bags around. The fans shouted, 'See ya at the gate!' and raced away to get their places. Tony came up to Long, looking afraid; they were all looking afraid.

'Where is he?' hissed Tony. 'Is he here yet? Cam said to ask if you got a phone call.'

'Not me,' said Long. 'He'll be along, stop worrying.'

Tony's soft 'Italian angel' face creased up as if *he* was

. . . .

189

going to cry. Long could see the headlines now: BAND WEEPS WHEN LEADER FOUND. He took his own hand luggage and led off for the check-in counter but he kept thinking of how it would be if James really didn't show. How would they be told? Just step in here for a minute, boys. He thought of Fiona, far away, swept into the awful mechanism of death at the Dorchester.

David Gould moved up and took Tony's place, walking beside Long. Remarkably integrated group, the Nightwings. Well, there was Cam, the drummer, who was black, came from genuine Jamaica, then there was Tony Morro on bass, umpteenth-generation English-Italian, and himself, old Gary Longworth from New South Wales, lead guitar, and David Gould, bass guitar and keyboards. Bit under-rehearsed sometimes, in Long's personal opinion.

David was Jewish, and stone-rich, went to the same sub-Gordonstoun public school up north as James. Hooray for the artistic, do-your-own-thing school, old Litchway. Full of pooves and cults and every kind of music, from the church organ according to Buxtehude to the pipe band, to rock, punk, rave and house, not forgetting techno from the German–Dutch push, the sauer Krauts of the Remove, or was it the Shell?

'He's here,' said David. 'They're in the Lufthansa VIP area. We could all go up, have a coffee. Or we could wait down here, let one of the Lufthansa girls take us through customs, give James a sort of welcome when he and Fiona come down at boarding time.'

'Well, let's do that then,' said Long. 'Tell the other lads he's here, for God's sake.'

Meanwhile The Creature and its companion were in blue aura. Yes, blue, which was by no means the worst, wouldn't even think the name of the worst colours. Look around, every-time-I-look-around, lovely tune from that Maori tribe in the red tourer, look around and you're in a big cosy room, somewhat institutional . . .

. . . .

'Jesus!' croaked James Raven. 'Fiona! Fee! Have they got me in the bin again?'

Fiona Graham wound him in her arms on the big private couch and held him, as if to shield him from the armies of the night. Her eyes were wide with terror; she didn't know what to do, whether to blow the whistle. She wished Gary was there or Frank, but there was no one and the helpful stewardess had no idea how bad he was.

'Just in the VIP lounge, at Heathrow,' she said. 'Jimmie-bird, please have a drink of your tea.'

He reached out his fine, sinewy young hand as if it were the scaly claw of a very old monster and seized the handle of the cup as if to snap it off. But he drained the cup and she was pleased. Tea, ordinary Ceylon, none of your Earl Grey or Darjeeling, worked wonders with him.

Drained the potion. Saw in the glass of the table top and in the eyes of the companion a reflection of a young man in black, with black hair and a bony, handsome face. The aura wavered into the dark, terrible end of the spectrum but then swung back. Into greenish. This meant pain but not unbearable pain, both in and out of the Creature's brain. Insane-in-the-brain, insane-in-the-membrane. Which meant less than nothing, he remembered, he remembered in his proper person, with a horrible pain boring into his left temple, how David had said this and they'd laughed in the dressing-room. And although he felt and the creature felt about as low and dark and down as they could be the James element tried to pull himself together. For the lads. For the fans. For poor old Frank slaving away at bloody Tempelhof Airport or wherever. The gig wouldn't take long.

'I'll have one of the ordinary painkillers,' he said to Fiona. 'Where's the red bag?'

'What have you had today?' she demanded.

'Nothing,' he said. 'None of the Specials. One Ritalin

....

from the damned clinic. You saw me take it at the hotel. Now I need one of their painkillers for my headache.'

'If you haven't taken any of the Specials,' she said, looking around to see that no one was coming, 'why are you so bad?'

'I told you,' he said. 'It's backlash or flashback or something. I go off into the equivalent of a very bad trip. And there's always a psy . . . psychic component.'

She turned aside and fumbled in her purse for the key and unlocked the red beauty case where they kept all the medicine in a whole labyrinth of secret compartments, jars, boxes, false bottoms and tampon packets that had been fooling customs men for years. She fed James one painkiller with the last of her orange juice.

Then it was time and the stewardess and a security man collected them. They marched off, smiling; James signed a couple of autographs outside the elevator and they were given a ride on a big charabanc trolley with blue upholstered seats. Customs was in a special empty place with noises off and they breezed through, gave the fellow some raven stickers for his kiddies. Then they were through the swing doors and there were the fans, right up to the barrier. More than James expected, must have been over a hundred of the wee buggers, and surely that was the fan-club girl, Jenny, and her committee.

There was a strain of music, and he knew what it was. None of the band carried guitars on board; the precious instruments went in their special customized container. But Long had a harmonica and Cameron carried this little old bongo. There were the Nightwings at the mouth of the tunnel, meeting their leader and his bird.

Long blew a long wailing chord of joyful despair on the old harmonica and Cam hit in with the beat for 'Demon Tamed' which was what James liked to sing at airports etc. Long felt a great rush of relief and love and pure annoyance to set eyes on bloody James. Like a mother seeing her child who had been late coming home. James was looking pale

. . . .

but OK, black frock-coat and ruffled shirt, touch of Willie de Ville, touch of Hamlet in Victorian dress. On his arm was Fiona, still everyone's idea of a supermodel, although she didn't like to be called that any more. Pale creamy pants suit, mane of beautiful dark-gold hair, absolutely natural.

The fans went wild at the bit of music and James, who could hardly make a false move when he was in front of an audience, twirled about, spread his arms wide and began to sing. He had a strong, classically trained light baritone with a mad edge to it which made the difference between Covent-Garden-and-the-Met and Madison Square Gardens and The Lorelei.

> Demon tamed – trust the shadows . . .
> Demons fading – like the mists of dawn!
> Demon tamed – this magic's better,
> Demons vanquished – by the rites of love!

Then, before the staff could get restless, James left the fans going wild and barrelled off to the plane, followed by his band. It was nice for them all, going aboard, because the passengers knew they were coming. Applause here and there and birdcalls and riffs of some of their numbers. They didn't have time to talk, really, because the band were in business class and James and Fiona in first, but this was par for the course. David went up and went over some arrangements.

Fiona could see that James was in what she thought of as Exhaustion Mode, in spite of the anti-depressant he'd taken. He lay back and shut his eyes after speaking to David and sending back cheery greetings to the lads. David said, with a wink at Fiona, that Frank had found a bodyguard this time.

'Ah yes,' said James, without opening his eyes. 'A Schwarzenegger clone.'

'You'll see,' grinned David.

. . . .

*

... slept, passed out, for no one knows how long then alone, deep in nightmare, very tactile, lying on sharp stones at the bottom of a deep, round pit, mineshaft or old well. The Creature writhed its scaly body and its scaly mind shaft locked into frail, fading, agonized James. Far up above was a round patch of light and when faces looked down the hidden James tried to scream warnings but could not ...

Then the dream took an abrupt turn and he was out of doors, free as air, in a meadow full of wild flowers. It was some kind of family picnic: Mum and Dad were there, and Helen and Tommy. It was fine for a moment but then the sun was blotted out by a heavy slice of iron-grey cloud and a roaring noise filled earth and sky—

Fiona was shaking his arm.

'Start waking up, dear,' she said. 'We can see Berlin.'

James perked up gallantly, took a sip of Sekt, the German champagne, then crawled off to the loo. He wondered why the one thing he never had was claustrophobia. Must be his back-to-the-womb tendency. Only problem was that you couldn't see out. What one needed, really, was a womb with a view. He went back laughing at his joke and told it to Fiona. He got back into his window seat and looked down at Berlin.

He knew very well how Berlin had looked from the air at the end of the war and for years afterwards. The ruins gave him a feeling of horror and a feeling of dishonour and discomfort when he thought of the Allies, *his* side, for Christ's sake, flattening the cities of Germany. Now he could see that the place had changed, lot of new stuff, roofs everywhere, green on the outskirts and the glint of water. Wasn't all that big, of course, not like flying over London. There was a big ragged green expanse where the wall had been and the border zone. Even from here you could see it was a huge building site. He tried to find the Brandenburger Tor and the statue of the golden angel on top of the victory column, the place where Bono of U2 had been standing in

....

his video. Great band. He and the lads had opened for them once in the Oakland Colosseum.

Then something happened, the plane banked, the morning sun dazzled off the city below and the bright bulk of the fuselage. James was plunged into the pit of death, he was plunged through the cold air down down into the city, which was dark and clouded. Death in Berlin. New number, yes, that was all it was. Popped into his head.

Frank wouldn't be too pleased because they were supposed to be keeping an upbeat image, jolly lollipops, more or less, after his trip to the clinic. Something funny-macabre, a person, Mister Death, no, Herr Death, Herr Tod – it would come to him. He lay back, with his seatbelt fastened and was so well behaved that Fiona thought everything might be all right after all.

Long saw that he had missed his chance to see James up in first class. David was talking urgently to the steward; he passed on the message to Long and Cam.

'Whole welcome demo has gone down the pipe. Bomb threat. Airport under heavy security. Frank will be mad as a bloody moo-cow.'

'Get someone to tell James!' said Long. 'Get the steward to tell him.'

He hoped their plane wouldn't be rolled into a corner somewhere but no, they were allowed off normally. First class got off first so James and Fiona had a few moments to stand and chat with the band in the congested aisle.

'Pity about the bird girls,' said Cam. 'Frank said they'd be really wicked.'

'I don't mind if there isn't a production number,' said James, grinning at Long. 'I'm in Creative Mode. How about a riddle?'

'Quick!' said Long. 'Spit it out, Boss!'

'What did they say to Jim Morrison when he stood in front of the telly set?'

'OK,' said Long. 'I'll buy it.'

The line started to move on and James said he'd tell him

....

later. Fiona reached out and pressed Long's hand and gave him a smile, but not a very good one. Last time they had seen each other was in one of the fancy waiting-rooms at the clinic. She had flung herself into his arms and wept and shuddered and sobbed. He'd held her tight and soon found that he was beginning to enjoy it all over again.

The band dawdled off the plane exchanging flashing smiles with the Lufthansa girls. Long could see into the halls, not empty as he'd imagined but full of subdued travellers. There were green-uniformed German coppers in their flat hats all over the place. The band, with James and Fiona, were neatly siphoned off into a small transit lounge. No one else but them and a soccer team from some sunnier clime getting a bit of a going over at a special customs table. They had their manager along, protesting vigorously: his boys took nothing stronger than good South American coffee.

A tall, balding, heavily tanned individual in a nonchalant raincoat came up and it was their manager, Frank Kleinfeld, shepherding them to the customs table in the wake of the Eldorados from Ecuador. There was the container with their baggage; everything went on oiled wheels. The four customs men and one girl went easy on the Nightwings, barely opened a bag. The bad news, as Frank said, from a safe distance, was a room full of reporters, just up ahead. How was everyone, how was James feeling?

'Marvellous!' carolled James. 'In the Creative Mode, eh, Fiona?'

'Sound a bit manic to me,' grumbled Frank. 'Keep it down a bit. *Leise, leise.*'

The footballers had a small party of management and expatriates waiting for them and Frank had been permitted to front up with a chosen few. Two pretty girls in black body-suits and feather jackets, carrying their raven head-dresses. Then there was Gunther from the Tour management, a fan, who shook hands with everyone, in the German fashion, while going on about the bomb threat et cetera.

....

Long became aware of the fourth member of the party, who had walked slowly all round the band, exchanging a few words with the policemen and LH attendants. She was very tall and solid, about twenty-five years old, with a broad, pale face and well-cut black hair. She wore a maroon leather jacket, black jeans and expensive basketball boots.

'Well, James,' announced Frank proudly, 'we have found you a bodyguard.'

The big girl, who was talking to Fiona, loped over to James and looked down at him with a lovely smile. She said in mellow tones: 'Whitney Houston, I presume!'

Cue for a big laugh. James sang a little burst of the film music and they all moved on. They were in a nowhere place, a grey space between two sets of doors. Long saw that the big Turkish girl, whose name was Taheer, took the job of guarding James very seriously. She looked in every direction up to the mezzanines, down the stopped escalators. Long saw her move very fast once, following a man in a long grey gabardine overcoat – could be a designer job. He had come from nowhere and circled round James, who was standing still, apart from the others. The man was young, tall, German you'd think. Gone now, in the direction of the meeting-room.

Long quickly moved up alongside James, who turned to him, frowning.

'What did he say? Did you catch what he said?'

James was nervous but controlled.

'That guy in grey?' said Long. 'Didn't hear anything. Was he a heckler?'

There were always a few loonies who cursed and swore at touring musicians.

'Said something about "*Freund*", friends, or a friend,' said James. 'Friends in Berlin . . .'

But Long didn't trust the man in grey any more than Taheer had done. He kept an eye open for him when they filed into the meeting-room and took their places at the long table with the microphones.

. . . .

They could all see at a glance that it was going to be a diabolical press conference. These were a bunch of tough old airport professionals, used to making mincemeat out of politicians, not the music writers and nice gals from MTV and VH-1. These fellas had been given the Nightwings or nothing, result of the bloody bomb scare.

Gunther went on, in English, about 'just a few quick questions! Boys are tired and have to perform tonight.' The bit with the venue was settled; yes, one of the new summer stages put up in the shell of the PROVOX building over on the Potsdamerplatz.

Then, per usual, there were some personal questions for James. Was Raven his real name? Well, it was now – he'd had it changed by deed poll – but his family name was Corbett. He came from Liverpool, yes, like the Beatles, and his father was in export–import.

Then the questions centred on what-sort-of-band-they-were, what sort of music they played. How close were they to, say, heavy metal? There were distinct links to Metallica and Black Sabbath, but were they more like Grufties, Death Lovers?

Long talked about Magic Rock, Gothic, roots in Folk Rock. James said no, the label Graveyard Punk didn't really suit their music, though personally he listened to a lot of punk. The band had a heavy law against criticizing any other bands or styles of music; solidarity all the way was the motto. They had heard too many snotty beginners being dismissive of hard-working chaps they just didn't fancy. No, said James, he didn't mind if they were called a cult band. They'd got a lot of that during their big American College tour.

This was too tame and positive for the hard-faced crew in the front row. A thin woman in her forties with an American accent leapt up and shouted, 'If that tour was such a big smash, *Mister* Raven, why did you come back to London and overdose?'

Two men shouted out back-up questions. Was it true

....

about the designer drugs? Had he been in a coma for forty-eight hours?

All hell broke loose so convincingly that Long was surprised. Frank, always the essence of cool, did his block completely. He sprang to his feet and cried out about 'broken promises' and 'the perfidy of the media' in German and English. Three photographers came in to the left of the long table and started blazing away. Long and Tony started yelling at them to leave James alone. Cameron, the biggest and toughest of the Nightwings, vaulted over the table and took on the paparazzi all by himself. A number of the media persons, wherever they were from, seemed to be siding with the band and calling for order.

In the midst of it all Long saw James standing very still with his head bowed. Order suddenly restored itself. Taheer helped a chap to his feet; he had made a dash for the table and she had strong-armed him to the floor. Another woman journalist spoke up, neatly changing the subject and steering round James. Could Herr Kleinfeld, Frank, tell them all some more about the Gould Resource Project in Kenya and the Music Temple?

So Frank was in his element and the others could sit and look like benefactors. Which they were, Long supposed. But after a visit to the Project and the little music school he always felt that the locals were doing the band a favour, just by being themselves.

Long and James exchanged smiles and James put an arm round Fiona.

'I'm all right,' she said. 'I just can't stop shaking ... because of the fight.'

The ordeal was over in a few minutes. They all escaped from the airport and were whizzed off to their digs in a big Mercedes station wagon. Long saw at once that Frank had done the right thing: months ago he had booked the whole top floor of the Pension Rosa, just off the Kurfürstendam.

It was an old theatrical boarding-house complete with retired ballet dancers Dieter and Hannes in the attic, some

....

hopeful girls in the front rooms and Frau von Fichte, the hard-eyed landlady. It was a great day for the Pension Rosa when they had a genuine rock band on the top floor.

It was still early, only eleven o'clock, even if they had lost an hour flying to Europe. So they had the whole of the rest of the day until rehearsal-plus-performance at six o'clock, curtain up at 7.45. Or 19.45, if you wanted to be fussy. So they all fell about in the big, comfy, shabby sitting-room of the suite and did what you did on tour, waiting for the show to go on.

They sent out for McDonald's and Chinese. Talked and laughed and sang and told silly jokes. Watched the German VH-1 and Viva and good old MTV. The bird girls seemed to have come along and Long had the idea Cameron and Tony did what *they* did on tour at least twice. The other bedrooms were spread out along a corridor. They all had a a couple of beers but that was all. Long was losing his taste for beer.

He was watching James closely; our boy was spacey and tense, not like he remembered seeing him before. Fiona came and sat with Long on the big flowery couch in the corner.

'What is it?' he demanded. 'What's wrong with his nibs? Is it some new Special?'

He saw her eyes, her perfect big light-brown eyes fill with tears which she blinked away – no one controlled tears better than a model-girl.

'He says it's a backlash from that d-damned designer shit,' she whispered angrily. 'He goes off into a bad trip.'

They watched James practising a segue with Cameron. On another couch opposite them Frank and David sat poised over a coffee table of paperwork and argued like an old married couple, which was more or less what they were. Taheer Cetin prowled from window to window, unrelaxed, fists in the pockets of her leather jacket. From the right-hand window you could see round the corner into the Ku'dam.

....

Long said: 'In the press talk just now did you see a tall bloke in a grey overcoat? Might have been stalking James...'

'No,' said Fiona with a gusty sigh, still holding off her tears. 'He's stalking himself, Gary. I mean he tries so hard but he's his own worst enemy.'

She got this out but no more because James came bouncing over to them.

'I get the feeling,' he said cheerfully, 'that everyone is watching me.'

He sat down on the other side of Long.

'Damn right, you old bastard,' said Long. 'We want to know how you're feeling.'

'Normal new gig jitters,' said James. 'I swear it. Hey, did you get the riddle?'

'Yes,' said Long. 'I got the bloody riddle. Let's do the riddle.'

'What riddle?' said Fiona, trying to cheer up.

So Long blew a loud blast on the harmonica and James said: 'We're doing a riddle! Turn down the telly. OK, Longworth, you chunderer from Down Under, answer me this riddle: What did they say to Jim Morrison when he stood in front of the television set?'

'Well, stone the crows, Raven, and starve the lizards,' said Long. 'I reckon they said: "Get away Jim, you make a better Door than a window!"'

There was loud laughter mixed with groans. James said he was going to lie down, have his nap after that. Long went to his single room. His gear for the gig had been hung up and brushed off already by Frau von Fichte and her housekeeper. He lay on the bed and felt depressed and fell into a light sleep.

The stage was good and the rehearsal had gone well. They were all on top, high, with the aid of strong German coffee, mostly, but Fiona had let James take one amphetamine and Cam had sniffed a pinch of some horrible Jamaican voodoo

....

powder. The two low tiers of seats in the PROVOX amphi-theatre were packed and the standing room in the front was full. James stood next to Long on the OP and they made signals to David on the Prompt. The lights went on in clusters and a huge feathery raven shape came up on the backscreen. The crowd went wild. Cameron and Tony were suddenly in position: drum warm-up, plus a rhythmic rumble from the double bass.

'Up there!' shouted Long.

He gave the walk sign to David and they took the stage, and Long felt as good as he had ever done. This was your life, Gary Longworth, and he was playing with mind and heart and soul and old David was hanging in well. This was their music, their setting of the Nightwings opener, of good old 'Dark Fantastic', their first hit. Then out came James, holding out his cloak with the midnight-blue lining, his raven cloak. He flung it off and went to the mike in his velvet long vest, carrying his special minstrel guitar with the red ribbons. He was off right on the beat. A cry of pain, almost, a cry of pain that turned into something mysterious, and thrilling.

> *'Take me into the night,*
> *Let me be your dark-time lover . . .*
> *There's this place in the wildwood*
> *Where mortals dare not go . . .'*

There were two short breaks and before the first one they played a cover version. It was 'Magical Mystery Tour', spooked up in their own style, of course, bit of a reggae touch from old Cameron. Then before the second break they show-cased their latest hit, biggest so far, with a sinfully expensive video made on location in darkest Oxfordshire. Everyone was waiting to hear 'Changeling'.

Long had never been too keen on songs with too much story in the lyric, but this one seemed to work well. James had done all of the text and then Long and James and

David had done the music. They ran a still from the video on the big screen with this waif-like actress girl, Kira, as the changeling, gazing into a pond in a formal garden. James sang solo, with only a wisp of sound from the keyboards:

> *'On Lammas Eve*
> *She sees her love in a dark mirror,*
> *He rides alone by the rushing river,*
> *How will she follow into the hollow lands?*
> *The lands of dream,*
> *Between the dawn and the day ...'*

Then they all went into the first chorus, dark and heavy, with a strong rock beat, with all of them singing and James drowning them out, like a damned soul.

> *'Lost child!*
> *Now take the measure of your ghosts!*
> *Stretch out your hand,*
> *Accept the ways of your lost land,*
> *The fires of summer by the riverside!'*

So it went on, with the girl seeing the knight, her suitor from the Summer Land, at Hallowe'en, and going off with him by New Year. The mortals she had grown up with 'treated her kindly, but she could not stay'. It was done well in the video, with not too much characterization of anyone but the girl. It came across to Long, always, as a sad song, maybe about growing up and leaving home. Or even about dying.

Of course it went over like a charm in the PROVOX amphitheatre, worth the price of admission. But they had something in hand for a big finale. The final section was short and the last number began with James off stage and a cunning arrangement, mainly from Cameron, of blues and bad-guy songs: 'Dupree's Blues', Stanislaus' 'Like an alley cat', plus 'Bad, Bad Leroy Brown'. Then the beat

....

changed and there was James in this tight-fitting single-breasted grey jacket, wearing a totally decadent dark-green slouch hat and snapping his fingers. Litchway had taught him a lot of good German: his teeth glistened.

> 'Und der Haifisch, der hat Zähne,
> Und die tragt er in Gesichte,
> Und Macheath der hat ein Messer,
> Doch das Messer sieht man nicht!'

The crowd carried on as if the wall had fallen all over again. Frank had been right when he said they liked a bit of culture and loved it when visiting artists had a go at German. They did old Mackie Messer through once and repeated the verse about the jailbait widow, *die minderjahrige Witwe*, as an encore.

So that was the programme for the Berlin gig and it had gone bloody well. All they had to do now was put in time until tomorrow night and do it all over again. They were far too buggered for a real party so they simply went back to the Pension Rosa, sent out for more food, had some Sekt, donated by Gunther, and sloped off to bed. The bird girls, Gisela and Silke, were still hanging in there. Long wondered if they'd turn up back in London.

It was suggested to him shyly by Gisela that she had a friend from acting school called Andrea but he thanked her and said he was very tired. He went off to his room, down the corridor and was woken up by Fiona, crying, in her dressing-gown.

She dragged him through the disordered sitting-room into the big bedroom of the suite. The lights were on and Taheer, in a fluffy blue track-suit, was standing with her back to the big window. James, in his pyjamas, sat on the bed clutching Fiona's red beauty case, where the drugs were stashed. And he was mad, he was out of his mind. A sort of throaty roaring sound oozed between his slack lips. His eyes were

....

horrible, glazed over, staring at things no one else could see; sometimes they rolled right back in his head.

'Tried to jump out here,' said Taheer gruffly.

'He's trying to get the strong sleepers from that bag,' said Fiona. 'He's right away, with someone, some*thing*, else. I don't know what to do . . .'

'Try to talk to him,' said Taheer to Long. 'Try to get through to him.'

Long knelt on the carpet in front of James and grasped him hard on both of his upper arms; he shook him and said fiercely, 'James! James, you fucking bastard, snap out of this! Talk to me! It's Gary!'

And to everyone's surprise it worked. James blinked and peered and said in a terrible far-away whispery voice: 'Long! Long! Get it away from me! Pull it off me or we'll both die!'

Long knew at once that James was seeing things but at first he stammered: 'What *is* it? What *is* it?'

The answer was very faint: 'Creature . . .'

James pulled his arms away from Long and Fiona secured the red beauty case. Now James was making feeble pushing movements in the air.

'Come on!' said Taheer loudly, nudging Long in the ribs. 'We'll get it away, James!'

She seized an invisible man-sized being round the waist and Long joined in the act.

'There!' he cried. 'We've got the bugger! Pull him away . . . Let James go, you Creature!'

Fiona joined in, stooping as if she was picking up the Creature's feet. 'Let him go! You see, Jimmie-bird, we've got him away!'

'Hold it!' ordered Taheer.

She whizzed up the metal jalousie on the window and swung it open. Then with a one, two and a three they flung their imaginary burden into the alley behind the Pension Rosa and slammed the window shut. There was an eerie, wailing cry, falling into silence, and it was a second before

....

they realized it had been made by James. He was on his feet now, teetering, still not properly with them.

'Take him to the bathroom, Long,' said Fiona. 'I think he might want to go. I'll make some tea.'

James went along like a good child, or a good-humoured drunk. Long wetted a towel and wiped his friend's face. James came back a little further.

'This is a bad one,' he said. 'This is very bad. Long? Did they come and get you?'

'That's right. How you going now? Fiona's making tea.'

'Tea always settles me down,' said James, sounding like an old-age pensioner. 'We went well tonight, didn't we?'

'Too right we did!'

'There's something I have to say to you, Gary,' said James, still in an awful quavering voice. 'Fiona shouldn't ... she shouldn't have ... I mean, I'm no prize package ... I can't even ...'

It was more than Long could bear. 'Stop it!' he ordered.

He led James out of the bathroom and they all sat round drinking the tea that Fiona had made with the nifty little bedside electric kettle and the teabags provided.

'Can I have one of the ordinary sleepers?' asked James plaintively.

Fiona had them in her purse. She fed one to James and he curled up in the big bed and drifted off before their eyes.

'Get some rest yourself,' said Taheer to Fiona. 'He'll be all right.'

At the door of the suite Fiona and Long embraced; he held her tight and tried to feel nothing. But this didn't work. He mumbled the same formula: 'He'll be all right!'

Taheer was prowling the windows in the sitting-room; she had a bed made up on the best couch.

'Carrying a torch,' she said. 'I know all about this band, don't worry. She was *your* girl.'

Long could not speak. He wished he was dead.

'I thought I saw the man in the grey coat,' said Taheer.

'What, in the street?'

....

He went over and peered out at the cold, well-lit Kurfür-stendam and the darkness of the alley.

'No, at the gig,' she said. 'D'ye know why Herr Kleinfeld hired me?'

'To keep James from hurting himself?'

'Because they had a letter,' she said solemnly. 'Some psycho talking about the death of the Raven.'

'Christ! Any ideas about who it is?'

'Could be the right wing, the neo-Nazis. Could just be some lone nut, a fan turned sour.'

Long popped another bottle of Sekt, wandered off to his room, and fell asleep in the end.

Next morning the joint was jumping. Good reviews on the news and in the *TAZ*, picture of Cameron hitting a photographer in the notorious *Bild Zeitung*, with the head-line KULT BAND MACHT KRAWALL. David translated it as CULT BAND CAUSES A RIOT. They all wondered what this sort of publicity would do for them but Frank was pleased.

'You'll see!' he chuckled.

It was a fine day and there was a tour of Berlin arranged. James turned up at breakfast, in the sitting-room, as sane as Long had seen him lately. He strode up to Long and shook him by the hand.

'Thanks a lot!' he said. 'You came and helped with me last night.'

'How're you feeling?'

'Pretty good.'

Fiona stayed behind, didn't go on the tour of the city, and James asked Long to go along with him and Taheer in the car. Cam and Tony and the bird girls all went in a Kombivan. It was a beautiful day; they saw the victory column, with Bono's angel, and drove through the Branden-burg Gate. They saw the Reichstag and the driver, a young chap named Rolf, swore it had looked better wrapped, by Christo and his lady, Jeanne-Claude. Taheer agreed: that had been a real *Volksfest*, a popular festival, with everyone

. . . .

having a picnic on the grass, hearing music and buying food and souvenirs.

So they came to the highlight of the tour and it was a three-storeyed red postmodern erection in the middle of all the hectares of damp, crane-cluttered building sites. The red thing was called the InfoBox. On the lower floors there were a lot of hi-tech features on all the building work – plans, simulations, informative little talks in many languages. In other words, a lot of slick, semi-interesting material as found at a trade fair. Then on the roof there was the paradise of the sidewalk superintendants – a viewing platform. You could look out through the viewers and be informed about the building work that was going on.

Rolf, the driver, was thrilled, he said, every time he came up here. Taheer, sensitive to the feelings and the politeness of James and Long, was apologetic. As they looked, obediently, the rest of the band arrived. The rooftop was filling up. Suddenly a high-school class recognized the band and surged over to them.

'*Es ist der Chames Rahven!*' they cried. '*Es sind die Nightwings! Menschenskinder! Autogramm Stunde!*'

So it was autograph time. Whole lot of signing going on. They went back to the pension after lunch and rested. When they turned up at the PROVOX amphitheatre there was a queue round the block; three extra tiers of seats had been put in, plus extra standing room.

The gig went every bit as well as the first night. They always made a few changes, to keep themselves fresh. Frank rehearsed the bird girls' dance before the opening and it worked well. Cameron and Tony did their special with 'Black Magic Woman' before the first break. The audience was even better than on the first night: they put in two of their own standards, including 'Demon Tamed', as extra encores. Then James introduced all the band, plus the bird girls, while all the stage crew came on. Frank brought on Fiona, in her blue Versace, and Taheer, in studded black leather. James thanked all their friends in Berlin and then

....

the whole amphitheatre joined in singing 'Auld Lang Syne'. Long got in a nice reference to a German cult classic: he said the audience could sing 'Da-da-da' if they didn't know the words.

Well, there had to be a party after all that. Frank had outdone himself again, hired the back rooms of a *Kneipe*, a pub over in the East, on the Prenzlauer Berg, an old hangout for writers and musicians. The food and drink were high-class but the whole district looked ancient. The crumbling tenements had dimly lit courtyards, reaching back into the shadows. At any moment a Mackie Messer type might come sidling out with his boys.

There was a jazz trio, friends of Cameron, plus old pals from the German scene, including Blixa Bargeld in a smashing Italian suit. The fashion industry had caught up with him. Everyone began to unwind. Frank and David did their exhibition tango; Taheer and the bird girls taught everyone the Macarena.

It was very noisy in the *Kneipe*. At last he realized that he had been claimed again; the Creature hadn't come back but something was pursuing him. There was the dreadful angst seeping across the sands like a purple-black tide. James went to the downstairs loo and splashed his face with water. In the mirror he saw that his face was expanding and contracting like some kind of mechanical doll.

He wondered if this might be the time to take his emergency special, which he had slipped into the cuff of his jacket ages ago. He was trying to fiddle it out when a face appeared next to his in the mirror. Good-looking young German dude.

'Don't do that, James,' said the man in grey.

His voice was clear enough but *altered*, as if it was being filtered through some strange device such as James's brain. He had a very soothing presence; he said that the concert went well.

There were two doors out of this downstairs loo. The man in grey took the second door and led the way to a corner

....

table in one of the non-party rooms. They drank small glasses
of German dark beer, a bit like Guinness.

James was feeling far-away but better, not so much high as
smoothed out, sort of thing that was supposed to happen
with *Sereen*, one of his dealer's horrible bloody Specials. His
new friend was telling him his name: he laid his card on the
table and said, 'There, you see?'

James didn't pick the card up because his hands weren't all
that steady. They both chuckled at the name.

'*Freund*?' smiled James. '*Heinz Freund*?'

'That's right,' said his new friend in that strange inward
voice. 'Freund Heinz, Heinz Freund. A friend to all.'

James felt happy and comfortable; he finished his beer.

'I haven't been doing too well,' he confided.

'Happens to many people,' said Heinz. 'This place we're in
has seen its share of misery. I live here now.'

Without the least scruple James went off with the man in
grey, Heinz Freund. Popping round to his place next door where
there was another party. The Irish had the word for it: this
was a wake. A bunch of fans were playing their seedies and
tapes; it was a wake for Freddy Mercury, who would have
turned fifty not long ago.

It was chilly outside but Berlin looked mysterious and
beautiful, with the night sky starless, wisped in cloud. James
saw yellow lights and blue, and a glitter of neon in the west.

He followed his friend's grey gabardine, which flowed out
behind him like a cloak. They went through the first courtyard
of a tenement, right next to the pub, and he saw that there
were lights in some of the rooms. A man and a woman were
kissing in a corner of the Hof and James saw that the woman
wore a long greenish skirt down to the tips of her laced boots.

They passed through a big brick archway under the second
tenement into the back courtyard. Two young boys ran past
them and James had the impression they were wearing forage
caps and some sort of uniform. The back building was even
shabbier than the rest and there was a light over the doorway.
They were inside and up two flights before James began to
feel apprehensive.

'Come on up,' said Heinz Freund, turning back on the

....

narrow stair. 'I've something most particular to say to you, James.'

James went on up, feeling cold and conscious of the fact that there was no music playing anywhere. He came to a big empty landing, swept clean at least. There was a counter with shelves behind it and next to it the stairs going on up. James went up two or three steps and was overcome with distrust.

'Where's the wake?' he demanded.

'There's always a death celebration going on somewhere,' said Freund.

He stood almost in the centre of the room under the only light, which cast odd shadows on his face.

'You wanted to die, James. Now you can have some help to finish the job.'

'You're bloody mad!' cried James. 'What the hell do you know about how I felt or what I wanted to do?'

'You tried to kill yourself . . .' said Heinz Freund.

James cast a glance up the stairs and this made his companion move very fast in a way that frightened him. The man in grey swept across the empty room, his cloak billowing out, and James raced up to the next floor.

It was the top floor: he could see the cloudy sky overhead through a hole in the roof. He had run into the big corner room but there was a normal corridor running off to his right. He couldn't tell if the place was tenanted or not. It could just have been some rough pad: there was a bed made up, as well as mattresses on the floor, and some kind of cupboard. There was electric light: a lamp shaped like an owl plugged into the wall on top of a box. There were candles guttering in the wind, stuck to an uncurtained window-sill.

James backed away towards an empty corner of the room as Heinz Freund walked towards him.

'*Vorsicht*!' he said. 'Take care!'

James tried to be calm; the man had been friendly, understanding. Could he trust his own senses? Was he imagining things that had been said? He made a great effort to explain, at last; he had not even done that with Fiona, with Long or David . . .

'Heinz,' he said, 'I don't believe I wanted to die. It was a bad reaction to a combination of designer drugs. I was hellish

. . . .

211

depressed, sure, and hallucinating. I was sure that we – that I
was going to die. But that is something different. I . . . I just
have to try and get clean.'

'I don't believe you!'

The man in grey spoke in a harsh whisper. All the lights
went out; James could not remember how this was done. He
spoke the name anxiously: 'Freund? Heinz?' But now he was
alone. He moved further towards the corner of the room,
heading for a long dusty curtain, a window with a faint gleam
of light from outside. His foot went through a soft place and
he sensed a great hole in the floor. As he dragged his foot
back, painfully, pieces of rotted timber went rattling down to
the floors below.

He crept on his hands and knees round the edges of the
hole and came to brickwork, the back wall of the room. At
last he stood upright and grasped what seemed to be a firm
place. But when he moved the dusty curtain it flapped into
vacancy; he dared not drag it away to show his plight. The
back wall had gone; he was on the edge of the abyss.

Taheer came up to Long, who was yarning to a German
drummer, and said to him, very quietly, 'He's gone.'

Long looked over at Fiona and saw that she knew; he
caught her anguished look. Frank was standing behind her
chair; he gave them an off-you-go sign. They collected Cam,
who was dancing with Gisela, fetched their coats and went
purposefully downstairs.

'I've got a tip,' said Taheer. 'James went off with a man
in grey. We think he's in the flats next door.'

'Does Frank know?' asked Cam.

'We're in contact,' said Taheer, showing her pink mobile
phone. 'Don't plan to make a riot, Cameron. We'll just
reconnoitre.'

A Turkish boy carrying a tea-towel met them at the door
of the *Kneipe* and held a conversation with Taheer. He
pointed along the street. They went marching out into the
cold street and turned into the courtyard of the nearest
block of flats. Taheer put her head into an open hallway,

....

almost a porter's lodge, and another Turkish youth came bouncing out. Kemal was a fan, thrilled to see two genuine Nightwings and he shook them by the hand.

He explained that only this front block was still occupied and that he saw everyone who came in. The block at the back of the courtyard was being renovated; it was covered with scaffolding. It had a brick underpass into the back courtyard: no one lived in the old block at the back because it was falling down. Only a few derelicts, *kaputten Typen*, crashed there and had hash parties, maybe, but they crawled over the back wall. Tonight he thought some people had gone by into the back courtyard. Just a little while ago. That was all he could say.

Taheer gave Kemal twenty marks. They strode across to the underpass. To Long the thought of James sitting around smoking hash with *kaputten Typen* was marginally better than James being mugged by a mad fan-gone-sour in a grey coat.

The back courtyard was a weedy, nowhere place, deserted in the powerful light of Taheer's torch. The old place at the back had a feeble light on over the door, illuminating a red and white Danger-Keep-Out notice. Long was becoming mad with anxiety.

'The hell with this!' he said.

He marched into the dirty hall of the building and let rip with a loud 'Coo-ee'. Taheer fiddled with wall switches and a few lights did come on. They all shouted 'JAMES!' very loudly and then listened. There was an answering sound, a mere echo, faint and far away.

'That was at the back,' said Cam. 'Come on!'

They ran along the hallway to the gaping back door and worked their way through tall weeds. Something moved overhead and Taheer shone the torch up to the ruins of the third floor. A curtain was flapping, and there was James, clinging to the broken wall of the corner room. There was nothing in front of him; the wall had crumbled away at his feet.

....

'Hang on!' shouted Long. 'Hang on, mate, we'll get you down!'

Cameron saw things differently. He walked backwards among the weeds with tears streaming down his face.

'James!' he pleaded. 'James, we love you man! We're nothing without you! James, keep still! Don't do anything foolish!'

' . . . hanging on!' said James.

'Stay here!' said Long to the others. 'I'm going up the stairs. 'Stay here just in case . . .'

Taheer pushed a second torch into his hand and he was off, flying up the stairs so fast that the place seemed to shake all round him. There were still a few lights and just below the last flight he came to a bigger landing, with shelves. Long crept up the stairs now and there was James, hunched oddly against his low, crumbling wall and clutching a rusty reinforcing-rod.

'Are you OK?' said Long.

He was surveying the half-furnished room, the gaping hole in the floor.

'Not bad,' said James. 'Did my foot on that bloody floor.'

'Can you crawl along until there's a bit more wall?'

'Could give it a try,' said James. 'Have a fiddle with that owl lamp on the box. It was on before . . .'

Long tested the floor as he went over to the lamp but it was firm. The lamp had fallen over but when he set it upright it came on again lending them a beam of light paler than Taheer's big flashlight. Long looked at the old iron bedstead on castors, made up with dingy bedclothes, and was visited by an idea.

'I'll just roll this bed a bit closer,' he said. 'You game to go down to Cam and Taheer if we can jack up something with the sheets?'

'I'll give it a go,' said James.

So Long went about things as coolly as he could; there was one tough good sheet, then a couple of threadbare blankets. James shouted out to the folks below and then lowered himself to the soggy floor. Long wheeled the bed as close as he could and threw James the end of the sheet, weighted with his harmonica.

'Lose that, Raven,' he snarled, 'and I'll belt you!'

That gave them the giggles. They snickered like a pair of hysterical idiots while James stowed the precious instrument inside his jacket and knotted the sheet round his waist. He crawled backwards a little, and reefed down the old brown net curtain. The back wall was a vast hole, rising up again where Long held on to the iron bed.

'Coming down!' sang James. 'Are you there down below?'

There were gargling noises which translated as take-care and what-was-the-sheet-tied-to?

'To the bed!' shouted James and Long together, as James rolled over the edge, grasping the sheet firmly. The bed held well, with Long hauling on it. There were all sorts of sound effects outside and at last, as he thought his shoulders would both dislocate at once, the weight went away. James gave a wordless whoop of 'Demon Tamed' and Long knew that his friend had reached solid ground.

Long left things just as they were, didn't even pull the sheet back up again or switch off the owl lamp. When he got down again Cam and Taheer were helping James through the hallway. James made them stop while he gave Long back his harmonica. And outside in the weedy court-yard there was a crowd of people standing stock still, like an army of ghosts. Long saw Fiona, Frank, David, Tony, a bunch of other people from the party, two uniformed coppers, couple of ambulance men . . . It had begun to snow quite heavily.

Taheer insisted that Long go along with James, first to get his foot seen to and then to make a statement about the man in grey. The foot was bruised but nothing was broken. They made their statements at the hospital in a private office, lent by one of the doctors. James was as sober and succinct as Long had ever seen him, telling it all as

. . . .

clearly as he could. He spoke in both languages and the young detective, Herr Simon, complimented him on his German.

James didn't spare himself; he spoke of his stay at the clinic in Kent, his episode of unconsciousness which had been played up by the media as a suicide attempt. If it was, he said, he hadn't been fully conscious of it. He was or had been dependent on certain so-called 'designer drugs' and now that he was trying to get clean he suffered agonizing 'flashbacks'. He declared – first Long had heard of this – that he was still a patient at the clinic, going straight back into treatment the moment he returned to England. He had been on special leave from the clinic in order to do the Berlin gig.

Then there was the whole vexed question of the man in grey. He had been seen by Taheer and Long at Tempelhof; they both described him. Youngish man, thirty to forty, tall, brown hair, well cut, pale handsome longish face, good bones, deep eye-sockets. Wearing a long, full grey gabardine coat, possibly a designer coat. James said he was sure it was the same man he had met in the *Kneipe*. He added some details: black eyes, real black eyes in which the iris could not be distinguished from the pupil. Underneath the grey coat he had worn a black sweater. The man had a very pleasant friendly manner, of that James was certain, but he could not be sure how much of the stuff he was remembering came from his own fantasy.

Herr Simon questioned tactfully and James agreed that he had been foolish to go with a total stranger. And no, not the least thought of a homosexual proposition had crossed his mind. They had been off to a wake for Freddy Mercury in a place where the man in grey was living just next door. But James had become suspicious; the man had offered to 'finish the job', namely to kill him or at least assist his suicide. Then he had been left alone in a dark and dangerous place where he could have fallen . . .

It sounded incredibly creepy to Long; it was surely only

. . . .

a kind act of fate that they found James teetering on the brink instead of lying injured among the weeds. Then there was the matter of the man's name, the card that James hadn't picked up. It was never found at the *Kneipe*. When James said that the man had given the name 'Heinz Freund' there was a reaction from Herr Simon; Long knew at once there was something in that name.

When the interview was over they found a couple of reporters waiting in the hospital lobby. James was all smiles, showing his bandaged ankle; one false step on the Prenzlauer Berg. He sent good wishes to all his friends in Berlin. When they got back to the pension it was three o'clock; they crashed and were up at sparrowfart again. The flight back to Heathrow was very quiet.

There was a hired car waiting at the airport to take James straight back to the clinic. No fans had turned up this time. James drew Fiona and Long aside when they came through customs and made them sit down with him on three plastic chairs away from everyone.

'What is it?' demanded Fiona. 'James, what is it? I can't stand all this . . .'

'I want you both to do something for me,' said James, looking at the ground.

Long had a sudden premonition of what was coming and he didn't know whether to laugh or cry.

'Long,' said James, 'I want you to take care of Fiona. I mean she's your girl, she really loves you, not me. We were just an episode.'

'Oh Jimmie-bird!' Fiona started to cry.

'You know it's true,' said James. 'I'm going into the clinic and I'll be there a while. I want you to do this for me. Long?'

'I'm willing,' said Long. 'Fiona?'

She nodded.

'Just sit here,' said James. 'See when they let me have visitors!'

He got up and walked off to where the driver of the

. . . .

217

hired car was waiting. When he was out of sight Long and Fiona moved together. Long felt as if he had died and gone to heaven.

In the next few years Long amused himself composing 'What happened to them next' captions. Long and Fiona got married and had two kids. Fiona wrote books for children; Long put out a solo album that won an award. James got clean and lived at his country place; Taheer came over to be his permanent bodyguard. Cam lived with Gisela Meyer, one of the bird girls, and they had a baby girl. Tony left the group and they got a new bass player, Roger, who doubled on violin. They put out two complete albums and planned a lengthy tour down under.

Taheer kept up with the investigation in Berlin: there did seem to be traces of a suicide club, a bunch of sinister types who helped young persons to 'finish the job'. They had shown interest in other well-known showbiz persons who had apparently made an attempt. She also showed Long a book entitled *Das Vornamen Buch*, 'The Book of First Names', a slim volume with a bright-green cover which contained 8000 first names with their origin and meaning. Under the name 'Hein', a shortening of Heinrich, it was pointed out that 'Hein' or 'Freund Hein' was a euphemism for Death, from medieval times.

Long and Fiona wondered about various aspects of their friend James. In bed at night Long took his true love in his arms and said: 'Do you think that Taheer takes care of *everything*? That she and James . . .?'

'Oh Gary-boy,' whispered Fiona fondly. 'Of course they do!'

About the Authors

....

Steve Aylett is the original South Londoner who thinks it's clever to say a word when belching. His books are *The Crime Studio* and *Bigot Hall* (Serif) – the former has also been translated into Czech. A third book, *Slaughtermatic*, is to be published by Four Walls Eight Windows/Turnaround. So that should teach you.

Michael Carson spent his late teens wondering if Bob Dylan was sincere, while his mum and dad sat in the kitchen worrying about the younger generation being assailed by false, overpaid prophets; his twenties listening to Neil Young in Saudi Arabia (and still wondering if Bob Dylan was sincere); his thirties – can't remember a thing, except he'd decided, sort of, that Bob Dylan, like everyone else, was awash with mixed motives; his forties trying to get 'Killing Me Softly' from going round in his head. Now in his fifties, he listens to Paul Robeson – certain that he was sincere – and worries about the younger generation being assailed by false, overpaid prophets. Over these decades he has written eight novels, including *Sucking Sherbert Lemons* and *Friends and Infidels*, and numerous short stories, some of which are collected in *Serving Suggestions*.

Laurie Colwin, born in 1944, was the author of five novels: *Happy All the Time, Family Happiness, Goodbye Without Leaving, A Big Storm Knocked It Over* and *Shine On, Bright and Dangerous Object*; three collections of short stories: *Passion and Affect, The Lone Pilgrim* and *Another Marvelous Thing*; and two collections of essays: *Home*

....

Cooking and *More Home Cooking*. She grew up in Chicago and Philadelphia, and later moved to New York, where she lived with her husband and daughter until her death in 1992.

Janice Galloway has written *The Trick is to Keep Breathing, Foreign Parts, Blood* and *Where You Find It*, clocking up mentions for Bowie, Elvis, Debussy, Dr Hook, The Ink Spots, a host of BBC radio medleys, Verdi, Mozart, Schubert, Britten, Burns and Kenny Rodgers. Her books have won the MIND/Allen Lane Award, the Cosmopolitan/ Perrier Award, the McVitie's Prize and the American Academy of Arts and Letters E.M. Forster Award. She wouldn't pay more than the prescription price for benzodiazepines or Prozac, would prefer not to make flippant remarks about her sex life, and lives in Glasgow.

Bonnie Greer was born in Chicago and has lived in London since 1984. She has won a Verity Bargate award for her playwriting and has dramatized the work of Walter Mosley and Terry McMillan for the BBC. Her first novel, *Hanging by Her Teeth*, was published in 1994. She danced topless to pay her way through college but had to stop when she discovered that eyelash glue gave her a rash. 'Stillness' can also be read in the short story collection *Eating Grits with Princess Di: Tales of African American Women Abroad* (Serpent's Tail).

Diana Hendry spent a good part of her youth dancing and smoking in the jazz clubs of Liverpool. She has now given up jazz clubs but not the fags. For penance she belongs to a health club. She is a poet, short story writer and children's author. *Double Vision*, a teenage novel, was going to include an Elvis lyric until the publishers found out the copyright fee. Her most recent poetry collection, from Peterloo, is *Making Blue*. She won the Housman Society Poetry Prize in 1996 and her junior novel *Harvey Angell* won a Whitbread Award. She lives in Bristol.

Philip Hensher lives, works, eats, sleeps and dances in South

ABOUT THE AUTHORS

London. His books are *Other Lulus* and *Kitchen Venom*, a forthcoming book of short stories, and an opera libretto, *Powder Her Face*. He writes for newspapers, too.

Christopher Hope's novels include *Serenity House* and *Darkest England*. But at heart he's a rock addict, hooked on the golden years, *circa* 1956 when, in South Africa, Calvin took on Presley, and lost. He has just completed a meditation on that best of all possible revolutions: *Me, the Moon & Elvis Presley*.

Ursule Molinaro is a night person in a night city. Although still double-breasted, she has released a number of arrows: eleven novels, thirteen plays, hundreds of stories, many translations and sundries. Her latest addiction: Personal Radical Shield Vitamins from California. She lives in New York City with a cranky Manx who bites her ankles to keep her hopping.

Joyce Carol Oates, long besotted by music, though not exclusively rock'n'roll (her first and most enduring love has been the piano music of Chopin), is the author most recently of the novels *We Were the Mulvaneys* and *Zombie*, and is the 1996 recipient of the PEN/Malamud Award for Excellence in Short Fiction. She is the only faculty member at Princeton University to be awarded the Bram Stoker Lifetime Achievement Award in Horror Fiction (1994). 'A Woman is Born to Bleed' is taken from her forthcoming novel, *Man Crazy*.

Michèle Roberts left home at eighteen to go to university, where she discovered drugs and rock'n'roll and tried to discover sex; and came across poetry'n'politics. The late sixties were a good time. Later on she became a writer, producing novels, poems, short stories, films, plays and essays. Her eighth novel, *Impossible Saints*, published by Little, Brown, came out in 1997.

Nicholas Royle wrote about rock'n'roll in his award-winning

....

221

short story 'Night Shift Sister' (for *In Dreams*, edited by Paul J. McAuley and Kim Newman), hiding forty-seven Siouxsie and the Banshees song titles in the text (a keen reader and Banshees fan later found another five); he took drugs as his subject in two stories for Pulp Faction anthologies *Technopagan* and *Fission*; but until now his approach to sex has tended towards the oblique, his first novel, *Counterparts*, being about a man who cuts his penis in half. His second novel, *Saxophone Dreams*, despite including a couple of sex scenes, features neither rock'n'roll nor drugs (though some readers might find them useful). His third novel, *The Matter of the Heart*, is published by Abacus. Born in Sale in 1963, he now lives in west London and is married to a doctor.

John Saul prepared himself for contributing to this anthology by being born in Liverpool, experiencing the 1960s, and later abstaining from anything to do with sex, drugs and rock'n'roll (emphatically opposite poles to writing fiction) through teaching English to London schoolchildren and writing fiction. Some of the latter has appeared in *New Writing 4* and 5, and in the Serpent's Tail anthologies *Sex & the City, Border Lines* and *Cold Comfort*. But along the way he did succumb to rock'n'roll, and wrote the novel *Heron and Quin* (published by Aidan Ellis), which is the story of a harmonica in search of a player.

Lisa Tuttle grew up in Texas, preferring rock'n'roll to the loathesome omnipresent country music until she moved to London in 1980 and got all sentimental about Willie Nelson, Ray Wylie Hubbard and George Strait, especially songs like 'London Homesick Blues' and 'All My Exes Live in Texas'. After a decade in London, she now lives on the wild west coast of Scotland, at least a hundred miles from the nearest possibility of a rave. Drugs and rock'n'roll seem remote, belonging to the distant life of cities; sex, luckily, is where you find it, and can be as much in the mind as in the body – otherwise why read stories about it, or write them? Her

....

most recent novel is *The Pillow Friend*; her collections of short stories include *A Nest of Nightmares* and *A Spaceship Built of Stone*.

Ivan Vladislavić was born in Pretoria in 1957. He now lives in Johannesburg and works as a freelance editor. He is the author of one novel, *The Folly* (published in the UK by Serif), and two collections of stories, *Missing Persons* and *Propaganda by Monuments*. His Elvis sightings began after a visit to Graceland in the early eighties, during which he fainted in the Jungle Room and was revived by a tour guide waving a still from *Viva Las Vegas*.

Cherry Wilder is a writer of science fiction, fantasy and horror, a New Zealander living in Germany. To deal in order with the theses of this volume she fancies old rockers, has stopped smoking and is a true fan of rock'n'roll. Her novels and stories are littered with players, musicians, ballad-singers, dancers and theatrical companies, often on distant worlds. Her most recent collection is *Dealers in Light and Darkness*.